STEAL IT ALL

DONOVAN: THIEF FOR HIRE

Chuck Bowie

MuseItUp Publishing
Canada

Steal It All © 2016 by Chuck Bowie

All rights reserved. No part of this book may be reproduced or transmitted in any form or by any means, electronic or mechanical, including photocopying, recording, or by any information storage and retrieval system, without permission in writing from the publisher.
The characters and events portrayed in this book are fictitious. Any similarity to real persons, living or dead, or events, is coincidental and not intended by the author.

MuseItUp Publishing
14878 James, Pierrefonds, Quebec, Canada, H9H 1P5

Cover Art © 2015 by DK Designs
Edited by Christine I Speakman
Layout and Book Production by Lea Schizas
Print ISBN: 978-1-77127-838-6
eBook ISBN: 978-1-77127-776-1
First eBook Edition *January 2016

*Steal It All is dedicated,
as always, to my wife and partner, Lois Williams.*

In this novel my approach drifted toward a police procedural.
Lois told me to follow the muse and see what the story would say.
It was a great suggestion.
Do stories write themselves?
Seldom, if ever.
Do drafts improve by themselves?
Seldom, if ever.
I am so grateful for my readers:
Victor Paul-Elias and Lois Williams.
I am so, so grateful to my editors:
Forrest Orser, Christine I. Speakman.
Special appreciation goes out to my son, Jonathan,
who researched 1980s-era Manchester Gangs for me.
And for the cover art, the first thing to catch the reader's eye,
I am thankful to DK Designs,
who turned words to images for my cover.

DONOVAN: THIEF FOR HIRE

Three Wrongs

AMACAT

Steal It All

CHAPTER ONE

London, England

IT WAS EASY ENOUGH TO enter Canada House, the embassy on Grosvenor Street just down from Trafalgar Square. He followed two young women carrying backpacks through the side door and into the main lobby. Once inside the stately building, he noted the security guard standing near the office across from the open concept desks. He and the guard watched the women read the information panel. A moment later, the taller woman moved over to a resource desk and began conversing with a communications officer. The second woman, shorter and darker-haired, dropped her backpack to the floor, and used a free-standing computer to gain access to the Internet.

His eyes wandered over to the trio of elevator doors. He located another self-service computer and pretended to use it, all the while keeping an eye on the elevators. Every few minutes, staff from Canada House would enter or emerge from one of the elevators. He waited until a lone, female staff member headed toward the elevator and followed her in.

The moment the door closed, the man pulled out a Glock 19 Gen 4, pushing the barrel tight against the silk blouse that covered the xiphoid cartilage of her chest. She gasped, eyes wide, holding the breath in. Her gaze didn't leave the man's trigger finger, even when he snapped the lanyard holding her security ID card from her neck. He touched it to the reader on the wall by the elevator numbers.

"I'm going to press three. Once we're there, you exit and go right. I will follow you into the women's washroom, ten feet from there. I'll tape your mouth and leave you unharmed. Any deviation from this and you are dead. Nod if you prefer to live." She nodded. Keeping the muzzle of the pistol firmly against her breast, he pressed three, and they waited for the elevator car to react, taking them to the third floor.

Her eyes flitted upward, for just a second, causing him to offer a grim smile.

"Security camera, I know. Yes, it will present an image of me after I'm gone. But I have no identity. Try finding someone who never existed, not that I really care." A half-moan escaped from her, and he saw a fine bead of sweat appear on her upper lip.

"I have a new baby."

"Then you have all the reason in the world to follow my simple instructions. By the way, I do not intend to blow up the building, so, no need for you to try anything desperate. It's show time. Your life depends upon the next seven seconds. As we leave the elevator, talk to me in a low voice about tomorrow's weather."

The third floor was comprised of a hallway leading to several private offices used by consular staff. Most of the office doors were closed, so no one heard the elevator door 'ping' or saw its doors open, and no one witnessed their arrival. A moment later, they entered the washroom.

The man quickly went to work. "What's your first name?" He pulled out a set of handcuffs, clicking one manacle onto her left wrist.

"Brenda."

"Brenda, I want you to sit on the toilet in the far cubicle." He produced two feet of wire cable and attached one end to the chain between the wristlets. Placing them on her wrists behind her back, he moved in closer to run the cable behind the toilet reservoir. He leaned in, straddled above her, in order to complete the wire attachment. Her knee came up, hard, making contact with his inner thigh.

"Ungh!" He didn't go down. Instead, he sat down on her lap and one hand closed off her windpipe. Squeezing hard enough to send a message, but not enough to break anything, he breathed out a terse statement. "That wasn't in our script. Bravery will make your child an orphan, Brenda." He released his grip and covered her mouth with duct tape, completing the task of securing her wrists behind the reservoir, and then stepped away. He used the tape to secure her feet at the ankles and then wrapped it around the toilet seat, effectively imprisoning her. "I'm sorry," he said, double checking the tape on her mouth, and then he left.

Once outside the washroom, the man continued down the hall, turned right and walked all the way to the back corner of the floor. He approached the door marked Director, Trade, opened it and walked in.

The corner office of Ian Gross, Director in charge of International Trade, was a study in cherry wood. The built-in bookcases surrounding the two windows were made from red cherry, as were the desk, the meeting table and all of the wood trim. The door, very solid, closed behind the intruder and the discreet click alerted the director to the presence of a guest. He swivelled around in time to receive a slug between the eyes. The man fired a second shot through the director's heart, but he was already dead.

Outside the office, the man could hear doors slamming and footsteps heading away from him, toward the stairwell. *I have at least twenty seconds. A minute, at the outside.* He went to a cabinet, sought a specific folder, pulled a file from it, and then smoothed the distance between folders so it appeared as if nothing was disturbed. Closing the drawer and returning to the desk, he lit the thin document, letting it burn to light gray ash on the surface of the cherry wood desk.

As soon as he heard footsteps drawing near, he placed the barrel of the Gen 4 in his mouth and pulled the trigger.

CHAPTER TWO

Niagara-On-The-Lake

IT WAS THAT PERIOD OF calm after the harvest, when the workers give themselves permission to relax and to shrug off that time-sensitive urgency that comes with the processing of the grapes. Tourists are gone, the harvest celebrations have been enjoyed, and, like the land itself, a lassitude settles over the property and its inhabitants. The bushes that brush up against the estate buildings thin with every leaf that colors and drops. The sun sinks earlier in the day, and the afternoon air is inhospitable and tired.

Sean Donovan worked the vines at Plenitude Winery. A thief for hire at age forty—was he really forty?—he had spent much of his adult life stealing things for people, no questions asked nor answered. The wear and tear on his mind and body, however, had caused him to re-think his vocation and he was currently a laborer in a winery in Ontario, Canada.

This morning, he sat on the side of his bed, dark whiskers shaved and his pale face scrubbed. He eyed the window and debated what to wear. Winter was never the season he looked forward to with anticipation. Skiing was unappealing and he'd never considered hockey, so winter was just five months of unpleasant excursions onto icy sidewalks, bulky clothing and cold, often wet feet. In fact, until he'd come to appreciate wine, he resented autumn for the frigid season it introduced.

He'd always chosen warmer climates to do business at this time of year, but things were different, now. He wanted to learn the business of winemaking, and to do that, it was necessary to follow the seasons, chasing the grape from soil to bottle. With warmth in mind, he studied the pale flannel shirt in one hand, a cream cable knit sweater in the other. Choosing between them might be his most challenging decision to make that day. The meteorologist suggested cold and damp and the window agreed. Almost December weather. He put the sweater on over his shirt, knowing he would be working outside until dark. The phone on the shelf in the closet rang. This was not his regular phone. He studied the screen before picking up.

"Hello?"

"Gaia speaking. You remember me, my friend?"

I remember that you're not my friend, and I'd better watch my back when your name comes up. Gaia Attanasio was a very rich art dealer whose business practices were always questionable. Donovan had done business with him in the past, and wished to keep future business to a minimum, if there was any at all. "Of course. What can I do for you?"

"I have a job for you, Mr. Donovan. In England. A collection of art has been placed in a home in Ambleside, in The Lake District. The collection belongs to an organization I represent. One of the items within the collection belongs to me and I especially want that back. Although the piece is mine, I wish to retrieve it, without necessarily alerting the organization of my action."

"Retrieve, as opposed to stealing it?" Donovan was intrigued by the possibility this wasn't a completely illegal endeavor.

"Yes." Gaia's tone was dry. "You don't need to know the details, only the description of the piece and its location, which I will message to you. When can you go, or are you in England now?"

"No, I'm not there at the moment. I may be able to do it. How much time do I have before I decide, and what's the fee?"

"Fifty thousand American and I will need to know in a day or so." He didn't sound happy. *You're used to getting your way without hesitation. I've half a mind to say no, just to piss you off.*

"Done. I'll let you know."

As usual, Gaia didn't bother to say anything before ringing off. Donovan shrugged, and finished getting dressed.

Over breakfast of melon, blueberry fritters, and coffee, he pondered the phone call. Assuming the item truly belonged to Gaia, which wasn't a given, the pay check would be appreciated. He had been thinking of a purchase, sure to clean out his bank account. Fifty thousand from out of the sky would be nice, thank you very much. His phone rang again, this time the regular one resting in his pocket.

"Hullo?"

"Mr. Donovan. Sean. It's Rory Thompson speaking, from London." Thompson was the Canadian High Commissioner to Great Britain: Canada's ambassador. Donovan had done some work for him the past summer, saving the life of his Director of Communications in the process. As a result, Donovan was on retainer as a security consultant for the embassy, called in when the need arose. Had the need arisen?

"A member of my team has been shot. Murdered at his desk. When can you come over to help?"

Donovan paused, surprised. Canadian offices, with the possible exception of the Swiss, had the reputation of being the calmest, most boring environments, perhaps in the world. What could have happened? "Are you looking for the shooter? It seems to me the police would be in the best position to—"

"The shooter is dead. He killed himself at the scene. What I need— what my team needs is a security expert who can get to the bottom of this. Why on earth would someone shoot a public servant in his office, and then shoot himself instead of trying to escape? And who is he? There's no identification on him and initial efforts are coming up blank. There's more to this than meets the eye, Sean, and I need you to figure out why this happened. When can you be here? Because now is what works for me."

"I'll be on a plane tomorrow evening. Best I can do."

Donovan heard a chuckle over the line. "Well, that's all I've ever asked of you. Get here as quick as you can. I'm assembling a team to support your efforts."

A team? Donovan had spent his entire adult life, on both sides of the law, working alone. What in hell was he going to do with a team? Heather, his co-worker came over, her paisley rubber boots squeaking on the hardwood floor.

"Time to hit the field, Sean. The vines aren't going to put themselves to bed for the winter." Smiling at her little joke, she sauntered off to cadge a final slice of toast. Donovan sat for another minute, pondering how it was perfectly acceptable to be part of a two-person team walking into a vineyard, yet perfectly awful to envision himself working with a team of police officials. How complicated his life had become in the previous half hour!

* * * *

"When Elliot says April is the cruelest month, it's obvious he knows nothing about tidying up Canadian grapevines, in the rain, in early November." Heather Donleavey, a master's English grad leaned her rake against the wheelbarrow and rubbed her sodden gloves together in a vain attempt to get the circulation going.

"Don't whine, Heather, it's unbecoming. Just be thankful those rubber boots are waterproof and, more importantly, lined. Besides, this is just temporary for you. You'll be teaching full time in January, right?"

"Well, there just seem to be days when I wonder what I was thinking when I took a fifty-cent-an-hour raise to leave the wine-tasting bar in order to work the fields."

"You said you wanted to learn everything. It's not just 'bottle to glass,' you know, it's dirt to vine to bottle to glass. Besides, look at the fun we're having." Sean Donovan straightened up, leaning sideways to shake a substantial rivulet of rainwater gathering in his hood, and then turned to face his co-worker. "Not to mention the view." He swept a hand across the brown field, up toward the winery.

With military precision, the vines, Pinot Noir and further over, Malbec, marched straight as a die for half a mile, up to an exquisitely appointed estate building. Down in the swale, a net-covered section of vines still carried the grapes that would be used to make ice wine. The nets kept the birds off, and periodically, a gun fired blanks to further discourage the more aggressive avian species.

While each worker was assigned an acre to put to bed, they were permitted to pair up while they worked. For some, the cold needles of drizzle were excuse enough to knock off for the day and forego their pay. Heather and Donovan were among the remainder who, for their own reasons, had teamed up and chosen to tough it out until quitting time.

"It's four, almost dark. Had enough?"

Heather had resumed raking. "Not yet. You go on in. I want to finish the row."

"I'm done my row. I'll go to the other end of yours and we'll meet in the middle."

"Sounds good." She gave him an appraising look, offering a full smile when he met her gaze.

He wheeled his cart to the bottom end, about fifty yards, pointed it to the other lone figure and began pruning and raking. They finished up just before five and pushed their respective piles of vine cuttings back up the gentle slope to the compost heap.

* * * *

Dieter Schmidt sat alone in his office, staring at the columns of denuded grape vines on the other side of the four French doors, the focal point of the room. It was three o'clock in early November, and he couldn't recall a quieter day. All but a few workers had come in from the vines. Tendrils of icy fog caught on the grape branches like rags tied to brambles, with nowhere to go. Even the fireplace seemed to be failing at its job. He crossed his legs and returned to a set of nine graphics, one of which would adorn the bottles of the new Malbec line. "They all look the same." The words came out half-hearted, like the heat from the fireplace.

His thoughts turned to the winery's finances, as they did a dozen—two dozen—times a day. What was he going to do? He remembered his father's caution to never spend what you don't have, and his thoughts crept, reluctantly, to the sale of the winery. A strong controlling interest in exchange for enough money to bring solvency to the company and ensure Dieter and Anna's retirement. *I wish I was retired right this minute.*

But he wasn't.

He got up to pace across the marbled tile and then back to his desk. *I'm still the boss here, for the moment.* He started. Had he said it? *Is it my intention to sell the place? Do I really have a choice?* And why did he fear that? Was it perhaps because he actually wanted to step aside, but didn't want to express this thought?

"Scheisse!" There was Anna to tell. She'd left him to think this through, hoping—what? What did she want? Well, until now, she'd been happy with their lifestyle. All they knew was winemaking, with perhaps some travel. Now, Anna wanted their son healthy and his massive medical bills to not stare at them. And she wanted a roof over her head. Ever the practical one, that Anna. And, although she wasn't one to make emotional pronouncements, he knew she wanted them to be happy. Debt did not make them happy. He'd lost many nights' sleep, working the myriad permutations that would lead them to a solution. Dieter would awaken at three, or three-thirty from a worrying dream fresh at the front of his cortex, like a movie whose soundtrack was too loud. Anna, who always seemed to be awake, would ask him if he had a bad dream, and was he all right. He always said he was fine, but he would lie staring at the ceiling for a half-hour afterward. There were many—a Plenitude!—of questions, but it always came around to a single answer.

Sell the winery. Keep a share, if possible, but sell it.

Then. The 'if' of it was settled. What about the 'when'? There was the matter of the American hospital. They had been patient as he gathered up half the cost of Kurt's treatment and care from their life savings. To date the hospital had been satisfied with his efforts. But where was the money for the second half of the bill to come from? It wasn't as if the value of the winery had sunk, but their only option at this point would be to take the balance from the contingency budget—half a million dollars—to pay the bills off. This would leave them working as if nothing untoward had occurred, but should there be an unexpected cost, a new roof, say, or a bad crop, they'd be vulnerable…still, they had to do it.

If he could close a deal within the next few weeks, everything would go well. But there were no takers, at this point. Not even a nibble from within his circle of owners. If wine sales slowed, or if something happened to the winery premises, or if Kurt relapsed… If, if. Dieter began pacing again, and then stopped to stare at the phone.

He punched in a three-digit number. "Anna? Can you come to the office?"

* * * *

Sean Donovan still felt the chill from the field, so he lingered in the steamy shower, easing the ague from his limbs. His thoughts vacillated between the meeting he had requested with the owners, Dieter and Anna Schmidt, and the trip he had planned to visit his friend, Beth McLean in London. In the case of the former, it would be one of those life-changing, career-altering moments that could go either way. In the case of the latter, there really wasn't any thinking to do. Donovan's original plan was to travel to London and spend some time with the witty, attractive, newly-appointed Director of Communications for the Canadian High Commissioner to Great Britain. His thoughts moved to a hotel room in London, to the memory of her bare thighs. The trip would be a very good thing.

Now, however, other reasons for traveling to England had come up, and they weren't of the pleasant variety. He'd accepted the security assignment from Rory, but what would he do to execute Gaia's request? He continued to think as he rinsed off and stepped out of the shower.

Dieter and Anna owned Plenitude Vineyards, from the fields to the estate building to the shower he'd just stepped out of. They had taken him on as unskilled labor, shared their knowledge of winemaking with him and treated him as well as he had ever been treated in his life. He accepted every chore no matter how menial and was learning every step in the process, from the ground up.

This was his second stint as a winery worker. A few months earlier, he'd taken a break from learning the wine business to resolve some issues. He had been called upon to deal with them because of his unique set of skills. His recent ex had been murdered, an acquaintance was being framed and his sister had become involved in art theft. All of these circumstances involved him, and his career.

Before entering the wine industry, Sean Donovan was a thief for hire. He had stolen items on a contract basis, and delivered them to individuals who paid him handsomely for this service. There were consequences to this vocation, not least of which was the challenge of getting out of the business. Donovan had found himself at a crossroads at age forty. He was without friends or anything resembling a home. It was a life comprised of constantly being beaten up, placing himself at risk and having no one in whom to confide. On the other hand, this career paid well.

Actually, it paid very well.

This last fact brought him to this moment. He dried off, exited the shower, shaved, and strode over to the closet to choose a suit. Donovan had acquired enough money that he had nothing material to want for. He could now do what he wished with his days, weeks, life.

Socks, underwear, shirt, pants. Tie, shoes. Jacket. He stood in front of the mirror, noting the first gray hairs forming a hint of caul by the corner of his temple. Do I look like a businessman? It's a very expensive, Italian-made suit. Will I be credible? Does it really matter, as long as I bring a shitload of cash to the table? Donovan glanced at the time before leaving his tiny room. As the door behind him swung tight, he noted the click—old habits dying hard—as he headed across the path from the laborers' residences to enter the estate building.

Dieter and Anna were in the office, awaiting their employee, Sean Donovan. Dieter had met there with him a few months earlier, to advise him his former lover, Nadia Kriss, had been murdered. This had precipitated Donovan's month-long departure while he had solved Nadia's murder. It hadn't brought Nadia back but Donovan had returned to the vineyard, just as he promised.

The office was a study in how to marry business savvy with design aesthetics. A solid mahogany wood door welcomed the visitor into a spacious, perfectly appointed office, and a set of French doors permitted visitors, if they chose, to walk out onto a cut stone patio, large enough to host cocktails for fifty guests. Today wouldn't be the day for such an event, though. The temperature hovered a few degrees above freezing, and the gusty rain resembled sleet, at times, as it flew left-to-right past the doors. Within the office it was toasty warm. The mid-wall gas fireplace pushed out blue flames above a five-foot wide, narrow bed of *Chateauneuf du Pape galets roulés*, the quartz river rocks for which the tiny French wine commune is famous.

Anna and Dieter avoided the massive double pedestal desk and sat in a nest of upholstered chairs nearer the fireplace. The couple was quiet. Anna seldom spoke unless directly asked a question—and an opened but un-decanted bottle of their signature Pinot Noir, together with three glasses sat between them. Early winter darkness had fallen and, just outside the exterior French doors, floodlights cast an ethereal light over the white granite patio and railing. A gentle rapping at the office door announced their guest, and they turned to greet their worker.

"Sean! Welcome. Don't you look nice! We're sitting by the fireplace where it's cozy. Take a seat, please, and have a glass of last year's reserve. It's a winner, if I do say so myself." Dieter took off his silver wire-rimmed glasses and set them beside his seat. He went over to the stereo and put on Sarah Brightman. "Too loud?" Anna shook her head. He took his seat and focused on their guest, smiling. "Well. You've been back to work for a few weeks now. Hopefully things are….calmer. What can we do for you?"

Donovan took a moment to pour himself a glass of the light red wine, before measuring his words and speaking. "I want to begin by thanking you for everything you've done for me, for your hospitality, the way I was treated when Nadia died, but equally for how much you've taught me about the wine business." He leaned forward, elbows resting on his knees.

"I mentioned to you both on the day I was hired I wanted to learn everything about growing great grapes and making great wine. Do you remember me saying that?"

Both heads nodded. "Yes."

"The reason I've taken such a great interest in winemaking is because I want to go full-on into business. The business of viticulture. But, knowledge-wise I'm not there yet. In the past fifteen months, I've learned a lot about the grapes, the vines, managing the fields, a bit about the processing, and I've watched how capably you two have managed your human resources. Your people."

"You get nowhere if you don't treat your workers like people. They are the biggest investment, besides the land and the vines, so they had better be tended as well as the product." Anna ended what was possibly the longest sentence she'd ever uttered to Donovan, leaned forward and poured herself a drink.

Dieter picked up his glasses and played with the wire bow. "We know how much you've learned here. Anna and I were talking about that just last week. And…we speculate, a bit. We were wondering if you might have wanted this meeting because you wanted a raise or a promotion. Because we can do that. Or were you possibly interested in taking wine courses nearby? Because, we, um, we haven't had quite as good a year as we would have hoped, and it probably wouldn't be possible for us to send you away to university. Perhaps next year…"

Donovan leaned back into his chair, the warmth of the fireplace and the warmth of the wine on the back of his tongue causing him to smile. "No, no, I may have got us off on a tangent. I'll be more direct. I am at the stage where I need to learn more about the administration, marketing, management, and overall care of a wine estate. I need to take my mind and hands out of the field, so to speak, and get them behind a desk for a while. Don't get me wrong, I've loved every moment with the production side, but I'm missing the entire other half of the business. You see, I want to invest in the wine business."

Dieter's eyes crinkled at the corners. He shook his glasses at Donovan. "Good fellow, one time a while back I watched a car salesman make a fool out of himself. He ignored a customer who he thought was too young and too poor, and as a result he lost a commission on a BMW. I wouldn't dare make that mistake with you, since I know you have… depths. But buying into the wine business is expensive. It's not like mortgaging a five hundred thousand dollar home, you know. The ante is a bit higher than that."

"How high?"

"I'm not sure at this moment, but, a lot."

Anna interceded, her voice aggressive. "Ten times that, to buy in. Almost five million. What do you think, Sean?" Her mouth formed a straight line, humorless.

He focused on her. "I want to buy Plenitude. I'm really fond of you and I'd love to work with you to make this vineyard even better. So, I want to buy controlling interest in this operation."

Anna spoke. "What makes you think we are interested in selling the winery, or any part of it?"

"Well, I've done my homework and I know you could really use a cash infusion. This evening wouldn't be too soon, as I understand things. Look, you wouldn't respect me if I came to you with no business sense. In fact, I haven't done that. Instead, I confess I know you have had some personal and corporate setbacks that have been a bit of a challenge. The personal challenges have eaten at your cash flow, and your corporate challenges have beaten up your equity. Neither one was avoidable, but I can stanch the bleeding."

"What?" Dieter looked upset. "How did you find out? That's very personal."

"I understand. But workers talk. They were—are—concerned. They mentioned you've been visiting your son who's had health issues, that he's in Florida at university, or he was, and he's been in an American hospital for some weeks now, and not likely to get out before Christmas. You may recall mentioning this to me yourself, in general terms. The other fact is you've asked two trusted friends from other vineyards if there was any possibility of a merger or a sale of shares, and nobody bit. Probably owing to the business climate, these days.

"Look. It doesn't really matter how I found out, as long as it wasn't by snooping through your books, which I haven't. The thing is, I have money, enough money. And I'm interested in buying in, but only if you two stay. I was hoping the ante would be five million to buy it outright, I'll be honest, but I can raise the extra couple of million to push it to seven million for an eighty percent stake in the company. You'll need some time to think things over, and I'll need a few weeks to raise the additional money." He stood up, watching their faces for any reaction.

"I've given you a lot to think over. Again, I'm really fond of you, and I respect you a lot. Your initial thought is some jerk is here, trying to steal your baby when you are at your most vulnerable. What I want you to ask yourselves is, what if you have to consider selling? If you do, wouldn't you rather sell to someone who cares about you and wants to be your partner, instead of some corporation wanting to nudge you completely out? Would you please think about it and come ask me anything you wish, any time over the next two weeks? I'm catching a flight to England tomorrow. Dieter? Anna? I believe we would be great business partners." With no one willing to decide anything concrete on the spot, they finished their wine and he let himself out.

CHAPTER THREE

MacDonald House, Mayfair, London

THE UNIQUE TRAFFIC MARKINGS ON the streets, the Guy Fawkes Day sales in the shop windows, the steering wheels on the right side of vehicles, and the quintessential skyline told him once again how much he loved London. And the rain fell. A bone-cold downpour escorted him from the building awning to the cab. The cabbie winked in the mirror and noted the 'London sunshine.' Chill rain in the fall was so commonplace the driver's comments made Donovan smile. He sunk into the immaculate leather seat, thinking about other instances when he found himself alone in another city, and the city streets flew past the taxi window.

Donovan texted Beth McLean as he left Paddington Station. In turn, he received a warm welcome confirming her invitation to stay at the Hammersmith apartment. Her cryptic note at the end of the text, referencing a security project was unnecessary, because the Canadian High Commissioner to Britain had caught him up with a phone call just before he left Niagara. Donovan was interested in her spin on the murder-suicide at the embassy, and how it matched up to the sensational reporting he'd seen on the news. They'd have lots to chat about that evening. Hopefully, their time together wouldn't be exclusively about work.

It being a weekday, Beth was at her desk at Canada House. She mentioned where her spare key was, joking that he could probably break in, regardless. The cab dropped him off at a restaurant where he tucked into a plate of eggs, sausage, fried tomatoes, and toast points. The coffee pushed back his jet lag just enough, and he felt sufficiently recovered to visit MacDonald House, home of Canada's Ambassador, the High Commissioner to Britain.

The circumstances around this visit differed from his two previous meetings. In the first, Donovan had paid a middle-of-the-night visit to discuss how he and the ambassador could extract Beth from a set-up created by a former coworker. In the second meeting, he'd received payment for having saved Beth's life and solving the scam that had swirled around her. This time, he arrived as an ex-officio service provider of the embassy, prepared to receive a briefing on the murder at Canada House and, equally important, to get his marching orders.

As before, he passed through security and took the elevator to the fourth floor, the ambassador's residence. The room was familiar to him, like the parlor of a favorite, very rich aunt. It was more than thirty feet in each direction, with tall, coffered ceilings and four Anatolian Turkish rugs mapping out opportunities for different occasions. Donovan liked the matching pair of cream leather club chairs, and he headed toward them. This time, though, five sets of documents had been placed at the oval boardroom table, so he was sure the occasion would be taken to be introduced to his team. Not looking forward to that…

A carafe of orange juice, pots of tea and coffee, and a plate of *pains au chocolat*, untouched, sat on a small table nearby. The air of suspense that had permeated the room in previous visits was gone. Donovan crossed the room to stand by one of the windows overlooking Mayfair. A somber tone enclosed him, and he noticed the mark of worry on the ambassador's face as he entered the room. He crossed two of the Turkish carpets to join Donovan and they shook hands.

"Sean. Good to see you. I wish we were meeting under more pleasant circumstances. You'll have to work through jet lag, but this can't wait." Donovan waved the comment off, and Rory continued. "Sit down, grab some coffee and I'll get you up to speed. The others will be along in just a bit, but I wanted a minute with you." He left the window and sat down, tugging his pant legs up just a bit, to reduce wrinkling.

"You have the docs over on the table, but I'm a talker. I want to tell you what I know about this." He pointed over to the boardroom table, to the documents that sat waiting. "On Friday the sixth of November, at two-ten in the afternoon, an unidentified man kidnapped a staff member in one of the elevators at Canada House. Using her ID pass card, he gained access to the third floor, where our International Trade unit works. He gagged her and tied her up in a bathroom cubicle and left her there, physically unharmed. A moment later, he walked into the office of our Trade director, Ian Gross, and, apparently without saying a word, shot him dead.

"Ian, by the way, was one of the few Brits working directly for the Canadian embassy. There does not appear to have been time for either of them to speak to one another. Within the next minute, we suspect he took a few pieces of paper from one of Ian's filing cabinets. These contents are still unknown to us. He then apparently burned them to ashes on the director's desk. After grinding up the ashes, he shot himself. The whole thing took less than five minutes from the time he entered the elevator. I have the video footage of the main floor as well as the elevator for you right here. Nothing, unfortunately, from within the director's office." Rory leaned over and dropped a flash memory key onto the table in front of his guest.

"I can tell you that the man hasn't yet been identified, although Brenda, the kidnapped staff member, thinks his accent was Canadian or American. Deep checks into our director's personal background have revealed nothing untoward about him. No, ah, complications that might have made him vulnerable to blackmail or murder, that we know of. You will have access to all investigative documents we have. Hopefully, you'll have better luck than my internal staff." He paused, his tone dry. "Not that you'll repeat that to my staff."

Rory swung his chair, turning so as to face Donovan directly. "You basically know as much as we know, at this point. I'm bringing in three specialists now. You've met Kevin Staal, our Information Systems director, who is sitting in for a few minutes. He will discuss security and access to the building. I'll introduce the others as they come in. Don't underestimate any of them, there's a reason I chose them." He tapped a folder lying beside him. "Beth prepared the briefing notes for us, so you can be sure she'll be involved as well. Ah. Here they are now."

The door at the far end of the room opened and a uniformed officer escorted three very different individuals into the room. Donovan recognized the man who had granted him security access earlier that year, when he was trying to clear Beth. The second person was a woman in her late thirties, angular looks with a matching athletic smoothness to her gait. She wore her hair blonde and short-cropped, sporting a navy business jacket and skirt, and carrying a briefcase with the Scotland Yard emblem above the lock. Her eyes were clear blue, her face a study in seriousness and her chin was solid and square. She kept her shoulders tight, suggesting a military background.

The third individual made Donovan take special notice. The man was a hard-fought sixty years of age, thick at the midriff and with a ruddy nose. Donovan noticed tiny white scars over the knuckles of his right hand. He was dressed in a white shirt and loosened tie under a rumpled jacket, and his hands were massive, as if he had been a boxer, or a meatpacker. He did not look like the guy who would back down from a fight.

The ambassador started without preliminaries. "You know why you're here. Let me tell you who you'll be working with. Sean Donovan is one of our private operatives. He's worked in security for several of our federal departments, and has in recent years moved to the private sector, as a security consultant. He worked on a job with us this past summer and will, I feel, contribute strongly to the team.

"May I introduce you to Gemma Trask? Detective Inspector Trask has been seconded from Counter Terrorism Command in Special Branch at New Scotland Yard. She's had assignments with MI-5 in the past, and brings that expertise with her as well. She comes highly recommended and sewed up a drug smuggling case just a few months back. Did I get that right?" She nodded, shaking Donovan's hand. "My IT Director Kevin has to leave us in a second, so let's get to his area of the chat quickly. But first I'll introduce Detective Miller. Jack is RCMP, on assignment with External Affairs. He has a background in accounting forensics, and an extensive career in industrial crime." Jack grunted and offered up a tiny nod. "Okay, Kevin?"

Kevin smiled, tugging his sweater down into place over a soft gut. As a computer scientist-turned public servant, his casual dress and clipped speech revealed a career behind a computer screen. There hadn't been a lot of time spent cultivating social skills, but his understanding of the role of bits and terabytes, spreadsheets, and programs in the workplace made him a valuable member of any project team.

"I'm afraid I'm the guy talking about closing the barn door after the horse has bolted. Before I begin, let me make something clear. I am a computer scientist who has security duties tacked on to my job description. I do not profess to be expert at it; in fact, it's apparent I am not. I know the ways that computers can be locked down, and I know how redundancies and secured measures can protect our servers. But what we've experienced relates, I think, exclusively to security. Physical safety issues. These are my responsibilities, but not exactly my area of expertise. We're a small group, here at the embassy, and to tell you the truth, I expect Sean, as our security consultant, will be more helpful in this area of the case.

"We're moving to entrance systems, versus on-site security, and we should have done so a year ago. This, in hindsight, has been a grave error on our part. Our approach has been to have security managed from Ottawa for all embassies. For countries like England, the presence of a security guard, we thought, would have been sufficient. Our plan had been to bump up security in the New Year. This plan is, ah, a little too late, and now, here we are. So, we're implementing stronger measures immediately.

"I've sourced out a Garrett walk-through metal detector that could meet our needs. They use it in the smaller airports and it's less intrusive than the ones that see through clothing. We are going to ramp up security. We can actually have something in place and our staff trained in less than a week." He folded the document he had been referring to, looking over to the ambassador for approbation. Rory nodded, and then looked to Donovan, one eyebrow raised.

Donovan met Kevin's gaze. "I was also thinking of the Garrett PD6500, as Kevin just described, or perhaps we'd be better off with a handheld metal and radiation detector. It's able to detect and locate both metal and radioactive substances. It can identify weapons from a one-inch hatpin to nine-inch medium pistols, and also identifies Cesium-137, Cobalt-60, and Sodium-22 radiation sources all the way down to one micron of Curie level. The downside is you have to have staff at the door at all times, but I suggest that's a price we should have to pay anyway, given the alternative. If one was to consider the number of instances of terrorism these days, we have to consider this for even the public area of the embassy in a friendly country like England."

"The alternative being a man walking in and murdering our staff." Rory nodded his head.

"Excuse me." Kevin interrupted. "What's Curie?"

"These are Curies. They're the decay rate of a sample of radioactive material. Not a big deal now, but I think being able to identify and measure Curies will help us prepare for tomorrow's terrorists as well."

"Okay, this is over my head. Since I'm not able to contribute beyond what I've already noted, perhaps you can excuse me? Sir, you've overbooked me for a second meeting, but I'm leaving this discussion in good hands. Gentlemen. Miss Trask." He shook hands and, taking his briefing notes, departed.

The ambassador poured himself a cup of tea, then spoke. "As you can see, I'm compiling a team, hopefully one with complementary skills. With that in mind, I'd like to talk about Jack Miller's skill set. Detective Miller is on loan to us from the Royal Canadian Mounted Police. He's an investigator, and this might be his last case. He brings thirty-five years of experience with him—the last twenty on the international scene—and his success rate is extraordinary. I've known him for a long time, and his skill set will dovetail nicely with yours." The ambassador paused to take a sip.

Donovan studied the man Rory was speaking about. Detective Jack Miller appeared to be in great shape for his age. He had a paunch, but there was no mistaking the muscular biceps and chest, the keenness in his eyes and the intentness with which he pursed his lips when absorbing information from around the room. In an alley, or in a bar, Donovan wanted to be beside him, not opposing him.

"I'm running this like a corporate meeting, for two reasons. One, this is what I do." His voice carried a tinge of humor. "But the other reason is this is the most efficient way to share information and get started. And time is not on our side. In fact, our respective…skills are so disparate, we almost need a translator to get some context here."

"May I interrupt, Mr. Ambassador?" Gemma's voice was low, and calm. "I think I can say that, with Mr. Staal's departure, our vocabularies have probably become a bit more…aligned. With one little issue, I believe we can proceed quickly toward getting up to speed and deciding on next steps."

"Little issue?" It was Donovan's turn to interrupt, his eyes narrowed.

"Yes." Her gaze remained locked on Rory. "I'm wondering, with all of the resources that Scotland Yard has at its disposal, why you feel it necessary to bring in, erm…additional folks to work with The Yard."

Jack Miller put a huge paw down on the table. It made an audible thump when it hit. "I'd like to respond to this." He leaned back, putting his hands in his pockets. "Detective Trask, this is the 'Canadian' High Commissioner to Britain. He presides over basically two buildings, here in London, and he—and those buildings—represent the entire country of Canada. Now, by population, Canada is a tiny country, not even forty million people. But it's a big country in terms of history, heart, and geography. We like to think of ourselves as everybody's friend. We say 'I'm sorry' a little quickly for my liking, and Canadians really—" He stopped, just for a second, "—really don't like to hurt people's feelings.

"But when we're backed into a corner, we don't go looking for another country to bail us out. That's our job. We kind of like to take care of our own business. Somebody takes a bottle to our buddy in a bar, well, we do our best to sort it out right then and there, ya know? So. Some guy walks into our building, kidnaps our staff and murders our colleague; what do you suppose we want to do with that? That's right. We want to close ranks and clean this up ourselves. So, if we look around this Canadian room and discuss this Canadian murder, who do you suppose we secretly think is the odd man out? The Commissioner? No. The guy who most recently saved our Director of Communications a month ago? Uh-uh. The RCMP? I don't think so." Gemma's face had blanched, now it reddened.

Jack continued. "But if we could just rewind two minutes, we'd be back to the part where Rory here was about to say that there couldn't be a better team than three or four Canadians and the entire might of Scotland Yard." The corner of his mouth turned up, just a bit. "Is there any chance we could begin again, but without the patronising tone?"

The room quieted, for a moment. Rory went to speak, but Gemma tried again. "Um, yes, I see your point. I—I may have presented the confidence of my department in such a way as to sound, perhaps, assertive. I didn't actually mean to…belittle the competence of Canada's resources. It's just that, well, if we're in London, we're used to representing, all…of London."

Jack's voice seemed loud, even in such a large room. "Does that mean we'll receive your full cooperation? You know you'll receive ours."

"Of course."

Rory stood, his glance meeting each of theirs in turn, closing off any more discussion. "Then, let's get started. My residence isn't really the best place to work from. You'll set up shop at Canada House in Grosvenor Square. Beth has arranged for a comms room to be made available for your use, twenty-four hours a day until further notice. It's not far from Scotland Yard's facilities, and their tools are world class."

Donovan's voice was low and firm. "Mr. Ambassador, if we worked out of Canada House, would we be able to gain access to off-server computers?"

"Absolutely. Anything you need, just ask Kevin if it's technological in nature, or me, if it requires a higher-level authority. There's one more thing. Every bus needs a driver." Thompson drummed his fingers on the table top. "I've given this some thought. You all work differently and you'll all need some measure of autonomy. And each of you has the requisite skills to lead this.

"Jack, you've got forensics skills, you should cover the business the director was working on. Gemma, you've got experience with gangs, so let's see if organized crime is involved. Sean, you're my X-factor. Beth will be your communications lead in all things going out. But I'm appointing Detective Trask to carry the ball. Let Gemma know what you want to work on, and I'm sure it'll find its way into the solution. She will also compile all of the information as it arrives, build the evidence board, that sort of thing. You two will report to her until further notice.

"And don't forget Beth. No one speaks to anyone outside of this team without checking with her. I mean it. Not even your former departments. I want to be on top of this, so keep me apprised about even the smallest of details. From today, your loyalty is to the case. By all means, keep your superior officers up to date, but make no mistake. I am the one who is looking for a resolution to this, and your organizations say to listen to me until you hear otherwise from them. Okay. Thank you for your attention, and for clearing your workload to accommodate this. The Government of Canada appreciates this."

The group rose, and Rory held them with one raised hand, his voice low and steady. "Do not for one minute think this is an easy case, an RCMP case or a Scotland Yard case. You need to focus on two elements: there has been a murder committed, and it has taken place on the most political of properties, an embassy. So we will not have individuals thinking they or their organization is larger than the team. You will succeed or fail only by leaning on each other. Donovan, here," his eyes darted from one to the other, "has spent his entire career working as a lone consultant. I'd bet a hundred pounds he'd rather do this alone. But I need you all, and I need you to be more collaborative. It's good to get this out of the way, but now it's time to go get answers. Am I clear?"

Donovan nodded at Gemma, and Jack offered up a huge paw to envelope Gemma's hand. "All right, then. Let's go someplace where I can get an early lunch and we can chat about this."

* * * *

Jack tipped a glass of orange juice in salute to his two new colleagues, and then quaffed a third of it in a huge gulp. "I am starved. When do you suppose the bacon and eggs'll get here?"

Gemma raised a bemused eyebrow. "As soon as they're cooked, I reckon." She lowered her voice so it carried around the table, but no farther. "It does make sense I'd get the nod to lead, given my department is here in London, right?"

Jack nodded. "He couldn't very well pick one Canadian and not the other. We'd be at each other's throat before the food arrived." His eyes twinkled. "I'm just teasing. You know London best, you've got Scotland Yard's resources in your back pocket, and Rory's got all the confidence in the world in you. You'll do fine, right?" He glanced at Donovan.

Without waiting for an answer, Jack dove right in. "Just so you know, I'll be calling you Gemma," he wiggled his empty fork in Trask's direction, "and you'll be Sean. So, what do we know about the shooter?"

Donovan leaned in. "Most of my information is from the mainstream media, so I'll need a few hours to get caught up. I just got off a plane two hours ago. Frankly, I won't be much good to you for a bit. Jack?"

The RCMP officer had received his meal and was in mid-bite when both heads turned to him. A full mouth didn't even slow him down. "The guy's still a John Doe. He's got a Canadian or American accent the kidnapped staff thinks, for what that's worth. His clothes have gone through forensics and are now being studied for location of purchase. His prints have been to hell and back. Nothing from that end of it. Dental records are being studied." He swallowed, and then continued.

"I don't like saying what I think, without a few facts. But I figure if he shot himself, the hit on the director wasn't traditional, in that sense of the word. Feels more like a grudge than a professional take-out."

Gemma nodded. "So, maybe we'll get somewhere if we look into the contracts the victim had been working on this year. You can do that, Jack. All right. I'm up." Jack nodded, loaded the fork, and recommenced chewing.

She sat quiet, her back to the door, and with feathers of spiky blonde hair partially hiding her blue eyes. Donovan motioned for her to not speak until a pub patron had passed, and then nodded for her to begin. "My people are working on the identity side. I expect it would be easier for you lot to delve into the contracts, perhaps pore over that filing cabinet to see what's conspicuous by its absence. This is especially true, given you, Jack, are expert in paper trail forensics." She sat back, staring absently, and then continued. "We're looking into facial recognition from passport photos and drivers licenses, but you know, that's a long shot. Nevertheless, we're giving it a try."

She changed gears. "The gun is clean, as you probably suspected. It had no serial number, no slug or casing patterns seem to be in our computer systems, and the only prints on it are from the lone shooter, who we don't yet know. Why would someone take the trouble to clean their identity, if they were going to shoot themselves anyway? My first thought is that it's a delaying tactic, which makes no sense to me. My second thought is—"

Donovan finished her thought. "He's trying to protect someone from all of this."

"Exactly."

"Who, and why?" The table went silent, until Jack finished their thought. "I guess we'll have to wait and see." Shortly after that, Gemma recapped next steps for each, they exchanged contact information, and then went their separate ways.

CHAPTER FOUR

Hammersmith

THE COMPACT LIMO OF THE newly-appointed Director of Communications pulled up to the curb in front of her apartment building in Hammersmith, London. Donovan rose from the low-slung wrought iron fence and stood waiting for Beth to retrieve a briefcase and a bottle of wine from the seat beside her. She thanked the driver and directed her full attention to her guest.

"You found me."

"Yup. I was looking for a cab. I didn't expect…"

"A car and driver? Yeah, it was a bit of a surprise to me as well. The first few times it showed up, I assumed it was because I was recovering from the gunshot wound. So I told Rory I didn't need it any more. He said it came with the job." She paused to kiss him. "He said in light of recent developments; that is, me getting shot, he'd feel better if I took advantage of an allowable perk of the position. I don't like the fuss, though. I'll probably stop next year, or the year after." She winked and they entered the building.

Once in her apartment, Beth opened the bottle of Gabbiano Chianti Classico, pouring it into fat-bowled wine glasses. Donovan raised an eyebrow. "This is a good start. Next on the list is food. Are you interested in going out, or would you like me to cook for you? A nice truffled risotto with chicken parm…what?" She'd given him a look.

Beth took a sip, smiled and placed the glass back on the coffee table, her lips fresh-stained with a wine blush. "Well, we can talk about that later. First off, I was thinking you may want to see my shoulder. You know, see if it healed." She took his hand and encouraged him toward her trim bedroom.

Sean poked his head in the doorway and took a quick look around. "Not a lot of room here. I may not be able to avoid brushing up against you while we study your war wounds." She had his sweater up and over his head, and was unbuttoning his shirt.

He pulled her in to him, and helped her to undress. "You recall that I, ah, wasn't actually the one who got shot." He kissed her now bare throat. "But if it will make you more comfortable if neither of us is dressed, then I'm game."

"I don't recall you talking so much last time we met." She'd unbuttoned the single clasp on the side of her skirt, and it fell to the floor. His pants followed and, a second later, she pulled back the coverlet.

He stopped, stricken by the fresh pink circle just between her left arm and sternum. His finger traced a pair of opposing, radiating lines of stitch marks that led away from it. "I'm sorry. I didn't realize it was so close to your heart."

The soft pad of her index finger met his lips. "Shh. You saved my career, and my life. So, my body has a tattoo unlike anyone else's. No big deal. And speaking of my body?" Her face was a question, while her finger dropped from his mouth to explore other lines, other angles.

"Yeah, we probably don't have to say anything else. Just one more thing."

Beth's face was buried in his neck, her words muffled, and she moved his hand over to cover a breast.

"I missed you, Beth. I'm awfully happy to be here."

"Yeah, yeah." She surfaced to offer an ear-to-ear grin. "Meanwhile, there are places in London you haven't visited, mister. Now, get to work." She followed her own advice.

* * * *

Sean had fallen into a brief, restless sleep, waking to Beth's movement around the tiny bedroom. He lay still, watching her lithe body as she picked up assorted pieces of clothing, straightening each with a fold and a swipe of her hand. Each time she dipped to pick something up, wings of hair beside her chestnut bangs swooped forward, hiding her high cheekbones, her nose, her brown eyes. She hadn't dressed, and he noted the raised weals they had caused during their lovemaking. Dermatographic Urticaria. Even light touches caused the skin to puff up and redden. Fortunately there was little discomfort from the condition.

Her neck appeared elongated, swan-like. He noted her collar bones, how they pronounced themselves in relief against her throat. Her breasts were small and round, like apples, he thought, noting her upturned nipples. Her abs and the long muscle bundles along her thighs rippled like a cat, just a little, when she stretched, and he remembered her hobby: Krav Maga, the Israeli martial art. She'd lost a few pounds since he'd first seen her undressed, that night they'd spent hiding out in London. Was she healthy? Recent evidence suggested so.

The circumstances in which he found himself seemed improbable at best. He was a criminal, a career thief, and, regardless of his efforts to seek redemption here he was, with a contract to recover an objet d'art on behalf of an unscrupulous art collector. And, to be honest, he had a winery to pay for and a half million dollars in new money wouldn't be sniffed at with disdain. Yet, the fantastical circumstance was he'd found someone. And every day seemed to bring her closer to him. To his heart. *For the longest time, I wasn't even certain I had a heart. Is she fixing me? I don't think I want to run from this.*

"Awake, are you? What are you smiling about?"

"Just happy that you've so obviously recovered. Sorry about the nap. Jet lag, I suppose." He shifted onto his side to face her.

Beth put her hands on her hips, unselfconsciously naked before him. "Glad you could rest. I confess I grabbed thirty winks as well. Not quite the full forty. Bravo, by the way. That was fun." She came over to sit beside him, and offered up a long and languorous kiss. "I've been dreaming about that recently."

"Look at you; all comfortable around me. I like that." He placed a hand on her knee.

"You do recall, we spent several nights together this summer, with only a couple of murderers coming between us. Nothing like almost dying to put things into perspective and nothing says relationship like crimes and misdemeanors. My mom says thanks for not letting me get disgraced at work, or get killed. She actually put those two events in that order. Imagine that!" She slid back into bed. "Sorry. My feet are freezing." She placed a cold hand on his chest, for warmth, and he winced as her feet found their way between his upper thighs.

"Make yourself at home. Um, can we chat about the incident at your office?"

Beth frowned. "Yeah, that was terrible. Ian was…crusty, but he never did anything to warrant getting killed. At least, not that I know of."

"Did he manage any contentious files? Were there any big arguments with anyone recently?"

She shook her head. "His job was to facilitate trade between Canada and other countries. These contracts don't always go smoothly, but the usual worst case scenario is lawyers from each side fire snippy letters at each other. Our shop doesn't often find itself in the middle. Oh!" Her smile was self-conscious. "I suppose you should know he wasn't, um, our absolute top notch director. You've heard the phrase 'best and brightest'? Well, he might not have been…either of those. And not to speak ill of the dead, but these last two years, toward the end of his career, he may not have…cared as much about the outcome of his decisions. We were kind of holding our breath he wouldn't mess up before he retired. We certainly weren't expecting anything like this, and in fact, his recent performance probably has nothing to do with this case."

She changed the subject. "You met the RCMP detective today, correct?" He nodded and she smiled, and then grew serious. "He's already looking into the contracts, files and so on. We've been told to give you and him our full cooperation, as well as to permit Ms. Trask full access, as long as you and Miller are aware of her activities. As Director of Communications, my job is to contain all information, release as little as possible to the press and otherwise muzzle everyone and their dog. Essentially, I'm the uncommunicative communications gal. I think they feel better to have no information than to release half a story or, worse yet, something that isn't accurate. But the press, especially the Canadian media, are right up my behind on this story."

"So, Trask and Miller are already pursuing leads?"

"Yeah. But you'll soon be in the thick of things, if I'd only let you get a few hours of sleep." She slid a hand up his thigh and held him. She whispered "What are you thinking? Sleep, dinner, or...?"

"Sweetie, you have them in exactly the wrong order." And he picked her up, placing her on his hips, and drew her down to meet him.

CHAPTER FIVE

Queens Park

JACK MILLER SAT AT A table near the back of The Rusty Spike, a pint of Guinness at his elbow, untouched. The pub was empty at four o'clock, and he could hear The Pogues over the speakers at each corner near the ceiling. He scratched partial sentences on a pad of hotel stationery with the nub of a pencil, and then lined up each filled page across the table top.

The server looked up from his crossword puzzle and eased over to his lone client's table. "You haven't touched your drink, sir. Is everything all right?"

"Yeah. The drink's for show. I'll take a glass of water and some more potato chips, though. Ah, crisps, are they called here?" He returned to his scattered notes.

Jack wanted to focus on the job at hand. He really wanted to play the part of an engaged, conscientious investigator. And he knew he'd be able to contribute, sooner or later. But he was struggling right now. Struggling with the untouched beer in front of him. Struggling with the loss of his wife, Arlene, who'd passed away six months ago, in April. Struggling with the need to wake up, get up, and put one foot in front of another for sixteen hours, and then doing it all over again the next day. Struggling with the effort to prevent himself from punching the next moron who said something stupid to him.

He remembered how small she'd become, just before she passed away. The final time, before palliative care when he'd bathed her, child-like, before carrying her to bed. She was asleep as she touched the bed, and he spent several hours watching her before he fell asleep, exhausted. He awoke, startled, swearing he heard her call his name. But as he studied her face, all bones and porcelain skin, she remained in a deep sleep. The ambulance attendants took her to the palliative care section of the hospital, and he'd followed in his truck. But she never awoke.

And he struggled with one other thing. The elephant in his own, personal room. Why was he called by his senior officer to work on this case? A case where the victim was in the morgue and the shooter was dead, by his own hand. It didn't appear to him he was really needed. Case closed, really. So, was this the RCMP's chance to cast an old bastard aside? Was he done, as a police officer? And what if, horrible, devastating thought, it was indeed time to go? Is this how it ends? Maybe it is.

A woman entered the bar, offered up a 'Cheerio, Tim' to the server, who poured her a draught without being asked, placing it at the end of the bar. She opened a newspaper and proceeded to ignore everyone. Jack reviewed his scraps of paper. What did he have? He had a victim, shot between the eyes during office hours. And he had the murderer, who had burned some kind of document before shooting himself with the murder weapon. Jack's fingernails scratched at the scarred table top, a nervous habit. The guy had contrived to obscure his identity before entering the Canadian embassy offices that day.

The man's identity would be resolved soon, of that he was certain. That would yield more clues as to the whys and the whats of the story. They had the how, the when, and the who, after a fashion. But why? Which would lead to more questions. Jack reached for the stout, instinctively, and then pulled his hand back. Knowing the beer was there seemed to provide him comfort, even if he couldn't enjoy it. How many had wet his throat since Arlene died? Far too many. With a sigh, he pulled a sheaf of papers from an oversized auditor's briefcase on the floor beside him. While he wasn't permitted to take the actual contracts from the office, he managed to get a copy of the master spreadsheet that chronicled the contracts negotiated or signed off by the late Ian Gross in the current fiscal year.

He studied the header: File Number, Contractor, Contract Date, Duration, Commodity, Dollar Amount, Status, and Comments. Straightforward. Below the header there were thirty-five agreements, each running above two million Canadian dollars, with the largest coming in just snug at forty million. What did they tell him? "Nothing," he growled, under his breath. "Not a God-damned thing." He pulled out a similar document, but for the previous fiscal year.

Same header, with the same kind of information. Similar dollar amounts. He pored over each agreement summary, looking for a difference. Forty-five agreements in total, with three uncompleted and forty-two closed. His forefinger followed the last column of each of the three contracts that hadn't been finalized or paid out. The comments were clear in the two earlier agreements, but the contract from the previous January seemed to contain deliberately vague comments in the last column. "Weasel words." Jack sat back, tucked all of his papers back into the briefcase and ordered steak and kidney pie with fries and gravy on the side. *I'd better get a closer look at these uncompleted contracts as soon as I get back into the office. The one for two million dollars in potato sales looks especially interesting.* Potatoes are not a very auspicious start for a murder investigation, but whole strings of murders have been committed for less. He took another glance at his glass of black stout, and then reached for the glass of water waiting beside the Guinness.

CHAPTER SIX

Westminster, London

GEMMA TRASK ENTERED THE WOMEN'S locker room of New Scotland Yard, just south of St. James Park. She took off her uniform, placing the jacket, blouse, and skirt on a pair of hangers. It had been some time since she'd been to her locker. Nothing like getting shot, to bollocks up a carefree summer. She spun the combination on the padlock and, out of the corner of her eye she spied a fellow officer rounding the corner.

"The newly-appointed Detective Inspector Trask. Felicitations on that, by the way. So glad you didn't indeed drop off the face of the earth. I haven't seen you for months, it seems, and now here you are, in your knickers. How has the recovery been?"

Gemma pulled a sweater over her head, wincing just a little, as her right arm lowered. She'd angled her face away from her colleague's eyes, to preclude having more personal questions asked about the shoulder. Forcing a smile, she turned to her colleague. "Hullo, Elena. Healing up. I've a new assignment. I reckon you've heard of the murder-suicide over at Canada House? They've called me in to represent the Yard on the case. I have a couple of Canadian characters to deal with—I mean, work with. Should be interesting, to say the least. At any rate, it's delaying a return to my usual work." She zipped up a pair of jeans and slid her feet into black loafers.

"Oh, they'll be all right, as colonials go, I expect. You've got a great track record, Gem. If they slow you down, you can always work around them. By the way, I bumped into the Chief. He's looking for you. Didn't seem too anxious, so I expect it may be about parking, or the Christmas party; summit like that. Just off your shift, are you?"

"Nah. I had a breakfast meeting with the Canadian ambassador and well, you know, represent the Queen and all. The boss says a uniform may not be necessary to wear every day. So I think dressing in civvies might be worth a try."

"Yes, yes." Elena nodded. "I quite envy you the luxury of jeans, I must say. At any rate, congratulations on the assignment, and once again on the promotion. Give 'em hell."

"Will do." Once her colleague left, however, Gemma sat on the nearest bench, thinking about the day, her newest colleagues, and what the next steps would be. She touched her right shoulder, the souvenir scar from her last case. Rehab from the slug that tore through her humerus had taken five months, and she felt she was about ninety percent. *It's more like sixty percent when I'm lifting weights over my head.* But here she was, back to work, yet not with her team. Promotion or purgatory? She wasn't sure some days. Today was one of those days, especially after the introduction fiasco. *I'll hold my tongue next time. No opinions, just facts.* It did feel good, though, being named team leader of an international squad. It's another line for the résumé, at the very least.

Before changing out of uniform, Gemma had visited forensics, and considered the information she had received. There was a little bit of progress. Most of the dead man's clothes had been purchased outside London, from three shops in Manchester. A detective was just heading back from there, and promised he'd bring a report to her later today. He'd begun by speaking with the city desk to see who might have recently gone missing. Working from that basic fact of location, X-rays of the man were being sent to dentists in Manchester. She had a good feeling about the direction the case was heading, but again reserved announcements. Facts, not opinions.

What was to be done with her team? She'd had junior detectives toddling alongside of her since she'd joined The Yard, some of them damned good. There was at least one officer she'd brought along and mentored, who was now working at the same rank she enjoyed. This was a small feather in her cap from the perspective of the Yard, but these two Canadians were the X-factor. They obviously weren't going to get her killed, but would they, in any infinitesimal way, be a help to her? She hadn't a clue. They both came well-recommended, so there was that. They brought skills, so they probably deserved a chance.

And what about her? Why was she not working the gangs division with her real colleagues? Was this really an opportunity or, as she feared late at night, when insecurities reared up, was she being sloughed off, handed a demotion without the cut in pay? She could ask, but that inevitably led to receiving an answer. Did she want to hear the answer? No. She didn't. She wanted to scream out loud, and have things go back to before she was shot. She wanted a do-over. "Is that too much to ask?" She challenged the wan Detective Inspector looking back at her in the mirror.

Gemma took a couple of over-the-counter pain pills from her purse, swallowing them with a splash of water, and headed for Gangs Division. She supposed she should check in for a minute before heading to her flat in Queen's Park. Jonny was working nights, so he wouldn't ring her up this evening. It's just as well. She caught herself at that. *Where did that come from? Don't tell me he's getting tedious already? It's only been two weeks since our first date.* She'd think about that later, over a glass of wine and the computer. For now, though, she'd better track down the Chief.

* * * *

Detective Inspector Gemma Trask sat across the desk from her superior officer, Chief Inspector Bruce Clark. He'd turned off his radio as she entered, snugged up his tie, which was askew, and motioned to a pitcher of water which she declined, with thanks. The office was austere, with two framed commendations and a bronze plaque of the familiar ER badge under the crown holding up the single slit of institutional green wall separating the windows. These three items rested between a pair of matching, floor-to-ceiling windows overlooking Millbank, but Gemma's back was to the better view. Her face, conversely, looked over to the steady gaze of her boss.

Clark began. "I know I asked you this during your re-entry interview, but I'll ask it again: How is the shoulder? Are you getting back up to speed?"

Gemma sat toward the front of the seat, back ramrod straight. "Just fine, Sir. Ninety percent, I'd say. I'm pressing hard to get it back to normal, and physio suggests, if I work at it, I can actually be stronger than before." She fumbled with her words. "Of course, I am working at it. My shoulder, that is."

He hesitated, his eyes suggesting he was making an effort to meet her look as he spoke. "And mentally? This is a taxing career, and if you're not at the top of your game for this case…"

There was no pause whatever from Gemma. "I'm fine, Sir. One hundred percent. I do have a question, though. It's about the case itself; the set-up, really. Here we are, technically on British soil, and the Yard is certainly, erm, involved." She hesitated, searching for the right words. "But because of the murder taking place at the Canadian embassy, there are non-British investigators involved. I…I don't quite understand why there is one rep from Scotland Yard, and two Canadians, as good as they might be. Why not three from the Yard? Not only that, I fear…since they don't know or recognize how Scotland Yard works, they might go off half-cocked and bollocks it up completely, excuse my language. It appears to be as much a babysitting assignment as solving a case. That's just my opinion, Sir." Her effort to soften her words with that last sentence didn't appear, even to her, to be much of a sop.

If his gaze hadn't quite met hers when asking about her mental health, these last comments certainly brought his attention straight onto her. "I hope you understand, there are protocols established when working with embassies. We have to tread a fine line between letting the embassy know we care about their concerns, while ensuring we take responsibility for solving the crime, or crimes, as the case may be. Sometimes, it has to be accomplished collaboratively. In fact," he paused for effect, "the very reason you were chosen for this case is because you have no experience with international issues.

"There may well be more to this than you think, so don't assume this is a…a practice assignment to get you up to speed. I know you're hard-nosed. You have a reputation for it and frankly, I'm delighted, most of the time. But not when dealing with embassies. These days, fifty percent of police work is politics. I've given you a complex case, I know it to be so. Part of your challenge is to walk a balancing act. Keep them happy, but don't let them get killed. Most importantly, we want to ensure the case gets a thorough run-through. The last thing we want is to leave a single stone unturned. Do not, above all, let that happen."

He stood. "Keep me informed as you proceed. I do not wish to be called on the carpet owing to a sin of omission. You were chosen because you aren't the kind to leave out steps. But, as you proceed, keep the ambassador, and by extension, his team, happy. And as I just said, keep me apprised of every twist and turn." He didn't ask if she had any further questions. She let herself out, as he turned BBC4 back on the radio.

CHAPTER SEVEN

Ambleside, The Lake District

NOEL MARTIN RIGG, PROPERTY BARRISTER, peered out of the train, his back to the universe that had been London, and prepared to re-enter the small-town world of Ambleside, in Cumbria, England. He picked up just as he left off the previous Thursday morning, his umbrella unfurled against the spitty November drizzle. One foot on the platform, the other on the ground, he smiled at a joke he'd heard on the train. A young man had been telling his companion that he dreamed it had stopped raining in London. She had laughed out loud at that. "Terra firma," he always issued those words upon exiting any vehicle, land or sea, and then he headed off to the Fox and Furrow for a pint.

It being half-noon, he paid strict attention to the rumblings from his soft mid-section and looked left, to the nearest public house that was, coincidentally, his favorite gastro-pub in all of the Lake District. He glared at his overnight bag, it being unseemly to haul over the buh-bump, buh-bump of the cobblestone sidewalk. A glance toward his residence suggested the walk all the three blocks home and thence back to the pub would have left him knackered for the remainder of the day. There was nothing therefore to be done, so he tugged it behind him, like a caboose. Off they chugged.

The pub was disgorging its noon-time crowd, the tables toward the back clearing first, the window seats following and finally, the row of banquettes along the sides nudging out their patrons. Noel chose a table that hadn't yet been cleared of dishes from the previous occupant. A creature of habit, he liked that table and considered it to be his. He'd been known to wait at the bar twenty minutes for it.

The server cleared the table, head down, dumping food scraps and dishes into a plastic tub. Noel tried to ignore her, reading snippets from the front of the real estate section of the Westmorland Gazette. A different server arrived and he ordered the poached haddock and a baked potato with mixed vegetables. He never ate the mixed veg.

"Beverage, sir?"

"A drop of cider, if you please."

The real estate section dispensed with, he moved on to the section 'In The Courts'. Not finding anyone there he knew or recognized, his attention returned to the lunch that had just arrived. He picked up the salt, frowned and put it down. He doubled up on the pepper and snuck a healthy dollop of ketchup, hiding it behind his potato. He struggled with the notion of using ketchup. No one in Ambleside used it much. But it was a habit—a bad habit, he reminded himself—he'd brought back from Maine, in the United States. *I won't order the ketchup next time.* He ate too fast, and then felt the onset of an acid reflux attack, but resented leaving even a morsel on the plate. Once the bill was paid, he stepped out of the pub and hailed a cab for home.

The taxi pulled up before a Tudor-style cottage, two stories, nine rooms, small detached garage, latched gate and enough space between the neighbors to avoid prying eyes. Behind his house one of the numerous rounded fells, or mountains, framed his roofline. In any other environment, the backdrop would have fetched an additional twenty-five percent price hike on a home like this, but urban Ambleside enjoyed a wealth of rounded fells: there was one for everyone. Fetching his luggage up onto the front step, Noel unlocked his door and stepped into the foyer.

Something was wrong.

His luggage tipped, and then fell forward, unnoticed. Walking-running from room-to-room, he noted a missing cabinet with its equally-absent television, a picture hanger, sans picture behind the spot where his Swedish stressless chair had been. Everything conspicuous by its absence. At a full, wheezy trot past one empty corner after another, Noel lumbered up the stairs and down to the last room on the left. Sweat slicked his upper lip and, with one hand on the wall to support his bulk, the other hand trembled as it reached toward the doorknob.

The eight-inch wide, hand-scraped oak plank flooring ran the length of the oblong room, from the entrance in which he stood, trembling, to the pair of windows looking out upon the cut stone walkway. Today, the floor was uncluttered by anything but the dusty outlines that marked where boxes had sat. Scores of boxes. Noel's hands went to the sides of his face to clutch at the part of his scalp just above his ears, that his hair had vacated years earlier. He moaned as he looked with greater desperation, from left to right, and then back to the left. Could he believe his eyes? Twenty-one feet by fifteen feet of nothing but floor. He whimpered.

I'm dead. I am so fucking dead.

Snuffling back a trickle of snot, he ran to his bedroom. *They may not have taken my laptop. If they don't see the inventory list, perhaps, the thieves won't know the value of...*

His bedroom contained a bed, and that was it. The chest of drawers was gone. The small Edwardian desk, handcrafted in 1878 just one county over, was gone. The laptop that had been perched upon it—gone. Noel felt his heart hit his throat, and he was no longer able to breathe. He sat down on the edge of the bed, holding his chest, gasping. This can't be happening. All those pieces, gone. All that money...gone. Automatically, he reached for his cell phone. The first five numbers to a London address were keyed in, but he cancelled the call. The phone trembled in his hand, and his breath came in ragged gasps.

* * * *

Noel Rigg burst from his traditional Georgian home with its canvas painting backdrop of Cumbrian hills, and waddled his portly ass down the picturesque streets until he came to the tiny offices of the local constabulary. Unfortunately, the effort expended to carry considerably more than two hundred pounds of loose fat and gristle across three blocks left Barrister Rigg with no air left with which to explain his predicament. He stood on the step, bent at the waist wheezing, with one hand holding the stitch in his side and the other braced for support against the door. It took him a full minute before he could compose himself.

Inside the office the lone occupant, Community Support Officer Phoebe Clark rattled hard candy around in her mouth and read an article she'd contributed to the Ambleside monthly newsletter. It concerned a crew of teenagers who had been tossing rocks at the occupants of the green, almost hitting one. She'd resolved the situation, in fact, by encouraging the offenders to clean up the green prior to the next bowling event. There was a rumor, floating around the neighborhood, hinting at a certificate of commendation from the town council, with her name on it. Wouldn't that be special! She'd trot it out just before Christmas, all framed in black, and place it on the mantel between her and her mother Jeanne's Christmas stockings. Her eyes closed, picturing her mother's look of approbation. Her ponderings were interrupted by the pop-eyed gaze of a wheezing, red-faced Noel Rigg.

"Mr. Rigg. How may I be of assistance? You look like you could use a glass of water."

"I've been bloody burglarized! Somebody's made off with the contents of my house." He sat down, charged his lungs and began again. "I've just got back from away, only to find my house empty of all its possessions. You must do something immediately." He slumped in his chair, certain of the tiny stirrings of a heart attack, or perhaps a massive aneurism emanating from deep within his brain. Or his chest, he couldn't be certain.

The benign happiness that was characteristic of Officer Phoebe Clark washed away from her face, to be replaced by a look of utmost concern. "Goodness!" she said, applying exactly the wrong word for the occasion. Out came a notepad from the top drawer of her desk. She rose up. "Shall we go have a look?" Rigg trailed in her wake, out the door and up the street.

* * * *

Noel Rigg could almost hear the reassuring tones of Officer Clark bouncing off his now-empty walls. She'd said all the right things, prior to abandoning him to his thoughts: it was a small town, the neighbors had eyes and ears, someone would slip up, and England's Finest would be all over the perpetrators like dachshunds on badgers.

Noel Rigg did not, however, believe these reassurances for even a minute. There was one little fact he'd omitted from Officer Clark's report. There had been no mention of the tiny detail of his spare room having contained millions of pounds of stolen art and collectibles. And it certainly did not seem the time to offer up the name of his employer, the consortium that had charged him with the responsibility of brokering these goods. For a moment—just a tiny moment—he pondered the relative advantages of throwing himself off Mount Fairfield. But even within the timid and the unworthy, there can at times be straws at which to clutch.

Noel opened his briefcase and located his short directory of friends and acquaintances, and his extensive list of associates. Hidden among the latter list, he scrolled through dozens of names until he came across the one he prayed would save him. Attanasia. Gaia Attanasia. All of the big cheeses have fixers, don't they? And this fellow Gaia was a big cheese, and by extension, the biggest fixer of all, wasn't he? And, as an investor in the former contents of his room, this man Gaia would be interested in retrieving his property. He might, perhaps, wish his property back even more than in punishing Rigg for allowing it to slip away. No matter. He had no choice. He rang a New York City number and presented the situation, his desperate words bouncing off the walls of the hollow room.

* * * *

Sean Donovan exited the train from London at seven in the evening and headed for the nearest Ambleside pub, The Fox and Furrow. He sat in the corner, avoiding eye contact, becoming the invisible man, a tactic that had always kept him unremarkable and therefore safe. He'd arrived in London a day earlier, having two jobs to do. With the call from Gaia, a New York art dealer he couldn't trust, he'd felt confident he could fit a little reconnaissance mission into his embassy work. There'd be a pretty penny in the job, retrieving a piece of art from a private home in The Lake District. It wouldn't take but a minute, he felt certain. A quick, facile excuse and he was able to scoot off for a day in the country.

He'd visited Beth as the first order of business, after meeting his new team at the Canadian Embassy. Now this. He smiled into his beer at the thought of all three activities having one thing in common: adrenaline. Pruning vines and cleaning stainless steel vats were important parts of learning the wine trade, but did they send that jolt of electricity through his bones? No. It was equally true that any one of these three tasks would have sufficed to raise that frisson of excitement, but that wasn't how life works. "Feast or famine," he muttered.

The Fox and Furrow was beginning to fill up, and a patron had already cadged the unoccupied chair across the small table from Donovan, carrying it across the pub to join a group of university students. He took another sip of Guinness and located the Rigg house from his cell phone GPS. Three blocks away. Gaia had noted that the owner was a barrister, fat and balding, not very bright and probably wouldn't even notice the missing piece, given that it was housed in a room chock-a-block full of similar-looking pieces. Donovan had watched the door until a man bearing that description walked in, a forlorn look on his face. When the bartender caught the man's eye and called out his name, Donovan was pretty certain the Rigg estate was currently absent of its owner. It was time to go for a walk. He tossed back the rest of his beer and ambled out into the cool November air.

The house was lovely, in part because of its Georgian style and the hills that framed it, and also, for Donovan, because it sat a good distance between the street lights. This bit of good fortune complemented the fact that the owner hadn't bothered to turn on the stately, authentic-looking gas lamp at the gate. The solitary light within came from the downstairs hallway. By this, and having seen the owner a minute earlier, Donovan gathered the house was unoccupied.

After glancing at the neighbors to see who may be watching, he walked up the path and rang the doorbell. There being no response from man nor dog, he jimmied the lock and entered.

The house was quiet, undisturbed by clocks or appliances. The parlor to the left was emptied of furniture. Odd. Donovan moved through the house, took the stairs two at a time and headed down the hall to the room identified by Gaia. He pushed the door open and cast a thin line of light across the floor with his flashlight.

Nothing.

He pulled the door shut and peered into the remaining four rooms flanking the hall railing.

Not a damn thing.

Not only had the artwork disappeared, but other than a garish painted bed in the master bedroom, there didn't appear to be any furniture anywhere. Had Rigg done a runner? Was the man at the pub a doppelganger and he was in fact in Argentina with the artwork? Or was there some other explanation? There wasn't time to ponder the state of the house, because one of the ground level windows at the back of the house was currently being slid open. He hurried down the stairs and stood in the shadows, watching a slender person throw a leg over the sill and roll to the floor with a deep exhalation.

"Not the most graceful entrance I've ever seen." Donovan stepped out of the shadows to stand a couple of yards away from the young man.

"You're a few days late, from the look of things. There's nothing left to take but a god-awful sleigh bed."

The youth jumped up, fumbling for his denim jacket pocket. "I-I've got a knife."

"No, you don't."

"I fokkin' do."

"No, you don't. If you did, it'd be out by now. Or, you'd be walking toward me, instead of slinking away. So, next time, yell at me to not fucking move or you'll cut me good. As you say it, walk toward me as if you were going to cut my balls off. Maybe make a low moaning noise, as if you were a little crazy. But don't worry. You'll do much better next time, I'm sure. What's your name?"

"None of your fokkin' business." He spat on the floor, rolling the sleeves of his jacket up past the wrists.

Donovan smiled. "Now, if you'd showed that attitude as you came up from under the window, you'd have been a much more dangerous-looking dude."

"Fuck off. So, what d'ya want from me?"

"I want to know why you picked this house. And I want to know why it's empty."

"Mr. Rigg is a friend of mine. I was just coming in to get something I'd left behind."

He looked at the boy, noticing the lack of flesh under the pale skin at the wrist and throat. It might be the metabolism of youth, but more likely the boy was hungry, and had been hungry for some time. Were there homeless people in the beautiful Lakes District? There are homeless people everywhere.

He thought of his father, beating him and his brother and sisters until Donovan's departure at sixteen. He wondered if this was perhaps how he'd looked at that age. What is it about parents that permitted some of them to forget their role as, well, guardians? He sighed. "Okay, let's say for some reason that you and our man Noel are best buddies. What's with the kitchen window? I hear there's a perfectly usable front door, just behind me and down the hall."

"He doesn't want me to—I don't use the front door. I only visit him…at times. He pays me to do, erm, odd jobs. He owes me a few quid and I came to see if he'd left it."

"I see. Perhaps he left it on his imaginary dresser in his imaginary furnished bedroom, eh?" *He's paying the boy for sex. Jesus Christ.* "Okay, forget about that for now. Tell me this. Where did the contents of the house go? Did Rigg get rid of it?"

"No. He went away for the weekend and after he took the train, a moving lorry with Manchester plates pulled up and cleaned it all out. I was goin' ter ask one of the movers, but they looked sketchy, so I held off. I should have told someone, but who'd believe someone like me?"

"Why d'you want to know who nicked the stuff?"

He could see from the boy's body language he'd decided to close up. Donovan reached for his wallet, withdrew a few bills and placed them on the floor, halfway between them. "Just another couple of questions. What was on the side of the truck; logos, names, that kind of thing? And are you sure they were Manchester plates? This is my last question: are you positive Rigg didn't know about this move?"

"Nah, he didn't know owt about it. I was watching him when he came home. He tore out of the house, straight for the peelers as soon as he got back. As for the lorry, they were definitely Manchester license plates. I used to live there, so I took note. As for signs, the side said Peterson's Freight, with a, some kind of swirly whirlwind where the 's' shoulda been."

"Like a cyclone or a tornado?" He made a mental note to look up the owner of Peterson's Freight.

"That's right." The boy hadn't taken his eyes off the floor where the bills rested. "Those mine now?" He was already reaching for them.

"Son?"

"I'm not yer fokkin' son." The response was automatic, devoid of animosity. Donovan ignored it, and continued.

"I'm not a very nice man, and I like my privacy. Since you haven't actually seen me do anything wrong, and since I haven't killed you yet," the boy's eyes widened at that, "an extremely healthy thing for you to do is forget you ever saw me. There's no reason to mention my appearance or to make eye contact with me if you see me on the street. Got it? I'm trouble, but only if you talk about me to Rigg or any stranger who might stop by here. This is clear, right?"

"For a few extra quid…" The youth's eyes looked hopeful.

"Don't even. And don't make me come find you, because I would. It won't be fun." With that, he left the boy standing by the open window and returned to catch the train back to London.

CHAPTER EIGHT

London to Manchester

GEMMA TRASK'S FLAT IN QUEENS Park was small, even by metropolitan London standards. It contained a single bedroom, a kitchen area within the parlor, a bathroom with a shower humorously described in the rental ad as 'intimate'—no tub—and a storage cubby. With no visible clutter, it was efficient and tidy. She'd stripped away all evidence of wallpaper and painted every vertical surface pale blue and every ceiling as white as she could find. As soon as she'd discovered computer tablets, she'd bought one and got rid of every book she owned, as well as her television. There were more austere residences than hers, but not many.

Jonny sat alone in the parlor, watching a comedy on her tablet. He raised his head as the episode ended. "Gem? Any chance you'll be done soon? I'll have to go to work in a couple of hours."

She lowered the papers from her file and made a face he couldn't see from the other room. "Sorry, Jonny. Look, this is taking longer than I thought. My colleagues need answers tomorrow, first thing. I don't think today's going to work out. I've got to go to Manchester and I need to take this with me. I'm really sorry about that. Come in and we'll cuddle for a minute. I'll try to make it up to you." She heard him leave the chesterfield, and followed the tread of his footsteps to, and then out the door of her flat. She listened as the door clicked. With a sigh, she pushed a spike of blonde hair away from her eyes and picked up the file. "Another one bites the dust."

Twenty minutes later, the phone buzzed in her lap. "Donovan here. I'm still in London, but I'm grabbing the next train to Manchester."

"Ah. Manchester. So you heard that's where our shooter might have come from. Where's Miller? Is he going with you?" *Don't be sensitive. Just hear him out.*

"No. He's still working on spreadsheets. Anyway, here's the thing. I've got to go to Manchester. Are you going to be...?"

Gemma completed his sentence. "Am I going to be all right alone in big, bad London without you?"

There was no annoyance in his voice, and she wondered if her sarcasm traveled over phone lines. "Well, sort of. I think if I looked around, I might dig up a lead or something to help us get everything wrapped up."

"You think you can do it yourself?" She bit her tongue, realizing by the pause after her words, that he caught the second bout of sarcasm. *Why do I do that?*

Donovan's voice was patient. "Look. I'm just now getting the hang of working with others, and I know I don't always do things in the right order. But I think you can help here. I'm not your boss, so I don't tell you what to drop and what to pick up. Do as you like."

"Right." It came out as a mutter.

"Gemma."

"Yes?"

"I think this might be a bit more complicated than we'd hoped." He rang off and she took another sip of wine, staring at the pale blue wall in front of her. *Why on earth do I do this to myself, every time? Am I so insecure I have to question the ulterior motives of everyone I chat with?* She thought about her relationship with her mother. There'd always been friction. Up until her sudden passing, mother could do nothing right in daughter's eyes, and daughter could do nothing right in mother's eyes.

Enough. Today's the day I quit feeling sorry for myself and start putting a better foot forward. I'll get on with these Canadian bastards if it kills me, starting now. Perhaps I'll go to Manchester after all.

* * * *

Next morning, Sean Donovan left an impromptu meeting at Canada House, heading to the nearest tube. He'd arrived back in London well before midnight the night before. Beth had waited supper and they ate a modest meal, chatted for a few minutes and gone to bed. In the morning, they went separate ways, with Beth meeting Rory at MacDonald House while Donovan got together with Jack at their office in Canada House.

The team learned several facts, each one pointing the investigation toward a particular English city. He exited the tube near Victoria Station and caught the next train to Manchester. The city was close enough to get there that afternoon, but far enough he'd have to find a place to stay that evening. He withdrew his cell phone to give Beth a call.

From the corner of his eye, he noticed a familiar figure gliding toward him. Detective Gemma Trask slipped into the seat beside him. "Canada House belongs to Canada, but bloody Manchester, well, I may know a thing or two about that town." She unwrapped a long gray scarf, tossing in on the seat between them.

Donovan had to smile in spite of himself. "I thought you loved London too much to leave her." He put down the paper he'd opened. "I have to be honest, Detective, I'm not used to working on a team, so it never occurred to me to invite you along. But I'm glad you're here." He explained his approach, inviting his new companion to take whichever part of the attack plan she wished. By the time the train rolled into Piccadilly Train Station in Manchester, Donovan knew considerably more about Gemma's career but little to nothing about how she'd been chosen to work on the Canadian case. Or anything about her personal life, for that matter. It felt very much like he had been steered away from certain personal areas. It seemed worth the small effort it would take to look into Gemma's life. Just a bit.

From the station, they grabbed a cab and traveled along the A6 to Central Park Northampton Road, just off Oldham Road. Once Gemma dropped a name to the desk sergeant, the chief inspector at the police station was able to see them right away. They walked into an office that had apparently been hit by a hurricane. It was challenging to see the top of Chief Inspector David Singh's head for the myriad papers, files and documents. He made a cursory attempt at straightening the papers up, but there was no hope and certainly no visible improvement. Abandoning the effort, he invited them to the break room for a cup of tea and a chat.

Gemma took a minute to apprise the inspector of the main elements of the case, finishing the briefing by explaining they were searching Manchester for information on the man who had murdered the trade director at Canada House.

"So, you think he might be from Manchester?" Singh took a sip of tea.

"A resident, yes. Possibly of Canadian nationality or origin. And we were hoping to read your case files and review any calls from the past week. We'd be interested in anything relating to folks who haven't returned home from a visit, houses no longer seeming to be occupied, that sort of thing."

David frowned. "Manchester's a big city, with lots of comings and goings. It could take a bit of time."

Gemma replied with a hard look. "We're prepared to take the time."

Donovan spoke up. "Here's the thing, Inspector. The man's identity will appear, sooner or later. Our concern is around this identity. Why did he hide it if he was going to shoot himself anyway? So, we're trying to get to the bottom of it, perhaps sooner than the mystery man would have wished. We don't know what's been hidden, but we suspect time is not on our side."

"That makes sense. How can we help, besides making our files available to you?"

Gemma leaned toward the table. "I'm glad you asked. Give us the transcripts of all reports for the past four days, and, say, one staff to work with us on them." She looked apologetic. "We would like to get started now, as in, this minute. It's presumptuous, I know, but as we said…"

"I know. Time is not on your side. Right, then. I'll get you three desks with computers connected to our server." He glanced at the clock. "Four thirty. We're in the middle of a shift change, so I'll snatch up one of the constables just coming on. He's supposed to be working car thefts, but he'll be pleased at the change in routine, I'm certain of it. Give us a mo." David left them to sip tea and wait.

A minute later, he returned with a man in uniform who was clearly too young to have seen much of life from behind a badge. "Gentleman, this is Constable Bryan Robertson. He looks young, but he's cracked three major cases this year and we're barely outside of October. Bit of a computer whiz, not that you'll necessarily need it for this job. Constable Robertson will show you to your desks and get you started."

Donovan and Robertson chose to scroll through the computer screens, whereas Gemma grabbed an inch-thick wad of computer spreadsheets. It took them an hour to weave their way through the possibilities and clear off the rejects. Gemma raised a manicured eyebrow at the young constable. "Might I have an update, please?"

"Ma'am, I have four possibilities, with two a bit more likely than the others. Two male teenagers presumed to have run away. One man, aged thirty, disappeared after a domestic dispute, and one abandoned house. That last one was rung in by a neighbor. That's it; that's all."

"Donovan?"

"I'm interested in just the one. An abandoned house in the north of the city. Wife overseas. Husband disappeared the day of the murder. I'll check that one out. I have a feeling. What did you find in the paperwork?"

"Just the one as well. I'm not too optimistic."

"Sirs?" The constable had raised a hand, as if in school. "You say time is of the essence. I've only just come on my shift. I was thinking… my uniform might come in handy, if you needed to wade through the four best possibilities this evening, with a minimal amount of explaining. Might I accompany you? I know the city and I have a vehicle at your disposal."

Gemma looked at Donovan. Neither wanted the company, yet both saw the advantage of mobile and uniformed support. After a moment, Gemma nodded. "Yes. Thanks. Go ask the Chief Inspector if he can spare you."

While Roberson was out of the hearing, Donovan asked if they should split up.

"You want the abandoned house, don't you? Rotter! Right, then. I'll take the Whiz Kid and three possibilities, and you can go your own way." Gemma smiled. "Pretty sure you won the draw, are you? Off you go, then. I'll wait for Baby-Face."

* * * *

Donovan took a taxi to the edge of Ardwick ward, getting out onto a street a short walk from the much wealthier City Center. He paid the cabbie and stood staring at the rows of unkempt red-brick tenement houses on the one side, with the nondescript, 1940s-styled homes raising the neighborhood standards on the other. He thought of his own upbringing, and knew from experience what the interiors of these tenements looked, felt, and smelled like. Turning, he walked toward a gray house with a rusty, wrought iron fence, covered for the most part by an untamed holly bush.

He paused before the gate latch, taking a moment to check each of the windows for movement.

"The fok you want?" The holly bush appeared to be talking to him.

"I beg your pardon?" He pulled a sprig of the thorny vegetation away and stared into the eyes of a grubby preteen girl. A curl of cigarette smoke wafted around her, and she didn't bother to get up.

"I said, what ya want? Are you dense or somefing?"

Assuming the tone adults use on children, Donovan began. "You know, that's not the language one uses to get on my good side."

This elicited a sneer. "Why on erf do I wanna get on your side? As if."

"It might be worth five quid."

"You pervie?" She pushed blonde, rosebush hair out of delft blue eyes. The open, curious look on her face revealed no fear whatsoever.

"I won't come near you. I just want a little information. Let's start with you telling me who lives in this house." He pointed to the modest, two-story Georgian building sitting behind the girl.

"A fiver for that?" She looked doubtful.

"No. A fiver for all my questions. Who lives there, how many, when was the last time you saw any of them, is there anyone at home now? That kind of information'll get you a fiver."

"You sound funny. American, are you?"

"No. What about my answers?"

She shrugged. "Ellie and Jess Campbell. They used to be Canadians. Ellie went away on a trip a fortnight ago and Mister Campbell went away…" she pondered a moment, "…maybe four days ago. Ain't anyone in the house, now. You can look if you like. No one 'ere to say you can't." She took a final drag off her cigarette, stamping it out with the heel of her running shoe.

"Any children?"

"No. Just me." The little girl's sing-songy voice went small. "Ellie used to make me tea, make me go to school. But she ain't been 'round. I dunno where she's got. D'ya think you could find them?" He could hear the wistfulness in her voice.

Donovan's voice softened in kind. "Where do you live?" The little girl with the blonde, rosebush hair pointed away from City Center, toward one of the massive, red-bricked tenement houses. He noted the sun had gone down and a chill had sprung up in the fall air. "Sweetie, would you like to earn another fiver?" Her eyes widened and she nodded, just a bit.

"All you have to do is stay where you are for a few minutes, and keep an eye on the street. If someone comes along, just sing out 'Tea-time, Mary.' Can you do that?" A pair of five pound notes floated over the holly bush to land at her feet.

He let himself through the gate and strode up to the walkway to the door, picking the lock without hesitation. On his way through the door, he emptied the postman's box and retrieved a fistful of bills and advertisements. He stepped in, went left, to the parlor, and opened the window closest to the little girl, to hear her better. Once set up, he crossed over to the kitchen table, looking for mail. There were another couple of unopened bills and one letter lying unattended beside its envelope. The letterhead advised that the correspondence had originated from the Trade Directorate, Canadian Embassy. Donovan sighed, reading the single page without touching it.

After a moment, he stepped back outside, and spoke with the 'tween. "Excuse me, Sweetie. What's your name?"

"It's Lexie Anderssen. Did you suss out where Ellie and Jess went to?"

"Not yet. You can go home, now. I'll probably be back here tomorrow. Maybe I'll see you around, Lexie. I expect I'll have more questions. But I'm calling the police, so you should go home now. If your mom asks where the money came from, you can tell her a policeman gave it to you as a reward."

This counsel garnered him another sneer. "My ma will get nowt of it. This'll last me a week, I reckon. I better go now." Her full, red lips were drawn to a thin line, and her eyes were narrowed, defiant.

Donovan re-entered the house and called Gemma, giving her the address and then sat down to wait. He nudged the letter around with the back of his fingernail and read it through twice.

* * * *

Robertson, the young constable from Manchester waited outside for his colleagues. Gemma Trask stood beside the table in the kitchen, under the light. A slender index finger jabbed at the letter addressed to Mr. Jess Campbell from External Affairs Canada, and then waggled in the general direction of the envelope that had carried it. "Ernest Hemingway once wrote a six-word short story. Saddest bloody story I ever read. This one comes a close second." She sat down on the edge of a kitchen chair and glanced at Donovan, who was staring up the street, in the general direction of police headquarters.

"I think we can put two and two together here. The gentleman gets a letter from government saying that his wife, who'd travelled to Romania to follow up on a failed potato contract she'd signed, was murdered. Then, it advised, despite refusing to go to check up on things on her company's behalf, the government was taking no responsibility for this, since they hadn't encouraged her to go."

She stood up, again, rubbing her hands on her arms to warm them. "But, the letter goes on to state that, again, it wasn't the government's problem if the potatoes got held up and rotted at the border. And it finishes with: 'Please accept our condolences.' I'm pretty sure if that's what went down, I might have been tempted to gun the rotter down in his 'Please accept our condolences' office as well. God. Damn."

Donovan turned back to the window, to watch the boy-constable who'd chosen to remain outside to wait for the forensics team. "There's one thing left that's bugging me."

"I know."

"Why did he erase his identity, in the short run? It only delayed things by, what, three days? Why would three days matter to three dead people? I think we need to figure that part out. And, I think we only have a few layers peeled back on this onion."

Gemma muttered. "I never liked onions, of the real or the metaphorical variety. Both kinds stink, in my opinion. So, we still have a case, then."

"Yes. Let's get Jack up here, unless he's peeling off another layer of his own onion, back in London."

CHAPTER NINE

London to Manchester

THE THREE INVESTIGATORS MET AT The Waterhouse, a clean, red brick tavern off Princess Street in Manchester. Gemma chose it because it had small rooms, and she felt they'd have a bit more privacy, it being noon. Donovan ordered water with his fish and baked potato, Jack ordered a steak and a pint of Guinness, the latter he studiously ignored through his meal. Gemma wanted to order a vodka cooler, but instead asked for water with a chicken Caesar salad. They sat beside a window overlooking a couple of chilly, forlorn patio tables on the sidewalk.

Gemma began. "I'll go first, since it was my people who honed in on Manchester. This is what I've got so far."

She leaned in to rest her elbows on the table, good manners be damned. The food hadn't arrived and her left arm ached above her elbow. "As you know, we found the shops not far from here, in the Piccadilly Shopping area. It's improbable the man—Campbell, was it?—came up here to shop for clothes, so it was dead-easy to conclude this was his home.

"I really don't have much to add, beyond that. I guess I'll take credit for leading you to Manchester and nothing more."

"Excellent. You pointed us here. That's the main thing." Jack's left hand reached for the pint, resting on it for a moment, but made no effort to hoist it. "I found out that Campbell's wife was involved in a potato importing contract that went down the toilet. The two-million-dollar shipment rotted on the boat, held up by Customs so the client couldn't take possession and the shipper couldn't retrieve it. Normally, shipping boats are climate-controlled, so I don't know how in hell the potatoes rotted. Anyway, the payment was made and then held by the Romanian government. When she headed to the port at Constanta to resolve things three weeks ago, she walked into a shit-storm. The Romanian client, or someone, it's not clear, shot her on the spot. Nothing in the files suggests that Canadian officials accompanied her, warned her, or in any other manner supported her through all this. She walked straight into a gun barrel. The guy is in custody, but that doesn't bring the wife back. And the insult to injury is our dead director mailed her husband what amounts to a fuck-off letter, disavowing his shop of any responsibility."

Gemma made a face. "Not cricket, that. So, Mr. Campbell receives the letter and heads for London. But not immediately."

Jack looked to Donovan, who picked up the tale at that point. "This is what you don't know. Ellie and Jess Campbell are Canadians. He worked here for City Parks as a rec director. She had a small, as in: no staff, brokerage company that imports crops from Canada and acts as a middle-man to resell them to Euro countries. All the risk fell on her, and all related labor was contracted out, so, no one on the payroll but her.

"Our Mr. Gross, International Trade director, carried the file for Ms. Campbell. He'd done so a year earlier, for a much smaller contract. This time, though, as soon as there were complications, he seemed to bail. I—we should speak with the ambassador to get a clearer picture of all this. But the files sure tell a specific story.

"And then there's the family life. They have no children and it seems, nothing much back in Canada in the way of relatives." He took a sip of water. "However, it looks like there's a kid involved after all. Her name's Lexie and she lives in the social housing projects across the street. A preteen smart ass." He found himself grinning in spite of his words.

Gemma spoke up. "What's the connection? Illegitimate child?"

"No. At least, I don't believe so. I think they adopted her as a sort of stray pup, you know? Shows up one day and keeps coming back as long as the food keeps coming."

"And how is this relevant, do you suppose? I see the tragedy, but in terms of Campbell's delay in going to London…"

"No clue." Donovan smiled a tight grin. "This is why we've channeled the power that is New Scotland Yard, to figure all this out. But all of our see-it-with-my-own-eyes witnesses are dead. I know that. If all we have is a little, non-related girl, it is what it is. I was thinking one of us could hang around the house this afternoon with a few chocolate bars on hand, and ask whatever questions we can possibly think of, to whoever shows up. In the meantime, one of us has to get hold of the ambassador or Beth McLean and get them up to speed before the press puts two and two together and blindsides them. What else is there to do?"

Gemma nodded her head toward the approaching server, and the table went quiet for a moment. She looked at the steam wafting up from the food. "Gentlemen, I am starved. But after I eat, I reckon I'll commandeer some local constables to check phone records, recent visitors to the Campbell house, witnesses who may have seen him leave for London, verify who are the next-of-kin, things like that. Got to be done. I'll assign the work, and then I'm heading back to London. I think I'm tidied up here, for the moment."

"There was a delay after Campbell received the letter. Then, there was a second delay he created by obscuring his identity. These delays may well have been grief. Or planning. But we won't know if we don't check it out. I guess I'll go hang around the house for a few hours. What do you think, Gemma?" Donovan kept his gaze on her.

"You tell us if you find anything at the Campbell house. I guess I'll head back to London, have a chat with Ambassador Thompson, tell him we all deserve a raise." She smiled a quick grin at her joke, and then was back to business. "I agree it's best to keep that Comms Director of yours in the know."

Jack nodded toward Donovan, a forkful of steak dangling. "Can't be easy, keeping the press at bay, especially the London press." He glanced at Gemma, to see if she was being sensitive about that, but she was nodding, lips pursed. "Right, then. Let's enjoy a good meal and go push this investigation along. If either of you think up something else for me to do in London, just give me a shout. Otherwise, I'll get back to the reports, I'll see Gemma tomorrow and you shortly after, right? Now, let's see what old-world cuisine is like." This time, he didn't bother to see if Gemma took offense, he just waded into his steak.

* * * *

Noel Rigg returned to his Ambleside home to think things through. He walked into his sitting room and was surprised yet again at the notion there was nothing on which to sit. He wandered through various rooms until he found himself in the bedroom. Why did they leave this behind? He was fond of his bed, having twice shipped it across the Atlantic. It was an oversized sleigh bed, originally stained mahogany, but he'd had it painted Chinese lacquer red, on a whim. He took possession of the edge.

It hadn't yet occurred to him his furniture must be replaced, not to mention the locks. He didn't want to think about it. In fact, he wished its arrival, tenure and mysterious departure had never happened. But every scintilla of his attention was pointed straight toward the room down the hall; the room devoid of everything but the dusty outlines of the boxes that had been stored there these past two months. Was this enough to get him killed? He pictured the alley beside the pub he'd been to for lunch. He saw himself lying on the greasy asphalt, between the garbage bins and the emptied lettuce crates. His cream business suit was desecrated by rat droppings and gravy stains, and his face had that sad, martyred look one sees on stained glass windows. Or perhaps the housekeeping company would come by on Friday and find him in bed, his throat slit, the top sheet now matching the red lacquered headboard. He shuddered and stood.

What was going to happen now? He thought of his long distance employer, the Omega Group consortium machine, and the tiny cog that he was. He'd heard The Omega Group was headed by a score of tycoons, none of whom was worth less than a hundred million pounds. But it wasn't about the money. He'd once heard a mid-level leader chastising one of his staff: "If you have to choose between money and power, always choose power. The money well can dry up, but power will always get you a first-class ticket back onto the money train." He shivered. With any luck at all, they'd think of his role as worth more than the bother of replacing him.

A second inspection of the storage room at the end of the hall revealed nothing new. The constable hadn't mentioned dusting anything for prints, but he avoided touching doorknobs, countertops or anything that his considerable knowledge of television might suggest contained fingerprints. Heading downstairs, he found one of the two kitchen stools thrown into a corner, returned it to the island and sat on it. The wonky one. Bastard! But it held him up, so he ignored its wobbly flaws.

What could he do to get his things back? Well, insurance would get him replacement furniture and appliances. He was primarily focused on getting back the consortium's things. He had two choices, neither of them attractive. He could somehow help the police find the perpetrators, or he could sit on his hands, waiting for Gaia's agents to do the work for him. In the scenario involving the police, he was at a complete loss as to what he could possibly say without winding up in Wakefield Prison. So, no luck there. In the second case, he was putting all of his eggs, indeed his life, in the hands of one of the leaders—a rich, powerful, ruthless stranger —who he had no doubt was capable of resolving anything and use any means that suited him. Rigg threw up his hands. He'd check with the constable in the morning, see if anything new had transpired.

And he'd await the arrival of Gaia's man, who would either save him, or murder him. He had no illusions about either extreme being a possibility.

CHAPTER TEN

Manchester

GEMMA DROPPED DONOVAN AT THE compact Campbell house across from the projects. He watched her continue on to the police station, and then turned his attention toward the property. He peered into the holly bush on his way past, but Lexie wasn't in hiding. A quick look around the back of the house and garden yielded nothing so he went in, this time with a key provided by Manchester's Finest.

The police had been searching the house all morning for anything that might offer more insight into the murder-suicide. As a consequence, Donovan didn't expect to find anything relevant. Still, a look around wouldn't hurt. He started up the narrow stairwell to the second story. Everything looked normal, as far as his understanding of married couples went, which wasn't extensive. His parents were so dysfunctional, he certainly couldn't use them as a template for, well, anything. A quick walkabout revealed the computer had been seized, together with the incriminating letter and most of Ms. Campbell's business documents. Not much else had changed since his previous visit.

While in the master bedroom, he opened the drapes to see if he could spot Lexie. He didn't see her, but his hand brushed against something cold resting on the sill. A cell phone. He powered it up and, while the battery was low, it still operated. It wasn't locked, so he looked around. The contact history was there. He noted several calls to London with the same prefix as Beth's office number. He suspected they were for Ian Gross.

There were also numerous calls to and from Ellie Campbell's cell phone. These calls had stopped three weeks ago. He felt a pang at that. Years ago he'd made a few calls to a colleague on a snowy morning. He found out later that the man had died in a car crash; he'd been calling a dead man. He felt a small touch of pain at the thought of what it must have been like, for Jess Campbell trying to raise his wife in Romania, only to find she'd already been murdered. The phone died in his hand. *Appropriate, I guess.* He rooted around, found the charger and plugged it in.

There was one other number that appeared to warrant investigation. It was a local call—no name identified—that Campbell received, on that last morning he went to London. Having consigned the number to memory, Donovan pocketed the phone. He'd noticed movement on the sidewalk beside the gate. Company was calling. He moved downstairs to greet his visitors.

"You must be Lexie's mom." The woman was tall, almost his height, with the dirty blonde, tell-tale rosebush hair of her daughter. She looked like Lexie, but grown-up. Her cheekbones were high and pronounced and she wore clothes that were dated, possibly from a used clothing bank. The garments were snug, revealing a person in excellent shape, if a little thin. Her face, beautiful at some point in the past, now showed those tiny traces of a life hard-earned. The woman's smile was nervous, and she had a tiny gap, between her front teeth. Her teeth, cheekbones, eyes and hair conspired to make her look Swedish.

"It's not that I must be, it's just that I am. May I come in?" The woman's accent was straight-up Manchester, and she was already moving past him, heading for the front room. "I suppose it would be forward of me to ask for a spot of tea."

"Yes, in the sense that this isn't my property, it's the scene of a police investigation and I have no idea where the tea is. What brings you here, Mrs. Johanssen?"

"It's not Mrs. My name is Anika. People call me Nikki. Yes, I heard about Mrs. Campbell, didn't I? It's a shame about Ellie. I didn't know her very well, but she'd taken a shine to my Lexie and that endeared her to me. Do you have any idea when Mr. Campbell will bring her remains home?"

Donovan was beginning to glean a picture of exactly how much the woman knew. He had no reason to disbelieve her, at this point. He was also learning a bit about her, as well. She had no trace of a Scandinavian accent, although she looked the part, and her daughter reflected these traits as well. But from it, he suspected Nikki may have had a previous husband from away, and they may have lived abroad for a time.

"We're still gathering information, at this point. My name is Sean Donovan. May I call you Nikki?" She nodded, and he continued. "As I said, we're still picking up the bits and pieces of this case. I'll be honest with you, there are holes in the story that we'd like to see filled in. For instance, we're curious as to who might have visited in the past week. And I was wondering, did you come by to see Mrs. Campbell, um, Ellie? Were you her friend?"

"As I said, we knew each other only through my daughter. A couple of months ago, Lexie stayed out too late and Ellie made her phone me to come get her. I made it a point to get to know them a bit, since it's impossible to keep track of my girl. She's very stubborn. Very independent." Donovan heard both exasperation and pride in her voice.

"Yes. I met her yesterday. She's charming and bright and maybe a little crude, like kids her age. So, you've come calling to see if Jess—Mr. Campbell—made it home from Romania?"

Nikki hedged. "Not…exactly. Well, yes and no. I received a call a few days ago, from Mr. Campbell. He said that I should be on the lookout for a small package that he ordered for me. He said I would be pleased when it arrived and to know that I deserved it. Does that sound peculiar to you? Because, the package can't be for me, but I have to inquire, you see. They didn't really know me very well. So, the reason I am here, sir, is to ask if it came here. He said it wouldn't take very long to arrive."

"And you have no idea what it is or where it's coming from?"

She shook her head. "I'm guessing it's a toy. I'm kind of hoping it's a computer of some kind. Lexie's very bright, but she's bored. She needs…things I just can't afford. But of course I'd be grateful for anything we can use as a reminder of Ellie. She was a very nice woman."

"Would you know what it might look like, if you came upon it? We could look around, as long as you don't touch anything."

Nikki sighed. "The problem is, I'd have no way of knowing what it looks like, because I don't know what it is. It would have to have my name on it for me to know it's actually for me."

Donovan shrugged. "Makes sense." He weighed the chances of her disturbing evidence, and then waved an arm at the house. "Why don't you have a look around? They really can't have you touching anything, but if you see your name on a package or whatever, point to it and I'll see if you can lay claim to it."

As soon as Nikki had rounded the corner to the other room, Donovan called Gemma. "Did I catch you at the station?"

"Yes, actually. I'm at a borrowed desk. What do you need?"

"Here's a phone number. Would you see if it can be traced? Secondly, if it can, I'd like you to come get me at the Campbell residence. Please dress in civilian clothes, the shabbier and more comfortable, the better. And Gemma? Bring a gun. We're going hunting." She said 'fifteen minutes' and then he heard her hang up without saying goodbye. Now, where was his houseguest?

* * * *

Nikki left shortly after the call. He noticed Lexie was waiting for her at the gate. The girl kept discerning eyes on Donovan all the while he spoke with her mother. It was as if she was trying to send him a message.

Or maybe trying to read him. Was he trustworthy? What did he have to offer, that she cared about? He knew he'd see her again, if he reappeared at the Campbell house tomorrow. What did she want? He'd find out.

Gemma's car pulled up in exactly a quarter of an hour. She got out and stood beside the driver's door, not offering to go up the walkway. She'd changed into skinny blue jeans, one knee presenting a two-inch horizontal gap of flesh. Up top, she wore a loose gray cardi over a tight T-shirt, and he saw a worn suede jacket thrown over the car seat. An old man's salt-and-pepper cap was pulled down over her head, so he could barely see the bottom of one blue eye and only a few wisps of blonde hair arguing their way out the sides.

She watched in amusement as he looked her up and down. "Will I do, 'til a better one comes along?"

"Fetching. What did you find from that number I gave you?"

"You might not be the safest bloke I've hung out with. That number's connected with a nasty piece of goods, from the heart of Ardwick, right over there." She pointed to the other side of the rows of brick housing. "He goes by the name Ace, as in: Ace of Spades, but his real name is Archie Hendricks. That would be from the Hendricks family. Three generations of crime, each one learning worse ways from the previous. They started with car theft, drugs, prostitution and it's been downhill ever since. The family's kept both the Manchester constabulary and Scotland Yard Gangs Division busy. We've managed to curtail much of the drug and car theft business, but lately they've added art theft and white collar crime like money laundering. That type of activity. They're a very unpleasant family."

"Manchester couldn't keep on top of them?"

"The opposite, more like. It's like digging a containment trench around a forest fire. You can certainly slow them down, but it's been a challenge, stopping them completely." She grabbed her jacket and they got into the car. She pulled away from the curb. "They employed this brilliant trick. Start the family business from a low-income neighborhood, never do any dirty work in that ward, and solve the occasional problem for the residents. You know, pay this one's rent, get that one's son a job. Make a telly appear at Christmastime. Robin bloody Hood. You wouldn't believe how much loyalty that buys."

"Does all the business happen out of the one house?"

"Nah. They've diversified, with warehouses in Moss Side, plus a couple of quasi-legitimate shops in the better wards. We cut the head off one snake and two more grow from the neck. I don't envy the lads here, I must say." She pointed to an intersection ahead. "If we turn left, we would be entering their neighborhood. They'll tag the car, the second we do that. Turn, or no?"

"Not yet. Let's pull over and you'll call him from here, if you don't mind. This is what I want you to say." His message took just a second, and Gemma nodded.

She took the phone, affecting an accent from North London. "Hullo, is this Ace, please? Brilliant. I'm calling about a friend of mine, Jess Campbell. You remember Jess, don't you? At any rate, I was wondering if the business you conducted with him recently 'as been completed. Oh. Right, then. I'll be there in a just a mo." She rang off, holding the cell phone in her lap. "He wants to see me. I couldn't read anything from his voice, so we'll be going in blind." He nodded, and she grimaced. "Well, this is all well and fine, but I'm calling the precinct to come looking for us in a half hour. That should give them time to find our corpses before we disappear off the face of the earth." She made another face at his grinning response.

Gemma eased the car around the corner and they crawled up the street. Three-quarters of the way, they spied a man, almost as round as he was tall, leaning against the entrance to a nondescript house. As the car approached, he butted out his cigarette and squeezed his hands in his pockets just as the first streetlights began to blink on.

The man's head was shaped like a bullet, shaved tight to the skin, with a flat nose and ears adding to the impression. His dark eyes were slits. His pants puddled on the ground on three sides around his work boots. Despite it being dank, early November, he wasn't wearing a jacket or overcoat, and his matted cardigan was open at the front. Once the car stopped, he stepped away from the building and waited, heels on the curb and toes in traffic.

Donovan had seen his kind many times before. One time, years ago, his father had brought home a man he identified as Ford, some barfly he'd met when drinking the family's grocery money. Ford smiled a lot when the family was looking at him, but his face became cold and expressionless when he wasn't putting on his act. Later that evening, teenage Donovan walked into his living room to see Ford groping his older sister, Mary. She made no sound, but tears coursed down her cheeks. The burly man put his smiley-mask on and asked Donovan where his father had got to. Mary rushed out of the room and Donovan followed without responding to the stranger. It amazed him, how powerless young people could be, and how adults—some adults—could be such...monsters.

He exited the car from the side closest to the man, while Gemma got out and stood peering over the hood, with her belly touching the outside mirror. Donovan nodded as he approached the large man. "You Mr. Hendricks?

The man leaned forward, just a bit, his smiling face a foot away from Donovan. He outweighed Donovan by more than a hundred pounds. "You don't sound English. Where d'you hail from?"

"Canada. You Hendricks?"

"Funny thing. It was a woman I was chatting with a moment ago, but here you are, taking charge. Are you in charge, Mr...?" His eyes flickered over to Gemma. "Are you from Canada, as well? Because, really, Dover Street is a very, very long way from St. Paul's and The Big Eye. You tourists might be, erm, off course."

Donovan brought his attention back. He spoke in a low voice, just loud enough to be heard. "I agree, but we'll be on our way shortly. It was a simple question my friend here asked you on the phone. Did you deliver the package that Jess Campbell requested? People are waiting for it."

"All in good time." He feigned puzzlement. "The curiosity for me is this. Why in bloody 'ell should I be bringing you up to date on an agreement I may or may not 'ave made with our Mr. Campbell? He could come and ask me himself." The smile he offered was sly, with little humor in it.

Donovan dropped his eyes to the sidewalk, his voice even lower. "You know why Mr. Campbell isn't here to discuss this. So it comes down to honor. Is there honor among thieving bastards, Hendricks? Not that Campbell was a thief."

The smile disappeared from the burly man. "I'd be very careful who I called a thief, Gov'nor. I like my chances of blowing you to hell, if you were to get on my bad side." He pulled his sweater back to reveal the butt handle of a pistol.

Hendricks heard two slight taps of metal on metal, coming from the direction of the car. Gemma had a police issue Glock 17 resting flat on the hood, just below the windshield. It was pointed at the man's ample midsection.

Donovan continued. "I have no idea why you're being so truculent, Ace. I asked a simple question about a package you promised to deliver. Today is Wednesday. Thursday seems like an excellent day to be delivering packages, doesn't it?"

It was Hendricks' turn to avert his eyes. "I suppose it could happen tomorrow."

"That sounds like a great idea. And this seems like an excellent time for us to be on our way, and you can have that dinner you so obviously need. Thank you for your time, sir." He turned his back, without hesitation, to get in the car. Gemma kept the Glock trained on her target until she was in the car and moving down Dover. Neither spoke until they rounded the corner.

"You've got balls, Donovan. I hope this was worth it. Let's go find a bar and you can tell me why you risked my life, and assure me it won't happen again without you actually telling me what you're up to."

CHAPTER ELEVEN

London

RCMP DETECTIVE JACK MILLER STOPPED studying spreadsheets and narrative reports to look up from the temporary desk in his temporary office at Canada House, in London. A pretty young woman in a navy business jacket and skirt stood at the door, a smile on her face and a cup of coffee in each hand. He waved her in.

"And who might you be?"

She strode over, set down one cup and shook his hand. "Hi, I'm Beth McLean, Communications Director here at the Embassy. I'm pleased to meet you. I was supposed to be at that meeting with you, the ambassador, Sean and...Detective Trask, but I had a press conference first thing. And frankly, we weren't sure what we were going to say to them about this. My job is the darndest thing: I stand up in front of the press, not telling them things I don't really know anyway, and then I follow up, not telling them things I only know bits and bobs about. I'll treasure the day when I can hold a press conference where I get to say things that are true and actually communicate something. At any rate, here I am now, introducing myself. How are things coming along?" She pulled up the closest chair and sat down.

"Well, something happens, and then you learn a bit. And then you learn a bit more." He took a sip. "This hits the spot." He waggled the cup at her, spilling a drop on the top document. "Actually, we now know who dunnit, as the detective novels say. A fella named Jess Campbell, from Manchester pulled the trigger. Our man Donovan figured that part out. We're working on the why, now."

The director smiled. "Donovan, eh? He saved my life, and my career, a few months back. I like him."

He watched her, half-expecting an elaboration of some sort, but it wasn't forthcoming.

Her follow-up came in the form of a question. "What else do we know?"

"We know that Jess and his wife Ellie are both dead, by gunshot, in two different countries. We do not know if the deaths are related. Not to dwell on our man Donovan, but he has…this way of looking at things. He sees things I don't necessarily see." Jack put his feet up on the opened, bottom drawer of his desk. "He found this little girl from the projects in Manchester, I have no clue where he dug her up. Next thing you know, he's chatting up the mother, who seems to have some sort of connection with our murderer. Now, how in hell did he find them? No one local saw the link."

Beth smiled. "The man does have resources to draw upon, not all of them…orthodox. But I'm on his side all the way. As I said, I owe him, big time."

Jack studied his coffee. "The girl—um, our person—from Scotland Yard is another one who's on the ball. She and Donovan visited Manchester's most notorious family last night. She was obliged to present a firearm to calm things down. That should make for an interesting visit, next time they call on that fella, Ace. But, they've got each other's back. It'll all work out. And again, we're not sure yet how the Hendricks gang figures into all this. We'll see."

Beth peered across the desk. "In the meantime, you're crunching numbers."

"Yeah." His eyes crinkled around the corners. "All through my career, I was a break-the-doors-down kind of cop, y'know? Run and gun.

And here I am, this past five years, morphed into a paper trail expert, cross-referencing spreadsheets. But there's a place for that, as well. For instance, look here." He pushed two heavily-marked reports across the desk with a meaty paw. "The wife owns a small import-export agronomy business. She takes supposedly high quality potatoes and ships them off to eastern European countries, pockets an honest day's pay for a hard day's work.

"Then one day, the shipment gets stranded at the border. We're talking big bucks here. The accusation was that the potatoes were rotten. But if you look at the date shipped, date of arrival at the border, and number of days quarantined in less than ideal storage conditions, if they weren't rotten on the date of arrival, they certainly were after sitting around for a month. She was fucked, pardon my French, right out of the gate.

"Here's the thing. If this case is merely about government red tape, then she just had a massive pile of bad luck kick her arse. But if someone, say, deliberately halted the shipment, we have a significantly messier scenario, wouldn't you say?"

Beth nodded, her face grim. "And what are the chances of that happening, and why? And if so, what are the chances you can track down the reason?"

Jack pointed a gnarled finger at her. "And that, Ms. McLean, is the sixty-four thousand dollar question. So, while our little firecracker Trask is pulling guns and cleaning up Manchester, I'll maybe put another few days into seeing if I can get to the bottom of the potato debacle. Everybody's got a job, right? And if my partners are full of piss and vinegar, well I'm happy to let 'em shoot bad guys. I'm not a big fan of bad guys." He spoke the last sentence to himself.

"Do you have any idea when Sean and Detective Trask are coming back to London?"

Jack put two and two together, offering her a full-on grin. "Oh, I expect he'll be back tonight. Tomorrow, at the latest."

She blushed, just the slightest bit. "Okay, thank you, Jack. If you want anything, give me a shout."

"Do you serve beer on break, here?"

Beth smiled, wagged her empty coffee cup at him and pulled the door closed behind her.

CHAPTER TWELVE

Manchester

SEAN DONOVAN AND GEMMA TRASK slid into a corner banquette in a restaurant on Canal Street, in the Northern Quarter. They had both ordered a glass of Rioja, but he cancelled the individual requests and asked to share a bottle. The walls were clad in aged oak, and the lights were so dim, it was a certainty some clients frequented the place for the anonymity. He noticed a couple of middle-aged men in the booth kitty-corner from them, eyes averted but feet brushing up against one another.

Gemma smiled. "It's going to take more than one bottle to get me drunk, mate. But it's a start." She wore an outfit similar to what she had on at Ace Hendricks' place. The jeans were snug against slender legs—darker indigo dyed denim and no tear this time—and she had a pair of brown leather riding boots whose uppers caught her just under the knee. She had a simple white blouse under her suede fall jacket, and her salt-and-pepper cap stayed in the car, leaving her short, blonde hair a little spikey. Donovan, in contrast, wore black dress pants, Blundstone boots and a cream cotton vee-neck sweater.

He didn't want to get off on the wrong note, so he steered the subject around to business. "I guess I owe you an explanation. Just like you, I'm trying to gather up a bunch of seemingly unrelated facts, and trying to make sense of it all. We have a murderer whose past doesn't seem to fit with that action. Yes, his wife was killed and part of the blame can be laid on Gross the director's shoulders. But most people wouldn't be driven to murder. Grief, certainly. Anger, probably. But a murderous rage? I'm not sure. So, I need to push a few buttons, and tease out a few more facts.

"I'm pretty sure Hendricks is pissed off at us right about now. He's a man used to running the show and we didn't let him do that." He leaned in, lowering his voice. "You're a cop and he'll have figured that out by now. Harming you will cause a shitstorm of grief to land in his lap. I did some homework on him, and based on that and what you've said about him, it seems his family always takes care of their neighbors and our hippie-mom Nikki is one of his neighbors. Or close enough. So, he would have delivered the package with or without me poking at him. As a non-cop and a non-neighbor, I'm the one he'll look to get revenge on, if anyone. He doesn't know me and it'll be a challenge finding out anything about me, at least in the short-term. So, we'll be okay for now."

"But, what are you after? I can't even see the connection between the Hendricks gang and the murder of a government worker in London. As a matter of fact, I'm beginning to think what we have may be all there is to understand, really." She sipped the wine, studying the deep red wine legs on the inside of the glass as they drained back into the bowl. "Bloke's wife gets killed, bloke kills the man he thinks caused it to happen. Couldn't it be that simple?" The restaurant was warming up, and she doffed her jacket, revealing a slender torso and long, lean legs. He couldn't help but admire how attractive she looked in the soft lights.

"It could be just like that. But if it isn't—if, for instance, someone encouraged or forced Campbell to pull the trigger, I'd like to know that. Anyway, I'll go see Miss Nikki to find out what was in the packet she received. As soon as I know, I'll head back to London. When are you leaving?"

The look on her face was calculating. He wondered if she wanted to help him see this through, or if, perhaps, she wanted to stay in Manchester. With him. Her reply answered the question.

"If I thought you needed my gun, I'd stay. Do you? I didn't reckon so. My plan was to go back today." She studied her watch. "Based on the time, I think I'll go back first train in the morning, and see what Jack's up to. Phone my room if you need a helping hand, would you? Now, what's for dinner?"

* * * *

Donovan thought about Gemma after they left the restaurant. She'd dressed up, but not to the nines, and although she appeared to be engaged in the conversation, it was clear this was a dinner between colleagues. He shrugged. *She treats me no differently than Jack. And that's as it should be. I think if I was in shit, I could count on her. Not that I want to find myself in shit.*

And then there was the tiny piece of information he'd failed to share with her. When he'd been right up in Hendricks' face, he'd tethered their phones, so that he could track the man on his own GPS. It was a simple enough procedure and the primary reason for annoying the man. And it could come in handy, knowing at some point where Ace was. He hailed a cab and recited Nikki's address to the cabbie, who sought confirmation through a wordless question in the mirror. Did the gentleman in the rear seat really want to be delivered there? Getting no response, he turned on the meter and headed for the part of a town having more than its fair share of bad luck and worse management.

The electronic pass at the building entrance was broken, so he let himself up to the third story, walked most of the length of the hall and stopped at 312. The door was pulled to, but not latched. He noted the wood around the latch was shredded, and reached into his boot top for the antique derringer he'd picked up on his first day in England.

He found Nikki sitting at the foot of her bed, weeping without making a sound. Lexie was curled up in the corner, arms around her knees, the mass of blonde curls shorn from her head and strewn across the lino floor. Equal parts rage and shame overcame him as he crossed over to the bed.

"Are you all right?" Nikki nodded, but he saw the blood across her sweater that had come from her nose and left ear. The top of her right hand was purple with bruising.

"Anything broken?"

"I don't think so. Maybe my nose. I couldn't stop them. One held me back while the other cut her hair off. Then they made her watch while the big one used…me for a…punching bag. A fresh stream of tears coursed down her cheeks. "What am I to do? What if they come back?"

"No, no, no." It was Lexie, rocking in the corner. "They said they'd… do things to us, next time. We have to go, Mom. We have to go."

"You're not staying here. Come on. Let's gather up the most important things and we'll go to London. Come on. I'll take you and Lexie to hospital first, if you like."

All hope had fled Nikki's eyes. "I have no money, not even for tea. I was hoping the packet from Jess and Ellie had a few quid in it, but there was no packet. I can't go to London, even to save my life." She raised her face to him. "You couldn't take Lexie with you, could you? I'd get a job and come get her as soon as I could?"

"No! We stay together or we go together. They'll kill you, Mommy." Fear escalated to terror in the little girl's rising voice.

Donovan sat on the bed, close to Lexie. "Nikki, you go wash up, see if anything's been broken. Lexie, you go sit on the edge of the tub, so your mom can keep an eye on you. As soon as you're both clean and changed, we'll grab a few necessities and then we're off to London. Okay. Go get cleaned up." He sat still for a moment, trying to quell his mortification at having been instrumental in causing this to happen.

Ten minutes later, they were in a cab, headed to Gemma's hotel room. Donovan called her from the car, explaining the situation. By the time they arrived, Gemma had requested room service and a tray of food and tea was laid out on the desk by the window. Ordering the mother and daughter to eat, Donovan took the inspector into the hall to lay out a course of action.

Gemma had two options. "There's a late train which puts us in Paddington at three in the morning. But let's go with a better course of action. I've booked a second room at the hotel here, near mine. They can get a night's sleep and we can all be off by half-six. What do you think?"

"Let's get the room." He handed her a wad of bills. "Here's a thousand pounds. Pay for the room and give the rest to the mother. I'll have more for her, once I get to London. Help her to understand that she's starting fresh, but she's not starting broke, okay?"

She hesitated. "Of course, I can do that, but if you're coming with us, you could give it to her as easily as I could. Unless…"

"I'm going out for a bit."

"Undertaking a little business, at ten o'clock in the evening? The kind of business that might get you killed?"

"I'm just going out for a beer. I'll see you on the train. I promise."

She rooted around in her purse, fishing out the compact Glock 17 he'd last seen across the hood of a car. "If this is fired in the commission of a crime, my career is over, Mr. Donovan. You will not use it to murder our Mr. Hendricks, and you will return it to my possession by oh-six hundred hours, do you understand me?"

"I'm just going out for a beer." He returned her stare, eyes flinty, and left without taking the gun.

* * * *

Assuring himself of the safety of the mother and daughter, he returned to his hotel room to pick up some tools, and ordered a cab to deliver him to the street before Dover, in Ardwick. As the car eased away from the curb, his mind traveled back to his youth, to numerous times witnessing his father beating his mother or his sisters. His forehead grew hot, and his eyes saw red at the memory of his powerlessness. But the trip allowed Donovan time to calm down, and a cold logic replaced blind rage. He thought of an approach he'd take, and sat back for the ride. The GPS tether on Hendricks' phone had come in handy, sooner rather than later. Ace was somewhere across the city. Once on the appropriate street,

Donovan wandered around the neighborhood, looking for access to Dover Street's back alley. He found it and worked his way, back door by back door, until he gauged himself to be at the Hendricks residence.

Slate roof, chipped brick walls, cobblestones slippery with the grease of at least four generations of back alley residents. He knelt, hunkered down between a matching pair of wrinkled dustbins. Scattered oblong shards of light filtered out of the occasional back building window, puddling on the board fences and abused trash bins. But there was no illumination from the back of the Hendricks house. Was anyone home? He wondered. Shrugging, he tried the latch and, finding it unwilling to open, jimmied the lock.

In he went.

An unoccupied house, one would think, is a quiet house. But if the goal is to be alone and unobtrusive, several kinds of noises spring up to contradict the common understanding of the house as an inanimate object. Boards, especially old boards creak at every change in temperature, and in November a heating system clicks and rattles. In this house, the grandfather clock in the hallway shouted out the passing of each second. But there didn't seem to be anyone human to hear these tentative sounds, with the exception of the intruder.

Donovan moved up the tight unlit staircase to the bedrooms. Every two feet his hand felt the seam where the sheets of wallpaper met. The house he had been raised in was covered floor to ceiling with wallpaper. He hated it. Wouldn't have it in any of his apartments.

He ignored the two smaller rooms and strode to the master, scanning the dowdy walls as he entered. A gilt shadow box next to the bed drew his attention. The plaque beneath it read: "Necklace worn by Her Majesty, Mary, Queen of Scots, Year of our Lord 1586." The zenith of the circle showcased an emerald, flanked by a half dozen rubies rising up either side. He thought for a moment. *That was the year before she was beheaded. What value might someone place on a memento like that, I wonder?* He dug into his backpack and took out an electronic sensor.

Passing it over the shadow box, he saw there was no reading. Not wired for security. *Careless.* He took the frame down from the wall and tore the back off, tossing the necklace and the corroborative document into his bag. Always good to establish provenance.

He looked at the remaining three walls. A deep, battered cabinet, not more than five feet tall stood guard in the corner. The face offered a dozen shallow drawers. He pulled the first open, and saw a dozen blueprints. The second drawer revealed the same type of content. Although they were unique, each invariably contained the same descriptor at the bottom right-hand corner: "Warehouse." With a set for each drawer, the blueprints represented warehouse plans for different parts of the city.

But storage buildings weren't what he was searching for. He looked at the wall to the right of the bulky cabinet. His eyes locked on a particularly tacky print of a dog. He lifted a corner and the metal edge of an old wall safe appeared. Setting the print aside, Donovan went to the bed stand, looking for an address book. There it was, in the top shelf.

With as much speed as he could muster, he went through the addresses. Under the Qs, he saw a number that didn't have enough digits to it to be a phone number. The combination. He'd read an article about the team of scientists who'd worked on the Atomic Bomb in Los Alamos. They'd been quarantined for months, and each had decided upon various hobbies to while away the time. One scientist, Richard Feynman chose the art of safecracking and, after six months, offered the theory that the easiest way to crack a safe was to exploit the frailties of humans, one of which was laziness. Folks like to write down their safe combination number in a handy place and keep it there, long after that number has been consigned to memory.

He was right. Donovan took the abbreviated phone number and used it to open the safe. A Phoenix wall safe, probably 1950s era. Its mouth opened without a sound. He reached in and pulled out twelve straps—more than a bundle—of hundred pound notes, a dark velvet bag of cut diamonds and a series of contracts. He set the documents aside to read later and pocketed the diamonds. The docs and money went into the backpack with the necklace. Time to go. He put the print back over the wall safe and straightened up the room.

Donovan slipped down, turned at the foot of the stairs and left through the kitchen door. He moved with no wasted time or effort, rectangular spokes of light lapping at his legs as he traversed the length of the back yard alleyways of Dover Street.

* * * *

Gemma was waiting for him, a pair of vodka and cranberry cocktail glasses sitting directly in front of her on the table. They were empty, and the one in her hand followed their status in a gulp. The top half of the one across the table was an ounce of alcohol swimming in melted ice. She pointed to his ruined drink. "You're late."

"Are they asleep?"

"I believe so. The little one is tough. Bright as a shiny penny, though. We'll get them set up with Family Services in London and they'll start again, I reckon. How'd you make out?"

"All right. I went out, had a beer and now I'm back. Nobody drowned and nobody died."

"What does that mean?"

"It's just a saying. I could use a drink, though." He called for two glasses of New Zealand pinot noir.

She looked at his backpack. "So, if I was to look in that bag, I wouldn't feel obliged to arrest you for anything?" She studied his face.

He held her eyes with an even gaze. "Gemma, you're a chief detective, right?" She nodded. "I understand that achievement to mean, since you're both smart and female, you're above average at what you do. So I have to ask, how do you suppose our professional relationship will go, if you push this?" His chin was tight, and neither blinked, as she pondered what he'd said.

"I reckon you wouldn't hang around long enough for me to fix anything I may break."

"It seems we understand each other very well. I've just bought you a drink and now I'll tell you half a story and you won't ask me the other half. And I'll begin by saying in all honesty that nothing I did this evening came anywhere close to affecting our case."

She said nothing, instead leaning over, as if to place a hand on his forearm, but then pulling it away. Gemma murmured as if to herself: "I'm sorry. I was worried about you. Right, then. Enough." Her hand returned to offer a little tap on his forearm and she pulled away once again.

"Okay. Let's talk about the girls upstairs, and then a bit about work. Will we all fit into your car or are we taking the train?"

"That was a Manchester forces ghost car, so it's the train for us. I gave Lexie my cap, which put her mind at ease about her looks. Nikki accepted your almost-thousand pounds and she promises to get her accreditation as a massotherapist back as soon as possible. Family Services will place her on a modest allowance as well and after that, it's up to her." The wine arrived and Gemma took a gulp and sank into the cushions.

"And now, work." Donovan slumped, laying his head back, to match hers, against the top of the chesterfield. "I don't know what else we can uncover in Manchester. Have you heard anything from Jack?"

Gemma nodded. "I got a text from him a few hours ago. There seems to be something up with the contracts coming out of Ian Gross's dossier. He says all of the correspondence from the Campbell file should have been scanned to the server directory, but when they did a match, one of the letters on the server didn't have a match in the cabinet. He set it aside and wants to chat about it, once we return."

"He thinks the mismatch is the document Campbell burned at the embassy? The interesting thing, I think, about that, is Campbell wouldn't necessarily be aware of the letter being backed up on a server. So he might think he'd got rid of the single copy."

"That's a good point. Jack also wants our opinion as to whether this case is closed, since we now know that Jess Campbell murdered Ian Gross." She studied his reaction. "I'm leaning toward calling it 'case closed', but you don't share my optimism, do you?" It was more a statement than a question.

He hesitated, mulling over what he was about to say, versus what he knew she wanted to hear. "I'm sorry. It seems to me there are more layers left to be peeled back. Hendricks seems to be lurking a bit too close to the principals in the case. It's still not clear to me why Campbell would go and kill himself, even if he did want to kill Gross. And we've got no satisfactory explanation for the delay between deciding to kill the director and actually pulling the trigger. But what really has me scratching my head is why Campbell would do anything with Hendricks? Why the mysterious packet for Nikki? Too many questions unanswered." He held his hands open, facing Gemma.

She ran a hand through her close-cropped hair. "I'm being foolish, trying to brush these off. The last thing I need is to be shown up by a couple of Canadians." She grinned. "Let's go home and see what Jack has to say. Okay, time for bed. Sleep tight." She downed the last sip of wine and was gone. Donovan lingered a few minutes longer, thinking things through.

A thought arrived, unannounced. With all of the activity taking place in three English cities, he'd completely forgotten about the possibility he would soon be the owner of a winery. Had Dieter and Anna made up their minds regarding the sale of Plenitude? Was it a yes or a no? Donovan threw up his hands and rose from the chesterfield. It was a discussion for another day.

CHAPTER THIRTEEN

London

BETH'S ARMS WERE FULL OF media releases as she rounded the corner and entered her office on the second floor at Canada House. She tilted in to bump Donovan's shoulder with hers as she circled the guest chair, stopping for a second to give him a peck. "Welcome back. You need a shave."

His eyes crinkled. "We sleep together for five seconds and you're telling me when to shave?"

"It depends, Sean. Want to sleep with me again?"

"Yes, please. Is now good for you?"

She rubbed his cheek. "Nope. Because someone needs a shave. You're very slow on the uptake today, honey."

He sighed. "I guess I'd better borrow a key, then. I'll throw in a shower, at no charge."

"You're a good man." She retrieved a key from her purse. "Do you have a minute to catch me up? Ooh, I don't like the look on your face." She kicked the door closed with a foot.

Donovan spoke through a scowl. "This whole thing is just getting messier. But the paradox is, we know who was killed, we know who killed him. It's just the details that are completely screwy. Gemma—the Scotland Yard elite cop, let me remind you—is convinced the case is solved. I haven't spoken with Jack, but I have too many questions that I don't know the answers to. I haven't worked with Rory before. Hopefully, he'll let me keep on, even if the other two bail."

Beth stopped fussing with her papers to meet his eye. "The ambassador has an analytical mind. He doesn't just look at the answers, sometimes even considering them irrelevant. He wants to know why and how things happen. He doesn't want your team to miss something and have this happen all over again. For these and a dozen other reasons, I expect he'll want to know why Mr. Gross was killed, and why the other man promptly killed himself. He'll keep on you, and thereafter keep you on until you have no more answers. Guaranteed. Well, I have to go into a meeting…"

"…and I have a shower to jump into. Got time for dinner, this evening?"

She dropped the documents and drew up to him, placing her arms around his shoulders. "I'm counting on it. See you then."

He left Beth's office and found the one Jack was working in. The walls remained bare, except for a not-quite-straight print of Cervantes' Don Quixote, who tilted at a windmill behind the room's lone occupant. Jack had hung it up on their first day, "to remind me, every day, not to be an old fool."

"Mr. Sean O'Shaughnessy Donovan! How come you don't have a thick brogue accent, with a name like that? Sit down, son, and tell me what you've been up to. Have you been getting cozy with the Hendricks gang?"

"Gemma's got a big mouth." Donovan's lips thinned, but he was nevertheless happy to see his new colleague, Jack.

"Now, now, all Gemma's doing is looking after her partners. Both of her new partners. And all she said was you took her on a tour of Dover Street, that's it. Being a little sensitive, are we?"

Donovan winced inside. Perhaps he had jumped the gun, a bit. "You're right. Jack, I'm still getting used to having partners. I've never worked with one before; never had the need."

"You don't say." He could hear the dry humor in Jack's tone. "So tell me seriously, what have you been up to?" Donovan took a few minutes to bring Jack up to speed, omitting the second side trip to Dover Street. He noted Jack's frown at the part where the mother and daughter were assaulted, and took pains to not reveal his shame at the part he played in implicating Nikki to Ace Hendricks. When the update was finished, they paused, thinking about the events.

Jack spoke first. "So, you and Gemma have discussed whether there are to be next steps?"

"Not really. What we agreed upon was we had to bring you up to speed, and then get your two cents' worth before anything else can happen. I think there are more things that need to be tied up, whereas she feels…"

"…that if she's investigating a murder where the perp and the victim are known, the case may be over with?"

"Exactly. But she says she's keeping an open mind. I believe she's waiting for your evidence to push her in one direction or the other."

Jack scratched his forearm. "That may be a problem, Seannie. What I turned up may not be the pivot point of the case, but I think it bears looking into. So…I booked myself a flight to Romania. I leave this evening, I'll be eating on the plane."

Donovan sat forward, excited. Had a few more pieces dropped into the jigsaw puzzle? Figuring the RCMP officer to be on the cautious side, this must mean something. A breakthrough? "Come on; spill it. What did those spreadsheets reveal? Or have you been nosing around other areas?"

The older man smiled. "Let's not get ahead of ourselves. Here's what I did, and here's what I found. I started with the spreadsheets, yes, and they told a tale of bureaucratic incompetence. We had case files for each spreadsheet entry. So I followed the electronic and paper trails—due diligence, you know—and as mentioned, I came up one letter short, between the e-files and the paper ones. That was the one Campbell burned, at least that's what I think." He pushed a single sheet, a photocopy, across the desk, and continued.

"It's addressed to Ellie Campbell. Frankly, it makes Gross look like an uncaring sonofabitch. If my wife was shot dead and this was the last letter she received before getting murdered, I don't know if I wouldn't have done the same..." He paused to look out the window, cleared his throat and began again. "Anyway, once I pieced the story together, here's the part that makes no sense to me. A contract goes sour in Romania. A tiny slip of a lady goes over to see why her potato shipment never made it off the boat, and some crazy arse shoots her. Over a load of god-damn potatoes. Why?" His voice lowered, as if he was thinking aloud.

"It's been my experience former Communist Bloc countries are expert at obfuscation. You ask questions, and they look at you as if they forget how to speak. They can repeat that until the cows come home. You get nothing from them, if they don't want to share it. So, why murder such a tiny threat this time? They don't deal with things that way. I'm sorry, but I don't get it." He held out his hands. "I just don't. So, I'm gonna go see for myself."

"Need help? I've been to Romania."

He looked wistful. "Nah. It'd be fun to have company, but you need to be in Manchester. I updated the ambassador and he's kindly offered to give me a letter that might smooth things after I get there. I've got this. I'll be back in no time." He changed his tack. "How about you, old son? What are you up to next?"

"Oh, all sorts of things to look into." He sounded vague, even to himself, so he tried again. "I want to know, more clearly, what Jess had to do with Ace Hendricks. I've got to get Nikki and her daughter into a place, with a few dollars and a plan in their back pocket. I don't want to think about them, so if they're set up, that's something off my worry list." He paused, thinking his words made him sound callous. "Look, it sounds selfish of me, I know. I am worried about what's to become of them, but once I have them set up, they'll be all right in London.

"At this point, I have to convince Gemma there's more to this case than meets the eye. I've got personal business rolling out, back in Canada. And there are, ah, always other irons in the fire." He was thinking of Gaia and his job in The Lakes District.

But Jack's mind had jumped in a different direction. "I know you're keeping it strictly business in this building, but, you and that McLean girl..." He left the question dangling.

Donovan had no intention of filling in the blanks. "Jack, there's an expression: *'Occupes-toi tes oignons.'* (Tend your own onion garden). That's French for 'Mind your own damn business.'" He softened it with a smile that was almost as broad as Jack's. "I will suggest that I probably won't have time for television while you're gone."

"Sounds like. Want me to chat with Gemma before I leave?"

"Nah. I've got it, as long as I can speak for you that the case isn't closed. I'll be honest. With you, Gemma and me, I'm still trying to find a way to interact more smoothly. It's not there yet, but I guess it's getting better." He pulled out his cell phone, pressing a button to check the time. "In fact, she should be leaving New Scotland Yard in Westminster about now, heading this way. I'll get her up to speed, she'll tell me what's up with the woman and her daughter, and then we'll divvy up the Manchester and London jobs to be done while you're away. Sound good?"

Jack rose. "That sounds excellent. I'll go pack a bag and head for the station." He divided the pile of papers, placing the restricted access group into the filing cabinet and dropping the remainder into his briefcase. Locking the cabinet, he handed the key to Donovan and marched out of the office. Donovan had noticed a text message while he was checking the time, so he sat in the nearest chair to wait for Gemma and to open the message from the Schmidts at the winery in Canada.

CHAPTER FOURTEEN

London to the Lake District

DONOVAN MET GEMMA AT THE entrance to Canada House, his arm guiding her straight back out into the late fall afternoon. "Come on. We won't get many more sunny days like this. Let's go for a walk." Wordlessly, she accompanied him, a bemused smile on her face.

They passed the lions of Trafalgar Square, walked through the Strand heading toward, and then straight into Old London. At one point they eased to the right, looking for the Embankment. Ten minutes in, Gemma looked sideways at her partner. "Look, I can walk with the best of 'em, and this is probably the most scenic area of my beautiful city. But come on! Where are we going, are we speaking to one another, or is this some sort of Canadian Outdoorsman therapy?"

"I just wanted us to get caught up, Gem. I'm on the hunt for a café." In response, she pulled her collar up to ward off the breeze coming in off the Thames, tucked her hands into her jacket pockets and, nose down, continued on another hundred yards.

"How about that spot?" He pointed to a café overlooking the Thames, oozing British charm. "Ever been there?"

"I think it'll do, if the coffee's really good." He maintained his pace, and a moment later they were seated on the warm side of the window, orders of Ethiopian coffee placed with the server. Donovan waited until he received his beverage, and then began by asking about the mother-daughter tandem.

"Nikki has rebounded amazingly. It's like she's got a new lease on life, and maybe she has. She's already registered in a refresher course, and Social Services has an apartment for her and her daughter. Lexie is still struggling, though. Nikki says she's not sleeping well, but that's understandable. Poor thing. Her gorgeous hair will grow back, but she'll be fearful for a long time, I reckon."

"Are they receiving any income from the state?"

"Welfare assistance?" Gemma's face clouded. "That's taking a bit to kick in. I expect she'll have used up all your money before it gets set up properly. I could give her a couple hundred quid…"

"No need. I've set up a trust fund. All I need is an address or a bank account to drop it in. It'll be about three hundred pounds a month, for five years. That's the maximum amount of top-up she's allowed to receive while they're on social assistance. And I've set up an equal amount for Lexie to use, come university time. It's not a lot, but they won't go hungry."

Gemma smiled, but her look was careful, questioning. "That seems like a lot of money."

"It does, doesn't it? I went and picked up that packet Nikki was waiting for, the one Jess was supposed to have set up for them. Unfortunately, it wasn't, technically speaking, wrapped or carrying Jess's signature, but I'm positive it was for Nikki and Lexie. One hundred percent sure." His look was even, it didn't waver, and challenged her to argue.

Gemma responded as if changing the subject. "Hey, remember when you told me there would be consequences to asking you too many questions? I feel a bit like that, right now. The by-the-book part of me wants to trot out of the café and bite my tongue. For a week."

He grinned. "And the rest of you?"

"It's hoping you burned the bastard's house down on your way out."

Donovan shifted in his seat. "Let's talk about Jack and the case. As his text to you says, he's off to Romania, to see what he can dig up. Well, I was speaking with Beth. She says the ambassador will want more answers. So, Jack and I are still on the case. Where do you sit?" He waited, watching as she shifted on the chair.

Gemma took another sip of coffee. "I've spent my entire career on the force. By the time I turned eighteen, I was in blue serge, and got my arts degree in criminology after hours while I was a Peeler. I've always had superiors telling me what to do. I never had to worry about whether I was still on a job. The issue was always clear. The case was either somehow resolved or it went cold. Those were the outcomes, every time." She stopped stirring her coffee. "This one, it's really not straightforward, and my commander isn't telling me when it's time to move on. He asks me what the ambassador wants. You say the ambassador wants more answers. We go get more answers, end of."

"You okay with that?"

Her voice was patient. "It's nothing to do with whether I'm okay with it. Nothing at all. It's what my commander and your ambassador wants. The pertinent question is what d'you do next, and what do I do next, innit?" She reverted to London slang, leaning on a North London accent.

He pushed his chair back, meeting her blue eyes. "I'm not your boss, so I'm not about to tell you what to do. But I can tell you some things that need to happen, and you can feel free to pick some of these." He took out a crumpled piece of paper, smoothed it flat and began to bullet out his thoughts.

-Potato load rotted and caused a shipper to be murdered. Why?

-A house in the Lake District gets cleaned out by a truck bearing the name Peterson's Freight. Owned by Hendricks. Anything special about this one? Tie-in to stolen warehouse loot?

-Hendricks supposedly using warehouses to fence stolen art pieces. Where? What? Why haven't searches turned them up?

-Jess promises a packet to Nikki, to whom he doesn't owe anything. Why?

-Hendricks was supposed to deliver a packet to Nikki, on behalf of Jess. Why? Where's the connection? Who owes who what, here?

Gemma stared at the paper, reading it upside-down. "You forgot one. I still don't understand why Jess chose suicide over a jail sentence. Any judge would have given him a light sentence for killing someone who most likely caused his wife to be killed. There had to be more to it than that."

Donovan looked up, a satisfied look on his face. "Ah. That's the partner I was looking for. Sounds like you're back on the team. So, which ones do you want? I want the Ambleside question. That's not far from Manchester, is it?"

"Not at all. As a matter of fact, folks who want to fly out of Ambleside would drive to Manchester to catch the flight." She studied the scrap of paper. "I want those." She stabbed a finger at the last two items on the page, the ones involving Nikki. "Our girl Nikki's on the up-and-up, but that doesn't mean she isn't hiding something. And if I can get that sorted, I wouldn't mind heading back to Manchester. Maybe we could do Manchester together?" She raised her head to gauge his reaction.

"Sounds good. I expect to be up there in two days. I'll head out to The Lake District first thing tomorrow morning and maybe later slide over to Manchester while I'm in the neighborhood. You?"

"I've got paperwork back at my office on Broadway Street. I'll pay a visit to our friend Nikki in the morning if I can catch her, and then take the train sometime tomorrow, I suppose."

"Then we'd best get back."

"Perfect. I'm having dinner with a girlfriend at six." She peered out the window at the unblemished sky. "Sadly, you are one hundred percent correct on our fall afternoons. Don't expect many more weather days like this. Bring a brolly from now on. There is nothing as bloody bone-chilling as November sleet in London, unless it's January sleet."

Donovan left some loose bills on the table, as they got up. "When I was a kid, I used to help my grandfather cut Christmas trees and wrap them in plastic mesh webbing called Vexar. They were for export to Texas, so we'd wrap them on November eleventh, Canadian Remembrance Day. As I recall, it always rained on the eleventh, except when it sleeted. That's my strongest memory of bone-chilling cold. The worst part would be about three o'clock, when you knew you had three more hours to go, but the rain was starting to leak down the top of your rubber boots, Wellies, you call them?"

Gemma nodded, offering a sympathetic look. "But you'd be a child. You could just go in the house and get dry and warmed up, right?"

Donovan gave her a sidelong glance. "My grandfather was in his sixties. I couldn't let him out-tough me, although he always did." He chuckled. "And he always underpaid me, telling me Russian kids did this every day of the year."

"Sounds like you had a happy childhood, Sean."

"Not even close." The thought soured his mood and conversation flagged on the way back to Canada House.

* * * *

Beth McLean pushed open the door to her apartment, breathing in the warm air and its complementing fragrances of coconut milk, garlic and veg, frying chicken and maple syrup. A bottle of Chateau Simard St. Émilion sat breathing on the coffee table. It was nestled between a baguette guarding a wedge salad, and a bread-and-butter plate cradling triangles of St. André double cream brie and tangy vlaskaas.

She dropped her briefcase by the door and headed for the microscopic kitchen, a piece of cheese in one hand. "Yes, the meal will be fantastic, judging by the aromas, but the fact that I don't have to decide what to prepare or cook it makes it ten times better. Thanks, honey." She stood on tiptoes to nuzzle his throat.

"I came back in a bad mood, and cooking almost always brings me out of it. Well, cooking and the sight of you."

"Bad day at the office? Gemma or Jack giving you a hard time? I can't imagine it was Jack." She took a step back, the better to read his face.

"Nah. Work's going well. I just had a reminder of my childhood, some shit I thought I was done with. And I got a text from Canada. A project I'm working on is falling into place, but the timing could be better."

"Is that bottle of French wine in there going to help things? Should we go to bed and relieve a little, um, tension before eating? I'm flexible, if you'll pardon the play on words."

"Oh, I'm already in a better mood now. Other than the fact that I'm going away for a few days."

"When?"

"Tomorrow. I have a couple of leads, and bad guys aren't going to catch themselves." He added another quarter cup of chicken broth to loosen the sauce.

"Let me guess. Manchester?"

"Yeah. And a nearby town as well. There's a lawyer in the Lake District I have to have a conversation with."

"Lawyer, eh? Who has the legal problem?"

"It's more of an illegal problem, and that would be said barrister. I did a little research on him—a guy named Rigg—and he's a perfect shitstorm. He's a combination of victim, crook, patsy, conniver if that's even a word, and I'll throw in asshole at no extra charge. I'm completely surprised somebody hasn't killed him yet."

"Why don't I pour us some of that yummy red in the other room and you tell me his story? That's a bottle of 2005." She nodded in appreciation. "Respect."

"Sounds good. These flavors have to marry up in the frying pan, and I just dropped some fresh penne into the water. You pour and I'll be right there." A moment later, they were seated on the chesterfield, comparing notes on each other's day.

She took a sip, licking her upper lip. "The media haven't let up on us. Seems it's completely Canada's fault our director didn't have a bodyguard outside his door. The rumor—get this—is he was doing industrial spying for some Eastern European country. Estonia or something. Totally ridiculous. But the media don't care about facts. Sell a couple more papers and slander the Canadians at no extra charge, who cares? Well, I bloody care."

"Bloody? Beth, you're becoming a Brit right before my eyes." He drew her nearer, almost spilling her wine. "You can't control the press, so you mustn't fret about whatever lies they tell. We'll have answers soon, and you'll have a response soon enough." He kissed her forehead.

"I suppose. But seeing the massive lies every day constitutes yellow journalism."

He grinned, the back of his fingers trying in vain to smooth the lines on her forehead. "And the Canada High Commission is the first victim of the British press. Shame on them."

She punched him on the chest. "You go get me some food. I'm out of sorts, now, and you have to fix it." Her laughter followed him out of the room.

That night, they lay in bed with all the lights off, looking out the window at the moon over the Thames. Donovan reminded her of the second time they'd met, how she'd pointed to the moon on the water outside her balcony window. Beth had suggested if he looked intently, he would see her career drowning at the bottom of the Thames. "And now, here you are, a newly-appointed communications director instead of a recently fired communications officer. And here we are, in bed together, getting to know one another."

"Intimately." She'd whispered, patting his abdomen.

"My grandfather used to say, sometimes a mishap can lead you to the next large space you need to occupy. This feels to me like it's happened to us, maybe brought us together, don't you think?"

She nodded, silent.

He told her about his pitch for the winery. How the Schmidts were upset at the notion of losing control of the company. Upset at the notion of losing their dream. "But they're going to lose control, regardless of whether I step in. It's just that, I like both of them and there'd be a place for them in the business, if it was me who bought in. I'm not sure someone else would accommodate them, you know?"

He decided to tease. "Hey, Dieter says our daughter just showed up the other day."

"What!" She sat straight up, eyes wide. "Our daughter? When did we make a daughter, and why wasn't I informed?"

He kept his voice casual. "Remember Claire, our young vintner from Arles? The one who was missing the barrel of Pinot? Apparently, she's shown up on Dieter's doorstep, looking for an apprenticeship. Says I sent her." He thought about the mystery of the missing cask of wine, of how he and Beth figured out where it had been cached. He remembered Beth and Claire huddled, speaking low in the wine cellar, sharing thoughts.

Beth's face presented surprise mixed with curiosity. "Really! What do you think of that? Did you send her, and if not, are you cool with it? She seemed like a serious young lady. I expect she'd probably learn a lot. But my real questions are these. Assuming Schmidt didn't turn her out into the cold Canadian autumn, is he upset with you for this? And how do you feel about this, assuming you didn't really invite her?"

"Okay, last thing first. I myself showed up on his doorstep a year or so back, looking for what was essentially a minimum-wage internship. So, this sort of thing happens all the time in wineries. And no, last time I spoke with her was at their picnic table, and you were sitting beside me. There's usually a more formal application process, but it's not unprecedented to have protégées pop in out of the blue. The first question is tougher. Here's what's perceived to be happening, from what I can piece together. A winery owner, in dire financial straits is approached by some cocky guy to buy him out. Next thing you know, what appears to be a ridiculous child-vintner shows up, saying the wannabe purchaser sent her. The optics don't look good for me, the guy who's trying to be sensitive.

"I'll call him in the morning, telling him it's just a coincidence and she would be starting at the bottom, just like I did."

Beth's voice was quiet. "It sounds like you're buying a winery, Sean. In Canada. On the other side of the pond. Up until now, you've been a bit more…mobile. Up until now, you could, for instance, come see me on a day's notice. Like when I was in trouble this summer. I suppose a multimillion dollar winery comes with responsibilities." They lay beside each other, still, an Atlantic Ocean of issues resting between them.

Donovan's voice was also quiet. "That's true. But Schmidt isn't going anywhere. The way I see it, as the majority owner, I can be anything from a silent partner, to a seasonal partner, to a fully-engaged general manager." His hand crept across the narrow gulf to rest on her flat belly. "If I needed to come visit my girl every month, or for a month, I could and would do it.

"When I was a kid, my home wasn't…pleasant. It wasn't really a home, except when my father was on the road. As an adult, I've mostly lived in hotel rooms around the world. I've got an apartment in Montreal —which you've been to—but it's really a storage place for my collectibles, nothing more. This is my chance to have a place I can call home." He put a finger to her lips to quell her protest. "Hammersmith isn't in any way my place, yet. I don't have my fingerprints on it, if you know what I mean. I'd like to stick around, be part of your life. But it's not just me with mobility challenges, right? As part of the diplomatic corps, you can get a call tomorrow advising of this amazing career opportunity starting Monday, in New York. Or Johannesburg. This time tomorrow night, we could be discussing how you're going to try to fit me into your about-to-change life.

"Now, I don't mean to be presumptuous, but I think you'd invite me to stick around, wherever your posting would be." He rolled over onto his side to face her. "But here's the thing. You and me; we're the lucky ones. If you wanted to fly to Montreal or Toronto tomorrow, you have the luxury of just pulling out plastic and buying a ticket. Same for me. I once knew a couple that broke up because he couldn't afford to take the bus across town often enough to sustain the relationship. Money problems are the single biggest thing that chips away at couples. We have a distance issue, which is big, but not as big as being poor and not together." He lapsed into silence.

"So." Her hand came up to rest on his. "What I'm hearing is, I'm not losing my man, I'm actually gaining a winery. That's the best argument in favor of long-distance relationships I've ever heard. Ever." She chuckled. "And let's not forget about popping out a daughter without me lifting a finger. You're the best." She leaned in to kiss him, a lingering connection that made him feel, if the juggling of cases wasn't smooth, at least their relationship was working.

"One more thing, and then I have to get some sleep." Her voice was casual, controlled. "When you get to Manchester, you're going be sniffing around Ace Hendricks' backyard, right?" She waited for his grunt in the affirmative. "And you're working with Gemma, right? Here's my concern. Hendricks has seen both of you, just before the mother and daughter disappeared. And, based on your dinnertime update, that was around the same time a bunch of valuables disappeared from his bedroom, right?" Another grunt. "So, what I'm wondering is, if someone has to chat with him, who will that be? Even ex-pats like me have heard of the Hendricks gang. Oh, I don't even know what my point is. I guess I just want you to be careful. You'll do that, right?" He felt her kiss again in the dark, as if sealing a deal.

"I can do that." Long after her breathing evened out and she slipped past REM and into a deeper sleep, he lay there, thinking.

CHAPTER FIFTEEN

Constanta, Romania

JACK MILLER'S TAXI DRIVER STUDIOUSLY ignored every stop sign and red light between the airport and the port of Constanta, on the Black Sea. Jack left the cab cursing under his breath.

He took in the massive land-and-seascape. The dockyards were huge, the largest commercial site on the Black Sea. He thought with gratitude of the diplomatic letter Rory had given him, and the doors it opened to Romanian officials. Thanks to their guidance, he had a specific dock to start with, as well as a local contact who spoke English. In front of him for the full length of the dockside, the late afternoon blue sky was prickly with scores of over-sized blue cranes. There's no time like the present. He trudged past the first warehouse, reading the numbers, memorizing the name.

He noted with surprise the English spelling on the signs: Constanta Shipyards, and remembered English, French, Romanian, and Russian were all taught in the schools. After fifteen minutes of walking, he passed what he assumed to be a coast guard boat, large blue letters proclaiming Politia de Frontera near the white bow. Jack gave a little wave to the Coast Guard sailor adjusting ropes, who acknowledged him with the tiniest of nods. He kept walking. This wasn't the correct pier. He felt luckier upon arriving at the next pier. A massive Maersk container ship large enough to hold five football fields sat under one of the ubiquitous cranes that emptied cargo. The ship took up one entire side of the pier, its prow pointing toward a warehouse with a familiar number.

Jack pulled out the sheet of paper containing certain Romanian phrases, as well as shipyard addresses and contact names, his hotel address and the phone number of the Canadian embassy agent in Bucharest. He walked to the white warehouse with the arched blue roof, staring up at the roof until he got a crick his neck. There was a door to the far left, but Jack chose to enter straight onto the shop floor through a pair of fifty-foot tall doors.

The warehouse was a holding spot for vegetables. The long, deep pad to the right was filled with ship and train containers, obviously brought inside to keep them away from the chill November nights. A few in the front were opened and inspectors perused the shipment of corn. The pad on the left contained countless fifty-pound canvas bags of rice. The cavernous middle seemed empty, save for a half-dozen dock laborers who were working at the very back.

The smell hit him first. Where the men were working, a twenty-foot wall of potatoes stared back. The angle of the mass of potatoes to the left and right was about forty five degrees, what one would expect of rounded objects piled in a heap. In the middle, however, the men were focused on a vertical wall of potato biomass. The tell-tale single stream of liquid emanating from the middle at the floor revealed the rotting center of the affected area.

The potatoes had congealed and shovels didn't seem helpful to move them, so the men were tugging at them with gloved hands. Jack guessed a front-end loader would ruin too many good potatoes, so the work had to be done by hand. Fruit flies swarmed around the men's heads and every couple of minutes, one or the other of the men would walk about forty feet away from the pile, presumably to catch his breath and reduce the tendency to vomit. But there was nothing wrong with Jack's nose, and he smelled the earthy, pungent smell of rotting potatoes, and thanked the person who decided to leave the bay doors open.

A few offices sat just inside the hangar doors, dwarfed by the massive storage area. He headed in that direction. Twenty yards from the office an armed guard stood in a little wooden shed the size of a toll booth. The guard studied him, his eyes the only kinetic evidence of life. Jack passed him, nodded, and entered the first of the two offices.

A thick, middle-aged man in a canvas work jacket looked up, a phone glued to his ear. A portable electric heater cast inadequate heat from one corner, and Jack thought the sun never reached this area. The building was probably cool the year round, but November added a new dimension to the coolness of the warehouse. The man slipped his hand over the phone's mouthpiece and grunted something. Taking this as an invitation to speak, Jack uttered the name of his contact: "Costin Pitu." The man resumed grunting, his whiskers scratching the ancient telephone receiver, but he nodded his head in the direction of the second office. "Multumesc," (Thank you), and he left.

The second office was warmer, cleaner and had no odours creeping in from the warehouse. Jack closed the door behind him and waited in the empty room. A toilet flushed and a minute after, a tall, slender man entered the office from the door at the back, drying his hands with a paper towel. He said something in Romanian.

"I'm sorry, I don't speak Romanian. Do you speak English or French?"

"Of course. How may I be of assistance?"

"Thanks for seeing me. In fact, I'm here on government business. Government of Canada. I have a few questions about–"

The man stood up, and then walked over to the window facing the guard. Jack couldn't tell if this was to confirm that the guard was still at his post, or if it was to hide his face, which was now turned away from his guest. Pitu stood, relaxed, yet his limbs were completely alert, as if lying in wait for the next ambush. "It's a bit chilly in here, don't you think? I'm going to turn on the heater, just enough to fight off the autumn." Jack thought it curious, as the temperature was fine, until he heard the click-buzz of the portable heater as the fan began to whirr. What a convenient way to mask a conversation!

Pitu returned to the desk, leaning over it to meet Jack's level gaze. Voice low, he asked a simple question. "You like beer?"

It seemed an odd question, but Jack was certain there was only one answer. "Of course."

"I'll be at this tavern this evening, after ten o'clock. You will join me?" He scribbled a few words onto a scrap of paper.

"Yes."

"I have work to do. Why don't you go look at the boats now." It wasn't a question, so Jack left without a word. Back out in the sunshine, Jack let his guard slip, just a little, and thought about a Canadian farm boy, wandering around what was formerly an Eastern Bloc country. What would his wife have thought of that, if she'd lived long enough to accompany him? She'd have loved it: the wild mushroom soup, the chewy, luscious red wines, the exquisitely sewn bed linens and tablecloths. He sighed.

Thinking about his wife got Jack thinking about his assignment. Was this an honor, to be the lone RCMP officer on this case, so far away from Ottawa? Or were they pawning him off on low-profile cases until he retired? He wasn't certain, but it didn't feel like a low-profile case. More like a case that could blow up any minute, spreading gory details across the front pages of papers in three countries. Don't over-think it, Jackie-boy. All you'll get is a headache for your troubles.

After checking into a nearby hotel, he spent the rest of the afternoon and evening walking around, choosing a place to eat, and asking hotel staff about the tavern where he was to meet Costin. It drew a rough crowd and lay within the perimeter of the dockyards, but with no history of trouble. Jack arrived a quarter of an hour early, standing in the shadows down the street, watching. At ten, he entered a tavern almost as dark inside as out, looking for a spot not too far from the door, not too far from a wall. One table fit the bill, so he took it, placing his Greek sailor cap on the table in front of the other chair. A few minutes later, Pitu came in and walked straight over to him without hesitating, and slid into the chair across from the Canadian.

"You are Canadian. Who do you represent, and why do you wish to know more about the potatoes that went bad?" He glanced over to the door, and then tugged his stocking cap a bit lower over his forehead, as Jack ordered a couple of beers. He left his untouched, eyes trained on the Romanian.

In response, Jack held his wallet under the table and flipped it open to reveal an RCMP badge. "I'm empowered by the Government of Canada to investigate the murder of Ellie Campbell. Folks don't normally get shot for a shipment of potatoes. Yes, the Romanian government caught the shooter and he'll be tried for murder. But this leaves all the details up in the air, and God is in the details, so they say."

It was Jack's turn to lean in, so he did, as he continued speaking. "I want to know the real reason why the potato shipment had to stay on the boat three weeks longer than it should have. What made it so special that everyone was concerned about this bunch of spuds? Why was this shipment alone singled out for quarantine? Finally, I need to know what the shooter had to say. That'll do for starters."

Costin Pitu slid off his stocking cap, rubbed the bristly hairs on his head, and put the cap back on. His face was all angles, high cheekbones and his hair was fine, with a widow's peak pushing the hair back off his forehead. And his face carried a worried look.

"The shooter, his name is Puiu, almost like my last name. He's a stupid man, a simpleton, and he has always been very gullible. Someone paid two thousand dollars, according to him, to shoot the lady. That's a year's wages for him. I don't doubt his word. Of course, he doesn't have any idea who paid him. All he knows is whoever paid him had a Western accent, probably British or Irish. The woman came around, asking questions about her shipment. It was on a Tuesday. The next day, when she arrived, he was waiting for her." Pitu made a pistol of his hand, mimicking the action of shooting Jack in the chest.

"As for the potatoes themselves, that was equally strange." He sighed, and then took a long draught from his beer. "I handle imports, exports, bills of lading, all of the logistics for my warehouse. The paperwork goes through me. So I was very surprised to see a shipment, just like all the other shipments, carrying the red X"—he crossed his forearms to signify the icon—"at the top of the import documents. It was signed by the port authority, with a second signature from Bucharest, from the Ministerul Economiei, the Ministry of Trade. The only other time I've seen something held up by them was because of a contamination. Some misguided freedom group. Protesters." He looked disgusted.

"The investigation took place and the port authority signature was valid, but the ministerial signature was illegitimate. In the time it took to uncover the fraudulent signature, the potatoes had begun to rot. Someone had tampered with the cooling systems on the boat." He opened his hands in supplication. "We couldn't very well accept the shipment at that point. So it was lost, the deal went to hell and the lady lost her money, her company, and her life, at the end of the story."

Jack looked up from a spot on the table. "Well, thank you for that. You speak English very well, by the way."

Pitu nodded. "University of Pennsylvania. Please let me know if you can figure out a way to get me back there, to Canada or the US. I never thought I'd find myself with a bachelor of fine arts, working in a potato warehouse on the docks. But here I am." He shared his first smile with Jack.

Jack said, "I find it odd we're meeting in this joint to chat."

Pitu fingered his stocking cap, a nervous gesture. "There's something you might be interested to know. My manager received some visitors a few days ago. They spoke English. From England. When they left, he came to me and told me to let him know if anyone comes around, asking any questions about the woman or her shipment. He looked frightened. I have a feeling they were, um..." His voice trailed off.

"Leaning on him."

Pitu nodded, silent. "There's just one other thing. My manager inspected the shipment while it was quarantined. He said he saw flashes of silver in among the potatoes. This was a few days before the woman arrived, but after the damage was done. He spoke with the port authority but they told him the food inspectors were already looking the shipment over and they'd address it. They were with the potatoes that day, and the next day, the day before the woman arrived, he sneaked—is that the word—back onto the boat. No silver flashes anymore."

"That's it?"

"That's it."

"No other details?"

"No."

"Are you going to tell the manager about meeting me?"

"He knows. You met him in the first office this afternoon. He didn't say anything to me, but that's not unusual. I didn't say anything to him, either. My wife will not thank me for putting my nose where it doesn't belong."

A worrying thought entered Jack's mind. "So, he knows I'm in town, and he may have told the Brits. We'd better be careful, from here on in. There's something more rotten than the potatoes." He reached into his pocket, and palmed five hundred American dollars, slipping the wad of bills under the table. "This is for the beer. Thanks, buddy. We'll just forget one another now." Pitu nodded, left Romanian lei on the table for the beer and they left the tavern, Jack holding the door for his Romanian host.

The door hadn't latched behind them before time blurred, and then ratcheted down into frame-by-frame slow motion. Three flashes exploded, followed by three more, all originating from the truck across the street. The first bullet took Costin in the face, exiting the side of his head at the temple. The second one caught him on the upstretched hand, pushed through the sternum and entered his heart, stopping it. On the way down, another slug pierced his side, laying waste to various organs before resting in his bowel. A final bullet missed the falling man, breaking the glass of the tavern door.

Jack, coming out directly behind, saw the bullet break against his new friend's head, and knew Costin was dead before he toppled. Jack didn't, however, see it, but rather felt the slug that caught him low in the abdomen, and the one that entered his upper thigh, severing the top of the popliteal artery and splintering his femur. Still conscious, Jack dropped behind Costin, a patch of shoulder exposed above his companion's corpse. The sound of the seventh and last bullet was hidden by the screeching of tires as the truck jumped out of the parking space and roared down the street. The seeing-eye bullet, the insult to the injuries, had only the barest fraction of yet-alive flesh and bone with which to connect.

But it did.

The round ripped through the shoulder like a knife through hot butter. The impact of the slug threw Jack onto his back, bleeding onto the sidewalk from a combination of entrance and exit holes. The last thing he saw was the distinct view of Orion's Belt—the Hunter—in the Romanian night-time sky. He heard voices and then...nothing.

CHAPTER SIXTEEN

London

SEAN DONOVAN SAT ALONE IN a coffee shop a few blocks from Beth's apartment. They'd awakened, made love, he fixed her breakfast while she showered and she'd coerced him into sharing the oh-so-tiny shower space as she finished. It was a good morning, so far.

He took a gulp of strong coffee, remembering the awful stuff he was required to drink in Bucharest. "Nice folks; horrid coffee," he murmured to himself, thinking it really wasn't a fair trade-off. He was heading into the weekend, as evidenced by the heft of the London Times he was reading. Friday's edition would be larger than today's, with Saturday's containing an immense number of sections. But he wasn't really absorbing the news, editorials or classifieds. He was thinking about Nikki, and her little girl, Lexie.

Nikki was doing fine. He had seen them the day previous, and she was glowing, ebullient, and full of plans. Lexie, however, had become a different girl. The sass was gone, she carried dark shadows under her eyes and she hardly said a word. Sean had tried to draw her out, with mixed success. He had made her smile twice, but it wasn't sustainable. What could he do to pull her out of this fearful funk? Keep her safe and let time heal things, if they would. What did he know about eleven-year-olds?

He smiled at the egg sandwich he'd ordered, noting the two slices of back bacon adorning the top. He hadn't ordered them, and wondered if his Canadian accent automatically warranted their presence. And he thought of Beth's last words to him, as she left for work. "Be careful." It was a reminder that he and Gemma had been 'made' by Ace Hendricks. That left Jack to be the X-factor. Nobody knew him, so Jack could still slip around Manchester, unidentified. He felt a little wistful, as a thought entered his head unannounced. He and Beth had worked well. But she was a senior diplomat; there would be no time for the new Director of Communications to support his games and schemes. Still, they were good together.

This worried him. With the exception of his relationship with Nadia, he had been a loner since he was a boy. Acquaintances weren't always safe around him, owing to the exigencies of his work. Worse, if possible, was his philosophy regarding friendship. He wasn't in favor of it. Trouble abounded, he became distracted, and invariably, mistakes were made. Variables were introduced with each new friend, raising by a full factor the possibility of trouble waltzing in the front door. Even in the better relationships, a chance comment could slip out. Feelings could get hurt and he'd certainly be the one in the doghouse.

With Beth, friendship seemed worth the gamble. They could argue, but agree to disagree. They could see things differently, but arrive at some answer that didn't make him crazy. And he liked her. She was fun. He smiled at the thought of her, realizing he smiled a lot, at the very thought of her.

He checked the clock on the wall. Gemma should already be on the train to Manchester. He'd be off to Ambleside as well in a bit. What would he be able to squeeze out of that soft pat of butter, Rigg? Lies, for sure. But Rigg was a desperate man, with the weight of a large syndicate leaning on his fulsome, lawyerly shoulders. Perhaps he'd wring a kernel of half-truth from him. We'll see.

The cell phone buzzed against his leg, and he pulled it out to study the screen. A Romanian number, but none of the ones he had stored in his eidetic memory. *It must be Jack. I wonder what he wants.* He answered the phone, and for some reason, waited before saying hello to his new friend.

"Hello, Mr. Donovan. My name is Dr. Luca, calling from Constanta, Romania. I have a slip of paper that I've retrieved from Mr. Jack Miller's clothes. The paper says to contact you in the event of an emergency. I am sorry to be the bearer of very bad news." Donovan's heart went cold.

* * * *

Beth, Gemma, and Donovan sat in chairs facing the ambassador's desk at MacDonald House. With a quick call, Donovan had managed to pull Gemma off the train just outside London. Scotland Yard sent a car to fetch her and she'd just arrived at MacDonald House. Rory Thompson stood nearby, leaning over the speaker phone. An official-sounding voice came on, in accented English.

"Hello, am I speaking with the Canadian Ambassador?"

Rory pushed a lock of red-blonde curls back over one ear. "Hello. This is Rory Thompson, Canada's High Commissioner to Britain. I'm accompanied by three of Jack's colleagues. Is this Dr. Luca?"

"Yes. Radu Luca. Some members of my medical team are here as well, together with a state official from our National Central Bureau. Mircea Bacu insists on being here to support Canada and this investigation. I noted that it is premature to initiate the investigation, since our primary aim is to save Mr. Miller. He, ah, suggested that criminal investigations have greater success when implemented at the first possible moment."

Rory interrupted Dr. Luca. "That's fine. We can discuss the investigation in a moment. Please tell us how Jack is faring."

"Not well, I'm afraid. He's lost much blood, and he's slipped into a coma. Fortunately, he is in excellent shape for his age, so we are… hopeful of his chances at regaining consciousness. He did say something before lapsing into unconsciousness. It makes no sense to us, but perhaps you can shed some light on it. The first person to reach him didn't speak English, but he heard something like Helix. Aches Helix." Does that have any meaning to you?"

Rory shook his head, looking over to his team for a reaction. Gemma and Donovan had locked eyes. Beth murmured a homophone for helix: "Hendricks." In response, Rory nodded, putting his finger to his lips and spoke, his voice unwavering. "I'm sorry, that doesn't seem to ring a bell. But we'll keep it in mind and confer with Mr. Bacu the moment we come up with anything. Let's get back to Jack. What can we do? Should he be airlifted to London?"

"No, no. He cannot be moved. You are well within your rights to send a doctor over to monitor our approach and his progress, that's up to you. But, in truth, we are doing everything possible to meet his medical needs. Our most renowned surgeon extracted the bullets and repaired the wounds. The microsurgery of the artery and sections of the bowel were accomplished with extraordinary finesse, and the broken bones—there were two in the shoulder and the femur in the right leg—were reset and pinned as well as I've ever witnessed. Unfortunately, his blood system went septic, but we have him on an antibiotic cocktail. In fact, all we can do now is to wait for Mr. Miller to regain consciousness. Is there anything else we can do for you or on his behalf?"

"No, thank you. We are most grateful for the extraordinary care being shown our colleague and friend. I'm sending a physician over but please be assured her role is merely to help with the workload. Every hospital I've ever seen has over-worked staff, and I'm sure yours is similar. Dr. Marie Kevler will be there shortly. She comes with the highest credentials and she'll be at your service, Dr. Luca. Keep us posted on our friend, if you please.

"Now, it is important that we exchange just a few words with Mr. Bacu."

"Bacu speaking. How may I help you?" His words were clipped, with just a trace of a Russian accent, and his question was perfunctory, void of emotion. Donovan was sure there wasn't an ounce of caring in the question.

"Thank you, sir. We've read your preliminary report and I'm wondering what else you can add to give us a more complete picture of the events leading to the shooting. Who was the man accompanying Mr. Miller? And how many shooters were there?"

"An analysis of the shells is not complete yet, but witnesses say there was probably more than one shooter. As for the man who was with Mr. Miller, he worked at the Constanta Shipyard, in the potato warehouse. He was an office worker, and we know of no connection with Mr. Miller."

"It doesn't sound as if a lot of information has been uncovered yet." The thin veneer of civility in Rory's voice was beginning to peel away, revealing frustration.

Bacu didn't sound sensitive. "There may not be more information to gather. He may have been mistaken for somebody's husband. It was an...unsavory part of town. But investigations like these take time. We have a guard on Mr. Miller's hospital room, and a team has been established to uncover additional facts."

"We'd like very much to send over a small investigative team to help with the case. Would that be helpful?"

Bacu's voice was almost a purr. "That will not be necessary. In fact, it would inevitably lead to delays in the investigation. I beg you to resist such an action." Rory swore he could hear satisfaction in the man's tone.

"Fine." The ambassador snapped out a one-word response that contradicted its meaning. "However, I will be sending one of my staff to keep an eye on Mr. Miller and to question him, once he regains consciousness."

"As you wish." The Romanian team rang off, leaving a tense silence hanging over the room.

Beth studied the telephone console, ensuring the green light had gone out. "I'm sorry, sir, but that's…bullshit." Beth squirmed in her chair. "I wonder whose pocket he's in, anyway."

"Well, you're going to discover that and more, Beth. I'm sending you and Donovan to find out. Take the next flight, if you can rework your schedules." He turned to Gemma. "I owe you an apology. I've just stolen your team. You're going to have to begin the investigation of Hendricks by yourself. I have faith in you, and frankly, my big worry is you not having a backup in Manchester. Think you can inveigle one of Manchester's Finest to lend a hand?"

Gemma Trask's response was crisp. "Absolutely. Mr. Donovan and I are convinced Hendricks is in it up to his thick neck, and if there's any chance he's responsible for Jack's condition…" She left the threat uncompleted.

The three looked to Donovan, who stood half-turned to the door. "Um, I was hoping to have a word with Gemma. In private, if that's okay." Rory nodded and the two left the room. In the hallway, Gemma raised her eyebrows, waiting.

"I'll keep it to the point. You, Jack and I have been thrown into this without ever having worked together before. It hasn't always been easy, trying to read each other's minds and tiptoe around sensitivities. Well, I think this whole case has gone up an entire notch, in terms of danger and the possibility of us getting killed.

"Here's the thing. Jack's chances of recovery don't change a whit, if Beth and I go there today. Finding his shooters might get harder with a delay, but what I want to know is this: Are you going to be okay in Manchester, without me? Hendricks would as soon kill you as look at you. More so, since I poked him."

Gemma leaned in as if to embrace him, but pulled back. Eyes averted, she muttered, "You're all right, mate. I feel like I've been more intimate with you this past minute than I've been with my last three boyfriends." She looked into his eyes, and back at the floor. "O' course I'll be all right.

If things get up in my face, I'll lay off until you get back. Look. I respect him like I would any junkyard dog. I'm not interested in ending up like…" The reference to Jack hung between them. She straightened her skirt with the flat of her hands. "Come on then, you're on a vacation to Eastern Europe, and I'm back on the next train to Manchester, yeah? Side meeting's over." He opened the door for her and they trooped back into the meeting.

* * * *

"So, what was that about?" Beth's voice was casual. "Was she being argumentative?" Beth and Donovan were on their way back to the apartment in Hammersmith to pack.

"No. The opposite, in fact. I think we've made a breakthrough. Until today, I was willing to bet she didn't trust me as far as she could throw me."

Beth grinned, gauging his slight frame with her eyes. "Actually, she could probably throw you a ways."

"Missing the point here, Sweetie. In the hall, I basically asked her if she'd rather I came with her to Manchester. She said no, of course, but she appreciated me checking in with her before assuming anything." He ran his hands through his hair. "Jesus! What I don't know about women could fill a book. But adding in women who are partners and it's ten times as bad." She raised a finger, but he jumped in before she could speak. "Which brings me to my next point. Until now, you've been the only person I've ever, and I mean ever, felt comfortable working with. So, I'm very happy to be working with you. As long as you do every damn thing I tell you, from the moment we get on that plane." He grinned as her fist slammed into his rib.

CHAPTER SEVENTEEN

Constanta, On the Black Sea

SEAN DONOVAN AND BETH MCLEAN had a helicopter waiting for them at Battersea Heliport, compliments of strings pulled by the ambassador. Both had packed overnight bags, so the chopper had them in the air and heading north out of London within minutes. They landed at Biggin Hill, a boutique airport where a silver and white Gulfstream G450 sat on the tarmac, waiting. "Lifestyles of the rich and famous," Beth murmured, as their bags were whisked from them and they were escorted to two of the six available seats.

"Sweetie, we're just hitch-hikers on the planes of the truly affluent." Donovan responded, as he spied another couple seated on a sofa toward the rear of the cabin. "And here's who we're hitch-hiking a ride from." He turned to face them. "Hello, I'm Sean. This is my partner, Beth. We're friends of Rory Thompson." He shook hands with a twenty-something couple, both flashing megawatt smiles.

"Well, say hello to Rory, next time you see him." The young lady lifted her feet off the floor and curled them under her. "My name is Téa and this is Marco. Uncle Rory said you needed to get to Romania in a hurry, and I've got a shoot there, so…" She waved a hand that encompassed the remaining cabin space. Her voice was languid, but her eyes danced, and her smile didn't quit. Her hair was impossibly blonde and her teeth were flawless. She seemed quite small in physique, yet her arms and legs were toned. "We're getting off in Bucharest, and I've got a hiking tour planned up in the mountains near Poiana Brasov. It's dead gorgeous there. The captain will fly you to Constanta, and you can keep the jet there for as long as you need it, or ten days, whichever comes first." She dimpled at her own humor.

"That's generous, thank you. Yes, I've been to Poiana. Be sure to eat local; the food and beer are wonderful. If you have time, the Biserica Neagra or The Black Church is worth a visit." Donovan chose a seat nearby and strapped in for take-off. Beth sat beside him, despite Téa's invitation to join her on the sofa. Throughout the introductions and small talk, the gorgeous young man said nothing, although he showed an interest in everything said.

Donovan watched Beth take in her surroundings. Her chestnut hair swayed as she turned from this wonder to that. The cockpit was closed off to the rest of the interior, separating the pilots from the passengers by a locked door and a wet bar. The six seats came next, arranged like theatre seating, but with considerably more space. Behind the seats a pair of leather sofas were placed facing one another, sharing a cocktail table. The setting sun flooded the trademark oval windows of the Gulfstream before dropping to dusk on the west side of the plane. Aft of the seating a compact office sat at the ready, and a kitchenette and washrooms completed the list of any services a passenger could want.

"I could get used to this." Beth sighed. Donovan thought of the last time he flew in a comparable jet. That time, he had been kidnapped; at the mercy, ironically, of one of his current contractors. The multi-millionaire Gaia had absconded with him, and they'd flown to Montreal to retrieve a piece of stolen art. He smiled at the thought that things had softened, to the point where he was now doing a recovery job for the multimillionaire.

With all of the murders in recent days, Donovan had failed to make progress on the piece of art Gaia had requested. He had to get back to that as soon as possible. *It's a funny thing. Although I seem to have lots of irons in the fire, there seem to be overlaps everywhere I turn. There are connections...* "Sorry. What were you asking?"

She smiled. "I was asking if you'd like a drink. The screen at my elbow was wondering. I told it 'Yes, please. Red wine, with some hard cheese.' What about you?"

"Please. New Zealand pinot noir."

She lowered her head and murmured into the screen. "Done. By the way, we should have a screen like this installed in my apartment, what do you think? Now, what were you fretting about, in your thoughts?" Her hand crept across the seat to rest on his forearm.

"I was thinking all of this stuff we're involved in is connected. In fact," he turned to face her, "the purchase of the winery seems to be the only thing on my to-do list that doesn't seem to be about the murders." He held out his free hand, raising fingers with each point, to count out the issues. "A corrupt lawyer gets robbed in Ambleside, and by all accounts the truck is from Manchester. A woman's business in Romania goes south and she gets murdered. Shot. She was from Manchester. Her husband, also a Mancunian, murders the guy who apparently bungled the woman's shipment. In the meantime, a nearby Manchester family is supposed to receive a packet, courtesy of the dead woman's dead husband."

He gently extricated her hand from his, and, while continuing to hold it, began pulling up her fingers. He continued. "Jack, on the case, goes to another country and asks Manchester-related questions and gets shot to hell. Through all this, woven right into the heart of everything I've mentioned, is this bastard Hendricks." He stared at her, his face intense. "Not. A coincidence. And there'll be a reckoning, soon, I think. Ah, here comes the wine."

A chrome salver arrived, but Téa high-jacked the attendant, directing that the drinks and appetizers be placed on the table between the two sofas. She pressed her hands together in prayer, facing Beth. "Please come save me. Us! Keep us company."

They sat in the sofa across from the young lady and her silent companion, Marco. Téa explained that she would be filming scenes for an indie movie in the mountains around Poiana, and then moving on to a fashion assignment in Bucharest. She asked how they knew Rory and, once that was out of the way, they settled into casual conversation designed to go nowhere and nevertheless be entertaining. When it was her turn, Téa asked if they had ever been to Bucharest. Beth shook her head, but Donovan nodded, wondering where the tale would go.

"A couple of years ago, I was modeling and the agency sent me to three events: Hamburg, Vienna, and Bucharest. By the time we arrived at the last city, there was no room at the nice hotels, at least for the first night, because of a NATO convention. So my guardian and I had to sleep in what I swear was the crappiest hotel in the country. Romania's not a rich country by any means, so when I say crappy, I mean B-movie, slasher flick sketchy. It was called The Capital. I'll never forget it.

"We walk up to the second floor, being careful not to touch the walls, which were dis-gustingly filthy. I swear, putting poop on the walls could only have improved them. As we go into our room, I noticed that the entry system—the door and latch—had been smashed in and not quite fixed. So we go in and push a chest of drawers up against the door." She raised one eyebrow. "Remember, we had no choice. The country was basically full of guests. So we look around. One bed, plus a sofa bed that we were afraid to touch. My guardian wouldn't go near it, and since I'd given her the bed, I had to decide: sofa bed or the floor? I opened it up and there was no mattress, just a bunch of springs that looked more like barbwire than a bed."

"So, what did you do?" Beth waited, aghast.

Téa's grin was rueful. "The closer I looked, the gnarlier those springs looked. I swear I saw bloodstains on them! So I argued with the woman downstairs to give me a sheet, which she did, reluctantly. I get back to the room and the sheet has a five-inch tear in the corner, plus a stain at the rip I sincerely hope was rust. Anyway, I spread it on the floor under the window and sat in the very middle of it until morning, my knees tucked around my ears, like this." She showed the compact posture she'd assumed that night. "You could hear the dogs playing all night, outside. The thing is, instead of being outraged like first-world brats would be, I suppose, I think of that every time I catch myself acting like a diva. It was a real lesson on how some folks have to live every day of their lives." Her smile faltered, and she glanced around the cabin, and whispered. "I'm a lucky girl, I figure."

After just a moment of silence, Beth spoke up. "So, Marco, do you have a story for us?"

He smiled, shaking his head just a bit. Téa tucked an arm under the crook of his elbow. "This is partly why I asked you to keep me company on the sofas. For my mental health." She winked. "Marco's on a 48-hour speaking fast, on behalf of a children's advocacy group: Who Speaks For The Children. Our friends and associates have agreed to sponsor him, since normally he's the yappiest one of all of us." She gave him a peck on the cheek. "He's raised a hundred thousand so far, for the children. I'm really proud of him." Marco's teeth glistened, and he pretended to wipe sweat from his forehead.

The attendant arrived, wheeling a tray with flat bread points and crudités, together with a half dozen Mid-Eastern and Asian-inspired dips. He returned with a second tray of hot foods, including butter chicken, rice and naan. While they ate, they discussed the Buddhist notion of taking time off from speaking in order to get in touch with your inner self. During the main course, however, the subject drifted to the concept of umami and whether it was a modern invention distinct from saltiness or if it in fact even existed. The flight attendant brought out some food that presented the notion of umami, and other, similar dishes that were delicious, but simply had a salty taste to it. The group, all smiles, were divided into pairs, one couple able to distinguish the difference and the other remaining puzzled by the concept.

After dinner, Donovan and Beth thanked their hosts and excused themselves, returning to their seats. The attendant lowered the lights, brought heated blankets and adjusted their seats to recline almost to horizontal. Beth had saved the crème brulée and tapped the glassy sugared top, the light blanket covering all but her hands and chin.

"Don't get used to this," Donovan warned. "We will not be treated this way for a long time, if ever again. All right if I interrupt this infatuation you're having with your dessert? Good. I wouldn't want to wreck such a strong love affair."

"Oh, Sean, you don't understand." Her spoon was upside-down, clenched between her teeth. "I want to march into the kitchenette and marry that chef. So good."

"Okay, then. But keep those noises down, or we'll get thrown off the plane." Her response was to scrape the sides and bottom of the ramekin with her spoon, a moan escaping from the back of her throat.

"Now. Back to business. As soon as we get to Constanta, I want to give the docks a once-over, but we really have to get hold of the widow of Costin Pitu. Jack wouldn't hang out with someone for no reason. Either Pitu was a suspect, or he knew stuff. Either way, he's dead now, and I don't think the police in Constanta want things to come out. That puts her first on my list. What do you think?"

Beth had attempted to put the dish down, and the attendant appeared and scooped it up as if by magic, leaving behind a pair of moist lemon-scented, heated cloths with which they could refresh themselves. She began with a question. "English and French are two of the four official languages of Romania, right?"

"Together with Romanian and Russian, yes."

"So the chances are a city girl would speak either English or French, right? I'm guessing, here."

"Probably. Where are you going with this?"

"I was thinking that, as a woman, I'd like to have the first crack at her, if that's okay."

"What approach would you take?"

She rolled onto her side to face him, her voice low. "Well, I'd appeal to her sense of us being women caught up in violence we didn't choose, assuming she's not in it up to her neck. You are aware I make my living by mastering communication channels with all sorts of people and organizations. But to be honest, my advantage here is I am a woman, communicating with a woman whose husband was just murdered. I am, however, perfectly willing to have you do the parts involving throwing yourself down flights of stairs and climbing icy water towers. I'll talk to women, you go fight armed guards. Deal?"

"We'll see. We won't land for another couple of hours. Let's have a nap." She felt him squeeze her hand. In a few minutes, they were both asleep.

* * * *

Customs was uneventful, and the airport was almost deserted at that time of night. The bored official unzipped Donovan's bag and pretended to look at the contents, but he spent much of the time watching Beth take off her belt and shoes. "Well played." Donovan murmured to her as they exited the terminal and entered the still-darkened night sky.

"All bets were off, once they shot Jack. I'll do whatever it takes." Her chin jutted out, just a little.

A cab took them to a hotel not far from the Constanta Dockyard and they checked in, and finished their night's sleep, a restless event. Next morning, they showered and set off in search of a diner. Once set up for the day, they flagged a taxi. Beth said, "There's no time like the present," and she watched Donovan drive off in the direction of the dockyards. She hailed the next available taxi and passed the address of the late Costin Pitu to the cabbie, and then headed in the opposite direction of Donovan.

* * * *

Beth stepped out of the cab, asking the driver to wait for her. There were gray buildings in every direction. She crossed a paved rectangle that led to one of the fifteen-story apartment buildings. After checking the slip of paper against the number at the corner of the edifice, she entered the closest end. She glanced into the elevator door and decided to take her chances in the semi-lit stairway. She passed a four-year old playing on the landing between floors. The girl had found a few shards of window pane glass and had fashioned a house from them. A tiny matryoshka doll lay within the glass box. "Tell your babushka not to throw stones, okay?" The little girl's face inclined upward, solemn. Beth continued on.

The number two hundred was affixed to the first door she came across. Beth's hand was descending to knock when a voice from within, in perfect English, stated that the door was open, and to come in.

"I've been following you through the window, since the cab pulled up. I knew you'd come for me. My only question is, are you here to murder me as well, or to help me find those fuckers?"

Beth, astounded, closed the door behind her and studied the slender woman sitting on a chair by the window, a light shawl covering her legs. Her face was long, oval, and seemed to be cold-chiseled from flint. Her hair contained touches of premature silver, but she was obviously the same age as Beth. Her almond-shaped eyes were such a tone of dark brown that the pupils had melded into the irises. Her lips, while full, were pursed into a narrow line, and her nose flared. "Well?"

"My name's Beth McLean. I'm a communications dir—officer with the Canadian government, out of London. I work with Jack Miller. He's the gentleman who was with your husband when he, when he…"

"Was murdered." The dark brown eyes continued to follow her, and Beth noted the drawn look along the cheeks, the darkness under the eyes, and the pain and sadness within them. "Canadian, eh? That's my only Canadian joke. So, you know the man who was with my husband the other night. What do you want?"

"I want to help. I want to find these men and make them tell me why they did this."

"A trace of a smile formed, but there was no room for warmth within it. "That's funny. We both want to find them, but for different reasons.

You want to have a conversation with them. All I want is to kill them. We may not be able to work together after all." She shifted in her chair, and Beth noticed something slide under the blanket, just above the woman's knees.

Beth tried a different tack. "I'm sorry, what's your name? Ava? This is how I see things. Two or three bastards swing by a bar and shoot a couple of people. Either they did this because they needed to silence them, or they were following orders. I think it's the latter. I want the man who told them to do this, and I can't get at him if we kill the shooters. And I believe if you think this through, you'll want the same thing."

Ava's reply seemed peculiar to Beth. She asked Beth to stand beside the laptop that sat on the kitchen table. When she rose, the shawl slipped to the floor, revealing an old Russian Makarov pistol. "I want you to go on-line and do a search on yourself. I'll follow the URL and then I'll decide if you're full of shit or if I will trust you. Your problem, however, is I don't care anymore." Her voice cracked, just a little. "So, if you make a mistake, I'll have no problem taking you out. Got it?"

A minute later, Ava seemed satisfied with the various references to Beth's personal and corporate life. "A director of communications? That seems like an odd person to send on a job like this."

"I suppose. But I'm on a small team that worked with Jack. Two of us are in Constanta, trying to find out what happened, and why. For me, the biggest thing is, what information did your husband share with Jack that night?" Beth paused. "By the way, I'm no more helpless than you are, so from this minute on, you are not alone.

"Have you eaten today? Because I have a cab outside, waiting. We could go grab a bite and share as much information with each other as we know. And we could work out next steps. Do you have any children? No? Then, you have no reason to stay cooped up here. Come on." A minute later, they were in the cab, headed to a restaurant near the dockyards.

On the way, Ava confessed that she had no money. "I buried my husband yesterday, and somehow the money came from several hundred

English pounds found in my husband's pocket. I don't know where he got it. It all went for the funeral, but I don't care about that. I'll go back to work on Monday, if I'm still around, and I'll be okay." Beth had nothing to say to that, so she remained silent.

At the restaurant, Beth picked lamb stew from a photo on the menu. Ava chose *sarmale*, or mincemeat wrapped in cabbage leaves, served with polenta. Both decided on *papanasi*, a kind of doughnut with jam and sour cream on top. She noted that Ava stopped in mid-course, asking the server to wrap the rest to take home.

Throughout the meal, Beth peppered her with questions. Ava pondered every one as if checking her memory, and seemed to answer everything to the best of her ability. It was in this way Beth learned of how Costin Pitu's supervisor had been visited by a pair of Englishmen, how he had seemed different after the visit. Beth also learned of Costin's suspicions suggesting Ellie Campbell's potato shipment may have contained more than potatoes. There were moments, tough moments, when Ava would stop, in mid-chew, her eyes wandering to the window, obviously thinking about her freshly murdered husband. Beth's heart ached for her, but felt certain that the best thing to do would be to pursue this.

Ava put both hands flat on the table between them, as they finished their coffee. "Any other questions?"

"Two more. Do you know how to use that gun? And, what do you do for a living?"

"Yes. I can shoot. I was in the military for two years." She sat back, looking around the restaurant as if seeing it for the first time. "Now, I'm an art dealer. I have a degree in fine arts from Penn State. That's where I met Costin. I specialize in the import-export laws surrounding art, collectibles, and historic pieces. For people I like, I know ways to smooth the passage from country to country. For people I don't like, I can snarl their acquisitions up in red tape for years." She allowed the trace of a smile to appear. "Why? Do you think you can get me a job back home?"

Beth gave her an admiring look. "I thought you were a well-spoken Romanian."

"I like to think I am also a well-spoken American. But I'm from the States, to answer the question you didn't quite ask. I'll go home as soon as I can line up a job and pay for a plane ticket." She tapped her purse. "But…first things first. We're fed. When do we go hunting?"

"Let's get in touch with my partner…Sean." She omitted the second half of the expression, thinking that the words 'in crime' rang too true. "He's been snooping around the docks and we promised to check in on each other around about now."

"Can I trust him?"

"I trusted him with my life, and except for the tiniest souvenir in my shoulder, it all worked out."

This elicited another smile, a real one, this time. "Now, that didn't really inspire confidence in me, Beth. You might want to leave that off his crime-solving résumé, in the future."

Beth paused. "By the way, I feel I should add this disclaimer. Neither of us is a cop. We have…interesting skill sets, but no policing authority. I have a letter from the Canadian embassy and the authorities are aware that we are in the country to look in on Jack, but that's as far as it goes. At the end of the day, all we have is us. Are you in?"

Ava nodded. "I expect the people we're seeking would know what I look like, as Costin's wife. So we'll have to factor that into whatever snooping you get me to do."

"I agree. But there are three of us. We'll work things out. Okay, let's get you back to the apartment and then I'll track down Sean. We'll get together at suppertime."

In the cab, Beth palmed a small wad of bills over. In a low voice, she explained the money was to grease the investigation. "It's not even my money. It can be used to proceed with the investigation, so all three of us need some. This is your share for the next few days." Ava said nothing, but accepted the bills, her head lowered.

****

The taxi entered the short street that housed the five apartment buildings, and Beth waited for the vehicle to slow. Her concentration was broken when Ava pounded on the top of the empty front passenger seat, crying out a short phrase. The taxi maintained its speed and drove past the buildings without slowing. "There's a man in my window." She followed it with a low oath. "Now what? Do we go back, and try to get the jump on him?"

Beth tried to keep a tremor of fear from her voice. "No. Now we head to a place near my hotel and we wait for Sean." She tried a smile, which came out lopsided. "He and I made a deal. He'd do all the grunt work while I look pretty and talk my way out of things. Let's go find him." She rubbed her now-sweaty hands on the sides of her thighs. "I guess we just got that break. Be careful what you ask for, eh?"

They got the cabbie to drop them not far from Beth's hotel. Halfway down the block, Donovan emerged from a shop with a bag of baked goods. He fell into step with the women and they continued on to the hotel. "Did you know Bucharest is known as the Paris of the East? And, like Paris, their baking is amazing." He reached in to the bag and pulled out an almond shortcake with three swirls of icing in the colors of the Romanian flag. "This one is called *sable*, which is the French word for sand. I've got *macarons* in here as well. We'll get caught up, once we get to the hotel," he added, his voice lower.

He had also bought some Ciuc and Ursus Black beers, having recognized the former from previous trips, and having been told the latter was the best rated Romanian beer. He opened three bottles, they sat down and Beth introduced Ava and presented their most recent discovery.

Donovan sat on the edge of his chair and looked down at the floor, elbows on knees and hands cradling a bottle. "Well, you'll stay here for now. I'll take out another room in my name. I think I'd better go visit your apartment. Got a key for me?"

"As if you need one." Beth tried to make light of his intention, but he could see the worry on her face.

"Don't worry." He looked up to meet her. "I wonder if you two are game for a little spying. Costin had a boss..."

"Fyodor Fyodorov." Ava looked from Beth to Donovan.

"Yeah, Fyodorov. It would be great if I knew where he lives and where he drinks. But it's hard to follow someone without using a car, especially if you don't know the city." He looked up at Ava.

"I can get a car, for a few lei. And of course, I know the city."

"We don't need anyone to approach anyone, got it? So, you see him and I don't care if he's with two Brits holding guns and a photo of Costin. Do not approach them. There's no need. Just see where he goes, who he meets, and come back to the hotel, got it? Ava, can you be trusted not to screw this up? Revenge is a powerful instigator, and everything is lost if you shoot one and let two plus the ringleader get away. We can't get caught up in the chase and forget what's at stake."

"I understand." Ava's voice was muted.

Donovan snapped. "I know you understand. You're not stupid. What I asked for was, are you willing to tail someone in such a way that they don't know it happened?" She nodded, eyes averted. "Good. Because it's not just about your vendetta. Anything less than what I ask, and you're risking killing Beth and me. I've thought it through, and I'm not all right with being dead." He stared at her until she nodded.

"It's almost five. Fyodorov will get off work in a half hour. Go get a car and get to the docks. The guy knows you, right, Ava? So Beth, you drive. If he spots you, get out. If he acts suspicious, get out. If you lose your nerve..."

"I know, get out."

"That's right. I have to go now. Here's some cash for the car and bribes. Give me the key and we'll either check in on each other, or we meet back here at eleven tonight. Sound good?" He left them to make arrangements for a car, and then he grabbed his green canvas back pack and flagged down a taxi to take him to the Pitu residence.

CHAPTER EIGHTEEN

Constanta, On the Black Sea

ON THE WAY TO AVA'S apartment building, Donovan was pleased to see the sun dip below the horizon. He reviewed the contents of his bag for ideas, which in turn made him think about the person or persons waiting within the apartment. If it was one person, what would he do? If it was more than one, could he get the jump on them all? Surprise was on his side, but they'd be on guard, so how much, really, was the element of surprise worth?

He also wondered about the degree of his reaction. Was it worth killing someone, given he didn't even know why the stranger was in the apartment? He may have been there merely to question Ava. That perhaps wasn't worth a death. And what was to be gained from this? He was two blocks away, so it was time for the driver to let him out. He saw the outline of the five buildings, noting how quickly daylight was failing. Taking the long way around, he entered the building from the end farthest from her apartment. Using the stairs, he climbed to the second floor, being as quiet as he could.

He peeked around the corner of the concrete landing and saw there was no one in the hall. Feeling exposed, he traversed the length of the hall and arrived at number two hundred. Her door. It had been left open a crack. Why? He reached into his pack and withdrew a realistic looking, three-quarter-size mechanical mouse. He activated it and moved to the stairwell, a few feet away. He looked up…nothing. He peered below him and there was a very young girl, playing in the dimness, beneath a window. As she glanced up at him, he placed his finger up to his lips in the universal signal to remain quiet, and winked at her. He placed a candy bar on the floor at the top of the stairs within reach of the little girl, and returned to his task.

Donovan put on a pair of computerized glasses and, using his voice, commanded the mouse to move forward. As the mouse moved, Donovan could see everything in front of the mouse's camera lens. He directed the mouse to follow the wall and to round the corner to the tiny living room. He peered through the twilight and could make out most of the features of the single individual seated by the window.

It was Costin's supervisor, Fyodorov.

He reached into his bag and pulled out a tiny glass vial. He broke the tip off it and poured it out onto the floor, just inside the door. Making sure the door was unlocked, he pulled it closed, making enough noise to alert the man in the apartment. Then, he crouched so his eyes were inches from the door knob. He waited, holding his breath and listening to the footsteps approaching the door. There was a pause of perhaps three seconds, and the door opened.

The barrel of a pistol preceded a hand, and then the door widened. Fyodorov stared down at the man outside the door, who remained on one knee.

Donovan said nothing. He put his finger to his lips, curling his other index finger in the universal gesture of invitation. The man stepped back, just a bit. In a moment, he bent down to see what Donovan was looking at, the gun trained on Donovan's heart. The fumes caught him and Fyodorov was out on his feet. Donovan, still holding his breath, took the pistol from the unconscious man as he fell.

* * * *

Fyodor Fyodorov regained consciousness in the kitchen of his former employee, Costin Pitu. He was taped to a chair that was in turn taped to the sink cupboard handles. Donovan sat on a kitchen chair across from him, a burner phone in one hand, a hypodermic needle in the other. He'd been staring at the unconscious man for three minutes, keeping his focus on the area around the eyes. Fifteen seconds earlier they'd begun to move from REM to semi-consciousness under the lids, but they didn't open a hair's width. Concurrently, the flow of blood through the vein in his neck increased its activity. His victim was fully awake.

"You are back with us, Mr. Fyodorov. Eyes open or eyes shut, you can hear me. I don't think you speak English, at least, not well. But I have someone on the phone, dying to speak with you. Just before I let her chat, you should know that I have administered SP117, the Russian variant of amybarbitol. Some folks call it a psychoactive truth serum. I call it your last chance to live beyond the hour. Let's chat with Ava. You may recall having murdered her husband, Costin, a few days ago." Donovan watched Fyodorov's eyes open at that.

"Ava, tell him about the truth serum, and then ask him about the two Englishmen who did the shooting while he drove. Where are they from? And where are they now?"

The man mumbled something while Ava translated. "He says he understands English, but he can't speak it." He uttered a series of grunts and guttural stammerings. "He says the two Englishmen blackmailed him into driving the car. He didn't know what they were going to do until they opened fire. He fears for his life, which will be worthless if anything gets out."

Donovan looked at the man, controlling him with his gaze. "This doesn't have to contain truth serum, buddy. I can put, say, nitrogen bubbles in it. Or air. Neither one is very pleasant for the body to process. It wants to, but after a few moments, it just decides that it's not worth the bother. I think you have to decide whether dying now is maybe worse than getting threats from people who I will be taking care of shortly. You look like you don't understand. Ava, can you help him to understand his options, here?" He waited, watching the eyes get rounder. The chance of a full hypodermic needle containing enough air to kill his captive was slim, but Donovan was betting Fyodorov didn't know this.

"Your choice is to die now, and not in a gentle way, or stand a chance of surviving by telling me a bit about our two Englishmen. What part of England are they from? Did they come here by plane or by truck?" Donovan pulled back the needle plunger, drawing in two cc's of air. Fyodorov took in an audible amount of air as well, as Donovan rested the tip on the top of his captive's taped forearm.

"No!"

Donovan smiled. "You know, that's a very Anglo-Saxon word. It's possible you speak better English than I gave you credit for."

"I spik liddle English."

"Then, tell me how close you are to dying within the next ten minutes, Fyodor." He scratched the man's forearm with the point of the needle.

"Close."

"That's correct. Here's the problem. There are two people with you right now. Let's ask Costin's widow what she thinks should be done with you. Ava?"

The voice over the phone was void of emotion. "Kill him now. Or wait ten minutes until I can get there to kill him myself."

Donovan shook his head. "She's not going to save you. And then there's me. If I am a policeman—politia—you might be saved. Am I a policeman, Ava?"

There was a trace of humor in her voice. "Not even close. In fact, it's my understanding you're a murderer. That's what I heard."

Fyodorov paled. "Don't kill me. I am married. I have…children."

"Jesus Christ. Really? You want to play that card while the wife of the man you murdered is listening? You've got balls, mister, I'll tell you that." Donovan ran a hand through his hair. "Tell you what. I'll give you twenty seconds to tell me something about the two men. Twenty seconds."

"Please…"

"Sixteen seconds. And after I kill you, I'll tell your widow what you've done to yourself and to her, just before I kill her as well."

Fyodorov began praying. Donovan stopped him at four seconds. "You happy with your decision, then?" He raised the syringe, his eyes never leaving the captive.

"No! I'll talk." He spoke Romanian as Eva translated. "I don't know everything. There are two men, from England. They came by truck. They didn't tell me from where, but the truck is from Manchester City. They are still in Constanta, until tomorrow morning. They took things from a potato shipment. I don't know what was inside, but they were in aluminum suitcases. They were supposed to leave two weeks ago, but their boss told them to stay—hide?—here until a search stopped in Manchester. Once the two men were shot here, the Englishmen became happy and they told their boss.

"I pretend I don't speak English too much, so they said things around me that they probably didn't want me to know."

"What else?"

"Nothing else."

Donovan told the women he'd be along shortly and ended the call. He turned his attention back to the man taped to the chair. "The more you tell me, the greater is the chance that I can stop them. Where are they, right this minute? What sort of weapons are they carrying?"

Fyodorov mumbled an address located not far from the docks, and then he volunteered a brief description of the men, together with the name of the bar they frequented. Each had a pistol as well as a semi-automatic rifle. Donovan emptied the hypodermic into the air and picked up a tiny bottle. Inserting the needle, he charged the reservoir with two milliliters of a clear liquid. Despite Fyodorov's twisting, Donovan plunged the needle into his forearm, emptied the contents into his captive's bloodstream, and waited until the man slumped to the side of the chair. He closed the apartment door behind him, and headed for the docks.

* * * *

They waited outside the bar until after midnight. Ava sat behind the wheel of the car, parked between the streetlights a half a block from the bar's entrance, her back rigid. Donovan and Beth stood in the shadows, just inside a nearby alleyway, watching the door. The closer to midnight, the louder and more crowded the area in and around the bar became. By twelve-thirty, the bouncers began an irregular stream of trips out the door, escorting drunken sailors and callow youths to the curb.

"Showtime. Are you all right with this?"

Beth took Donovan's hand, bringing it to her belt. He felt the compact pistol. "And I've got the little dart behind my ear. I'll be fine." She undid the top button of her blouse, reaching up to graze his throat with a gentle buss. "If I knew I was getting into the seductress business, I'd have gotten a breast augmentation."

"Don't ever change, Sweetie." His forehead carried a worry line. "We can do this another way, if you're..."

"I'm good. In my mind, I'm across town, in a hospital, watching Jack right now. This is for him. Here goes nothing." She stepped out of the shadows and strode to the door of the bar, spike heels clicking on the cobblestones and hips swaying like he'd never seen until that moment.

* * * *

Once inside, Beth headed straight for the bar, not bothering to look anywhere but at the bartender. She held up one finger. "Ciuc." The bartender cracked open a bottle of the popular Romanian beer. She paid in Romanian lei and then sat near the end of the bar, head over the bottle. Her long dark hair swooped forward, masking her face.

After her first sip, Beth listened intently, trying to deconstruct the roar of the crowd into disparate conversations. She sought non-Romanian speech, as well as any sounds that weren't compatible with the general cacophony of an Eastern European bar. Only once did she hear a single English word, and she waited a couple of seconds to lift her glass and point her ear in the direction of the out-of-place sound. After a minute, her eyes followed the sounds she had isolated.

Two men fitting Fyodorov's description of the Brits sat at a table along the wall that led to the kitchen. Both men were in their late twenties or early thirties, and the stockier of the two had his head swaying over a fresh pint glass, showing all the signs of having enjoyed a full evening. Beth made a small show of taking off her jacket and folding it over her left arm. She took another pull from her draft and sauntered over to the table, eyes locked on the more sober of the two.

"Did I hear you say something in English?" She offered her most brilliant smile, her words slurring, just a bit. "I am so fucking lonesome for a joke or a laugh in my own language. I swear I'd even listen to a chat about footie, for cripes sake." She leaned down, exposing a bit more cleavage, and placed a hand over his forearm.

His words oozed oil. "Where ya from, darlin'? I haven't seen ya around." He placed his free hand over hers, pushing an empty chair out as an invitation.

She took another long gulp of beer. "I"—she belched without trying to cover her mouth—"just got in yesterday, from Kiev. Jus' looking for some fun, y'know?" She half-slid, half-fell onto the proffered chair. "I work too hard. A girl needs some fun, sometimes, amIright?" Beth put a definite slur on the last few words.

"Right, you are, darlin'. Let me get you another beer."

"That's an excellent idea! I'll pay. What…" her eyes narrowed, unfocused. "What'll you have?" She fumbled with her purse, pulling out a small wad of bills. "Here, Baby, You keep track for us." As she handed the money over to her new companion, he pulled his arm back, as if stung.

"Bloody hell! You scratched me. Mind those claws."

"Sorry." Beth smiled, dropping the used dart to the floor and affecting an abashed look. The Brit looked at the money, and Beth looked at the Brit. "Baby, you look tired. Is it time for us to go home?"

"Nah." But his face looked confused. At the sound of the word 'home', the drunker of the two Englishmen became a speck more alert, mumbling the word, "Perhaps." She continued to study the first man's face.

"Sorry, Baby, but I think you're done for. Let's all go home—she practically threw her last word at the drunker companion—and we can have more fun there. Sound like a plan?" The man she'd been hitting on grew sleepier, more confused. She helped him up, dragged his mate to something approximating vertical, and the three stumbled toward the door, one on each of her arms.

"Madam?" It was one of the bouncers, speaking in English. He handed over her purse. In English, he asked, "Are you going to be all right, with these gentlemen?" His face wasn't judging, but his tone registered concern.

Bringing her voice back to sober, she replied: "Perfectly fine, thank you. I'm their boss and I'm just seeing them safely home." The drunk opened one eye at the sound of the word 'home', and she marched them out the door and up the street to the waiting car. Donovan caught up in time to keep the drugged Brit vertical and help pour them into the back seat. Doors slammed and the five drove off.

* * * *

The women occupied the front seat, with Ava driving, while Donovan sat with the men in the back. He had placed the drunk by the locked door, hands tied, with the drugged Brit in the middle. After rifling through their pockets, Donovan found a scrap of paper with addresses on it, and then asked Ava to drive them to a warehouse.

They arrived shortly, and Donovan walked over to a lorry with British plates, unlocking it with keys he'd taken from the men. The pistols and rifles were in a low-slung metal case, just behind the truck seats, in the cab. He closed the lid of the case, taking care not to touch the weapons. Moving around to the back, he unlocked and then unlatched the back, lifting the overhead trailer door.

He shone a flashlight into the gloom of the box. Scores of reflected points of light flew back, startling him. Peering in, he noted dozens of aluminum suitcases and briefcases, many of them dusty or with streaks of mud across them. Grabbing the nearest one, he opened it, and then stared at a painting. He lifted the artwork to reveal a second, and then a third within the case. The next suitcase contained similar pieces. *When opportunity knocks, I'd be a fool not to answer.* Donovan sighed, slid the overhead door back into place, and locked it.

"Nothing significant, except for their guns. Let's go to your apartment, Ava."

* * * *

With three sets of hands, it was easier to escort the pair of Brits up the stairs of Ava's apartment building. The drunker of the two was beginning to sober up, so they taped him to a chair first. After securing the drugged Brit, their attention returned to Fyodorov, who still showed no signs of returning to consciousness. Donovan hadn't said much, but his eyes kept darting from prisoner to prisoner, as well as to Ava. As a consequence, Beth was the only one who was surprised when Ava opened her purse and pulled out a pistol.

She stared at Ava. "What are you doing? Don't ruin your life now. Come on."

"What do you know about a ruined life? Is your man dead yet?" She waved the barrel of the pistol toward Donovan. "I have a gun. The three men who murdered my husband in cold blood are right here in front of me. In one minute, Costin will be avenged. I don't care what happens to me. I…" She stopped when Donovan began to approach her, moving between Ava and the three seated men.

"Stay where you are. I'll shoot."

Donovan kept walking. As she brought the pistol up to the general location of his chest, he batted it aside with his left hand and punched her square on the chin. Beth caught her as she slumped.

"That was harsh."

"You're welcome."

"So, do we tie her up as well?"

"Nah. She wasn't going to kill anyone. She was just processing her grief, I think."

"You think." Beth's voice was flat, incredulous.

"Well, you can never be sure. Listen. I'm going to need a minute to work out our next steps. Can you keep an eye on things?"

Donovan went into the bathroom and phoned a brownstone on the Upper West Side in New York City. "Hello, Gaia. I have a truckload of stolen art that needs to be moved. Yes. Still in the truck. No, nothing related to my primary gig. In Constanta, Romania. Do you have a way of getting the goods out of the country? A conservative guess would be seven to ten million, but I only looked at one-fiftieth of the pieces of artwork, so I'm guessing. Here's the thing. They really can't be resold, as they're murder evidence. A trick like that would bring all kinds of trouble down on my head, and yours as well. We'll recoup our investment from the thirty-five percent insurance reward, so that's where our money will come from. It'll be legal, for a change. But they absolutely need to get out of the country. I am thinking of a thirty-seventy split in your favor, so are you in? Great. Here is the address and the plate number. Do not have your men come get it until I retrieve four weapons from the cab. They were used in a murder, so your men wouldn't find it helpful to have border guards find them. Give me an hour before your truck arrives." He rang off and returned to the parlor.

"Beth? There's something you need to know. There were numerous pieces of art in the back of that truck. I didn't want to tell you in front of Ava. I've just made arrangements to have them taken out of the country, and the police can deal with it later. I just don't trust the government officials in charge of this case, after we listened to that government slime ball over the phone in London. But we need the guns as evidence, so one of us has to go get them. Here's the million-dollar question: do you want to drive yourself to a warehouse and pick up some murder weapons in the middle of the night? By the way, there is a time limit on that. Or, would you rather babysit three murderers and a bat shit crazy woman, all of them desperate to escape and do you harm?"

She came closer, putting her arms around his waist. "Sweetie, on normal dates, the guy shows the girl the hot tub and a bottle of tequila. When are we going to have normal dates?" Sighing, she pulled back. "I'll babysit the crazed murderers, you go get the toys. Do you suppose her pistol actually works?"

"I'm pretty sure, but they're tied and taped, and two of them will be drugged for another hour or so." He took out a vial from his backpack. "This will cause their hearts to race up to three times the normal rate, up to two hundred and twenty-five beats per minute. If any of them come at you, drop it on the floor and hold your breath as long as you can. If you breathe it in, you won't have a heart attack, but you'll feel like you are. So at least you'll know that but the others won't. I'll be back in an hour, tops." She issued another sigh and sat on the remaining chair, and he left without a backward glance.

CHAPTER NINETEEN

Constanta, Romania

BETH STOOD IN THE QUIET apartment at three in the morning, listening to the breathing of her four captives, and inspecting the Russian pistol she held pointing toward them. The handle had four tiny notches hewn into it. *I wonder if they represent four dead people?* She shook her head, denying the possibility.

Ava groaned, just a little. Beth trained the gun on her, waiting for the eyelids to flutter. A moment later, they opened and Ava spoke while rubbing her jaw. "I'm sorry, Beth. I probably wouldn't have shot them."

Beth grinned. "That's exactly what Sean said. But you do understand why I'm keeping the gun pointed at you, right?"

Ava nodded, a doleful look on her face. "Where did he go?"

"He had to go pick something up. He'll be back any minute. In fact, I think I hear him now." She backed toward the door, the gun pointing in the general direction of her captives. When she turned the knob, four policemen trooped in, with three pistols out, the proximal point of each barrel five inches from Beth's face. The last officer to enter surveyed the room. With a smile, he advised her in a perfect English voice she was sure she recognized, everyone was under arrest. She dropped the gun and put her hands up without saying a word.

* * * *

Two of the police escorted the Englishmen down the stairs, half-carrying them. One officer returned, and he and the remaining policeman half-carried Fyodorov to the paddy wagon below, while the officer-in-charge held the two women. When the lone policeman arrived back at the apartment, he and his superior officer took the two women out of the building. They'd left the lights on and the door unlocked, having got their quarry and not worrying at all about the state of the apartment.

When Beth got to the back of the opened police van, she peered into the darkness. The vehicle was empty. "Where are the Englishmen? And where is Fyodorov?"

The officer in charge smirked. "There were no Englishmen. There are just you two women. You must be imagining things." The smirk vanished. "Get in. We have a long distance to travel tonight."

"Where are you taking us?"

"We are going to Bucharest. You are being arrested for spying against the state."

"What? Who are you?"

"You don't remember me? We spoke on the telephone the other day, with me in Bucharest and you apparently at the Canadian embassy in London. My name is Mircea Bacu. I am the one who told you not to come. You cannot just waltz into a country and do whatever you wish. There are...consequences, the smallest of which you are currently experiencing. We'll see if these consequences...escalate, as I believe they will. Now, get in." Beth and Ava climbed into the rear door of a black police panel van. They clung to the narrow wooden bench as the van accelerated, and a moment later they were headed out of the city.

* * * *

Donovan opened the cab of the British lorry, took all of the weapons together with the steel case and stored them in the trunk of Ava's car. He started the car, but after a moment's hesitation, turned the ignition off. There had to be something in the cab of the truck, some clue that tied the men to the artwork, and ultimately to the potato shipment. To Ellie Campbell. He went back to the truck and climbed in.

It was a standard British vehicle, with a GPS on the dash, sheepskin cover on the driver's side seat, and logbook tucked in the door slot. There was nothing in the glove box and little else but snacks behind the seat. He flipped open the logbook and started with the entries from mid-October. Nothing. He sat behind the driver's wheel, thinking. *If not here, where? If it was me, I'd have it within reach of this seat.* He looked up, right and left.

Donovan looked down to the grotty floor mat. With his left hand, he reached under the mat, pulling out a large plastic pouch people pack their sandwiches in for work. He widened the opening at the top, but was interrupted by the sweep of a set of headlights passing across the hood of the truck. *They're early. Or they might be visitors I really do not want to meet.* He shrunk lower in the cab, opening the door farthest from the visiting truck and slipped out without latching the door. Tucking the plastic pouch into his shirt, he walked straight toward a dark wall with the silhouette of the lorry between him and the new arrivals. In a moment he'd slipped around the corner, and only then dared to turn back to catch a glimpse of the new arrivals.

A military truck had drawn up alongside the British lorry. Two men and a woman dressed in army fatigues hopped out. The first man strode up to the corner of his truck and stood look out. The second man and the lone woman each chose a truck and opened the back of their respective vehicle. The woman hopped onto the bed of the lorry. Donovan couldn't see what she was up to, but what scuffling he could discern suggested she was checking out the goods. Her partner came over to the back of her lorry and whispered something. The man at the front issued a curt, single-word command and all three stopped communicating, with the exception of hand signals.

A moment later, aluminum-sided suitcases began flying out of the back of the lorry. They were caught by the man and moved, fire brigade-style, to their vehicle. *I wonder if they are actually army? I doubt it, but it's brilliant, if they are challenged.* The hundred suitcases were shifted in exactly two minutes, fifteen seconds. The box of the military truck was latched, locked and the man and woman hopped into the cab. The guard left his post and reached behind the gas tank of his truck. He retrieved a package and separated it into two components. He stuck one onto the trailer area, at the bottom of the overhead door. Moving at a lope, he tossed the second one into the cab of the lorry, closed the door and hurried back to his truck. Off they went, and Donovan, knowing what was coming next, sprinted to Ava's car.

He pulled away from the lot and sped off, not hearing an explosion, not seeing the sky light up behind him. But seeing nothing doesn't mean something wouldn't happen shortly. *I'll read about it tomorrow.* He drove to a spot under a streetlight, pulled on a pair of latex gloves, took out his package, and read it.

It was a set of instructions, and it was clear. The two men were to go to the Constanta dockyards, and intimidate the supervisor at Pitu's warehouse, to impress him of the importance of keeping his mouth shut. With what was apparently a different pen, he'd scratched a final message, directing them to stay in Constanta for two weeks, and to track down and kill anyone who showed up, asking questions. Donovan looked at the first message, and then back at the second.

Both were scratched with the same handwriting, although neither was signed.

He folded the scraps of paper, using the original creases, and placed them back in the plastic baggie. Putting the car in gear, he pulled out and headed back to Ava's apartment. A sixth sense overcame him as he pulled up to the gray building. Something's happened. He left the car and eased over to the shadows of the adjacent building where he could peer at Ava's window. All of the lights were on, but he could detect no trace of movement within her place. After two minutes, he walked over to her building and entered.

A moment later, he stood outside of the door to Apartment 200 listening. Nothing. *If they've been shot, there'd be police, and a crowd gathered. Something else is going on.* He pushed the door open. Again, nothing. Everyone was gone.

"Shit."

He took a quick look around the apartment, locating two purses. Ava's pistol was kicked behind the apartment entrance door. *They left in a hurry. Or, rather, somebody took them away in a rush. Was it the Brits? Did the Romanian, Fyodorov, get the jump on Beth? I don't think so. No. Somebody came and took them.* He looked through the purses, and found their passports. They were still in the country, but where? He heard a scuffle outside the apartment.

Although he opened the door immediately, there was no one in the hall, nothing visible to make the noise. He stared at the door—201—across the hall. The shifting scuffle had stopped, but he continued to stare at the eyehole in the door. Donovan appealed to the invisible watcher. "*Va rog. Unde este Ava Pitu?*" (Please. Where is Ava Pitu?) He waited.

After a pause, a small voice passed through the door. "*Politia. Patru politia.*" Four police. Then he heard small steps walk away from behind the door.

"Shit." He said it for the second time in five minutes. It was not shaping up to be the best evening he'd ever had. "Multumesc." Thank you. He pulled Ava's door shut and headed for the car.

* * * *

As Donovan sat waiting as the sun rose up from the horizon, the police station clock hands swept past hours five, six, and seven, with no answers to show for his wait. The first hour had been consumed by finding someone with whom he could basically communicate. As the shift changed at seven, however, several officers arrived who spoke English. What was not helpful were their answers. No, they hadn't picked up four individuals. Yes, they had communicated by radio with all officers on the beat. No, none of them had taken in anyone.

Donovan sat on a bench in the reception area, holding half a cup of undrinkable coffee. He rolled over every scenario he could think of. Were they dead? Who knows? Were they picked up by local police? Apparently not. Was he being lied to? Who knows? Were they picked up by individuals posing as police? The thought of that made his skin crawl. A few hours earlier, he had witnessed a truck with military personnel at work, and couldn't tell whether they were imposters, so the thought of people posing as police was a distinct possibility. *I need a shower and some time to think.*

His musings were interrupted by his cell phone. He pulled it out and peered at the screen. Rory Thompson. He touched the green button, and Rory began speaking without waiting for a greeting.

"Mr. Donovan. Are you missing anyone? Look around you. Who's conspicuous by their absence?"

Donovan was as willing to receive sarcasm as Thompson was willing to offer warmth. "Is she all right?"

"As all right as anyone would feel if they found themselves in a Bucuresti prison, accused of spying. How did you let this happen to her?"

"It's complicated."

"Yes, well, it's more complicated now. We've got to get her out of there, and there are two ways I can see. The first is the diplomatic way, which is the long, hard way. Two weeks to eighteen months. Beth wouldn't prefer that, I expect. The second way is to present compelling evidence that would exonerate her. What have you got? And from what I've heard in the past two hours, I'm not holding my breath. To begin with, I had a chance to speak with Beth for thirty seconds. The shooters were released. In fact, the Romanian authorities are claiming they don't exist."

Donovan went numb. "Beth had them cold when I left her. Weren't they taken with her?"

"They were not." He could hear the concern in the ambassador's voice. "Maybe you'd better get to Bucharest, and see what can be done. Can you speak freely now? Do you trust your phone?"

"No."

"Well, the Romanian government offices will be no better. What can be done, in terms of relatively safe phone calls to me?"

Donovan took a second. "I know someone."

Rory's voice was dry. "I knew you would. Call me when you get there. And watch your back."

CHAPTER TWENTY

Manchester, England

GEMMA TRASK SAT AT HER desk in New Scotland Yard looking out into space. She wasn't exactly staring outside, as the nearest window was located through a glass wall and across a phalanx of detectives. It was more a case of staring off into the distance. She was on special assignment with nary a Scotland Yard inspector to bounce ideas off, nor a fellow detective with whom to set up a game plan. It was the damndest thing, being overcome by this strangest of feelings, to be surrounded by a cohort of Scotland Yard officers, and yet to be alone. For her entire career, she'd had superiors, and later, subordinates, but for this case...a few strangers, none of them even her countrymen. Her ostensible colleagues—an RCMP officer currently lying in a coma in a Romanian hospital bed and a police consultant flitting around Eastern Europe—were of no use to her now. And she'd been asked to go snoop around a viper's nest. Alone.

I don't think so. Even on the telly, the actor-bobbies get back-up. I am not going in alone. She thought about who was available. It would certainly be dead easy to grab a security officer from the Canadian High Commission office. After all, the murder in the Canadian embassy was why Scotland Yard was involved. But would they be familiar enough with Manchester? Or would they stick out like a sore thumb? No, this time it had to be one of her own kind. She headed for the chief's office.

The chief agreed Gemma needed support, and questioned her closely on Donovan's whereabouts—he'd return from Bucharest any time now—and how soon did she predict they'd have evidence on Hendricks? Evidence being in short supply, and being oh-so aware of Ace Hendricks' lawyers and their horrible track record against them, he'd split the difference, offering a bright young detective to accompany Gemma to dig up something, anything they could use in evidence against the Hendricks gang. Satisfied, Gemma left the chief's office, feeling better. An hour later, she was briefing Detective Max Caldwell, a good, solid copper.

* * * *

The trip from London gave them time to set the scene and flesh out the characters. What was needed, however, was a starting point. They arrived in Manchester, dropped their kit bags off at the safe house assigned to undercover agents in the area, and she waited while Max picked up an unmarked car. They headed for a pub to develop a strategy.

"I'm convinced the warehouses hold the key to this whole mess." Gemma took another bite of her steak and mushroom pie. "Hendricks has had his house, as well as his warehouses searched before, and it always comes up empty. Nothing from our local sources suggests there is a hidden warehouse or what-not that can be used as a holding tank for stolen goods."

Max watched his colleague, hardly blinking. He was tall and slender, a marathon runner in his off-hours, and he was wearing an athlete's hoodie at the moment. Although young, Scotland Yard had been quick to snap him up when he'd requested a transfer from the Surrey police department to London proper. "I'm originally from up here, as you know. Hendricks' gang is a legend, and not in a good way. We've tried to pin him down a hundred ways, and he always floats to the top, like sewage in a fresh lake. He's arrogant and with just cause. The locals won't give up anything on him. To date, he's bullet-proof." He put his sandwich down, untouched.

"Nobody's bullet-proof. You won't catch me raising the white flag before we even get into his part of town." Her voice carried a reproving tone.

Max raised a hand. "Please don't get me wrong. I want to be the bloke who brings him and his empire down. I just think two things, at the moment." He placed both hands on the table, his eyes clear and unwavering, his voice confidential. "On the one hand, this could be tricky and we have the deck stacked against us. On the other hand, you've got a great long list of shite that seems to be beginning to stick to his arse. If ever there was a time to catch the bastard with his hand in the jar, it might be now." He sat back. "And you've a got a good reputation for this sort of thing." He frowned. "Erm, about your last case, your shoulder is one hundred percent, correct?"

Gemma smiled. "I probably won't be able to out-point you on chin-ups for another month, if that's what you're implying. Nah, I'm all right. I'm good." She went back to her meal.

"I didn't mean anything by it. You and I, we need to know everything we can, going into this, that's all." He picked up his fork, spearing a chip. "So, we're going to visit a warehouse, are we?"

"Yes, indeed we are."

"But they've been checked."

"Not by us."

* * * *

The warehouse they chose, probably the smallest used by Hendricks, was a ramshackle plywood and sheet metal box, propped up by a stout welding shop to its left and a condemned boarding house on the right. Every building was jammed so tightly together, if a fire was to happen, nothing on the block would survive. They waited until dusk to move in.

The front door was chained. Gemma nodded to her right. "Let's take a stroll through the Ritz Hotel." The door to the abandoned building was padlocked, but the entryway was in such bad shape that the pair was able to squeeze between the door and the frame. Once over the rotted sill and inside, they took a moment to listen for sounds emanating from the building, and to peer back out at the street, verifying they weren't followed or spotted.

They flicked on their flashlights and headed to the very back of the building. The wall separating the boarding house from the warehouse was solid the entire length. They exited the back into a dank alley, and moved along the back side of the warehouse, looking for an unbarred window or under-secured door. Nothing.

"Now what?" Max looked at Gemma, waiting.

"Nothing down here." She looked up, above the top of the warehouse. "Let's go upstairs, see what's there." They hauled an excuse for a ladder from within the shop around to the back wall. Many of the rungs were missing, but they clambered up and stepped onto the flat roof.

Communication was a series of hand signals and the occasional whisper. Windows from a nearby multi-story building were an issue, so they kept the use of flashlights to a minimum, and only in a direction away from that building. At one point, Gemma knelt, a shielded light tracing a line across the back of the roof.

"See that? They've done a major reno to the entire back of the building." She motioned to Max to get closer. "Look. The last ten feet of the warehouse has new roofing, yet the outside of the back is original, including that ratty ladder we climbed. I wonder why." She dropped to one knee to feel the demarcation between the old and new roofing.

"The building itself doesn't look worth the bother. Why invest in it, I wonder. My dad's a contractor. The trades would normally recommend a whole new roof, if they had to guarantee it. The inside's dead-empty and looks like it should be condemned, so again, why? I'm missing something here. Let's go back down and check out the inside back wall again. Wait. I want to text the photo to my partner Donovan, maybe see what he thinks. Shine the light on my phone." The message took only a second to send.

They started down the ladder, Gemma first. Max had made it down five feet when he heard Gemma curse from below him. He changed direction and pushed upward. He had his head and arms over the roofline before the slug from a silencer caught him in the side, passing between the third and fourth ribs and piercing his heart. His foot caught Gemma's shoulder on the way by, but he was gone before he hit the ground.

"I've got you dead to rights. Come down slowly, keeping your hands where I can see them. The ladder rungs will do nicely."

Gemma cringed. She knew the voice, remembered the stocky, fireplug body and shaved head belonging to it. Hendricks. Half of her brain thought of Max, of how she'd been the one to have chosen him to work with her. And half of her brain was frozen in fear, for she knew exactly what her new circumstances were.

She was alone with a murderer, in his backyard, in his neighborhood. In his town.

Dropping one step after another, she arrived all too soon, to stand beside her fallen comrade. She knelt, once again, to check for signs of life.

"He's dead, and soon you might be following him, depending upon how forthright you are with me." Hendricks grabbed her arm, pulling her away from the corpse. "I know you. We've met before, haven't we? You're the copper that threatened me. Is this your Canadian mate from that day? He doesn't seem as cocky this evening." He booted the rib section of the body, not bothering to roll him over.

Gemma tried to stall for time, to steal a chance to think. "How'd you find us?"

Even in the dark, she could see the smugness. "I got eyes and ears everywhere, ain't I? Folks across the street gave me a call, put me in the know. You are mine, now." He took her service pistol and pointed to a spot ten feet from anything. "Be a darlin' and sit there. You know the rules. If you have to move, I have to kill you." He pulled out a phone. "David, bring a bag behind the warehouse, yah, on the Sproul Street side. On second thought, bring two, in case this cow here has second thoughts about arguing with me." He nodded at her, his stare significant. "Two of you should be good. Yeah, the usual." He rang off.

Hendricks walked over to Chief Detective Trask, the pistol in his right hand pointing toward his prey. He looked up at the sky, perhaps gauging the amount of time left before dawn. "All right then. Up you go. You like this warehouse? You're going to love your new home. Get up, I said." Kicking her in the thigh, he took the cell phone from her jeans pocket and ground it to pieces with his heel. Pushing her shoulder, he herded her toward the rusty ladder she'd just descended. "Climb it. Me mate Neil, here, and I'll be right behind you, but don't be daft and try to kick me." She moved from the ladder to the roof, and then turned to face her captor.

"Over here." He pointed to a spot at the rear corner of the repaired warehouse roof section. As she turned, he hammered the back of her head with a vicious blow. The silencer snapped away from the gun barrel, hitting the roof several feet away, and Gemma dropped like a stone.

"You owe me for a gun, but you'll give me no grief on this wee trip." He grabbed a heel, hauled the unconscious figure the width of the warehouse roof as if she weighed nothing. Tearing aside a strip of tarpaper to reveal a trap door, he opened it, and dropped the unconscious woman most of the way through the hole, still holding her upside-down by one heel. Slowly, he swung her unconscious form back and forth, back and forth in the dark, until her torso took on a pendulum's path. Once the momentum was to his satisfaction, he took her to the extreme amplitude, and then released her. She swung away from him, first the head and shoulders swallowed by the dark. Her hips and legs followed into the pitch black hole, and he winced at the thud her body made as it hit the concrete floor.

He stood up, strode over to the roofline, and watched a panel van marked with the city logo ease into a narrow driveway opposite the back of the warehouse. A pair of men in coveralls brought a vinyl bag over to the spot where the corpse of Detective Max Caldwell lay in a crumpled heap. One of them grabbed a pair of heels, while the other unzipped the bag.

CHAPTER TWENTY-ONE

Bucharest

Sean Donovan sat behind the wheel of Ava's car, the morning sun peeking over the roof of the Constanta municipal police department. Now what? He had two Brits on the loose, doubtless on a plane back to England. Beth was in a Romanian jail, charged with crimes against the state. He had to smile at the ridiculous, frustrating situation he was in. He'd lost control of the whole situation, and still managed to legally make almost a million dollars. Crazy stuff. Shaking his head, he pulled out of the Constanta police station parking lot, accompanied by a pair of orphaned purses on the dusty passenger seat beside him.

He arrived at Bucharest's Majestik Hotel just after noon, had the concierge put away the car and, using a burner phone, called his friend and colleague, Maria Cuza. She was pleased he was in town and agreed to meet him for a late lunch.

He was seated in a red leather banquette toward the back when at precisely five after one Maria walked into the Chinese restaurant on French Street, in the popular Lipscani district. In keeping with her style, Maria wore a cream pant suit over a crisp white blouse. She proffered each cheek to be kissed, and after a warm hug, sat down and smiled at him.

"So mysterious, Sean! This isn't exactly your neighborhood. What brings you here?" Until recently, Maria was the Director of Systems in the Romanian Ministry of Labor. As director, she'd managed several systems security contracts with Donovan, and they'd become friends over recent years. She'd left Labor this year when she was promoted to Deputy Minister of Agriculture.

"I'll get right to it, Maria. I'm in trouble, or, at least, a friend of mine is. She's somewhere in Bucharest, in jail for spying." He held up a hand to quell her words. "No, she wasn't spying. I'm afraid she's stirred up a hornets' nest, um, political in nature. A friend of ours was in Constanta, investigating the murder of an English woman. A potato exporter. You heard about her?

"Anyway, he gets shot and Beth and I came over to see what we could do to help. We found the shooters and were in the process of rounding them up when Beth gets arrested by regional police. In the meantime, the two suspects either got away or were released. Frankly, we think the police let them go."

Maria's face was solemn. "Do you know where she is right now?"

"In Bucharest. I'll know shortly, as soon as I chat with my ambassador."

"Jilava Prison, I suspect. And do you know the arresting officer?"

"Mircea Bacu. I was on a call with him a few days ago. He didn't seem very…empathetic to our circumstances at the time."

She shook her head, her face serious. "He is not a nice man. He's very ambitious, very self-serving." She thought for a minute. "The Minister of External Affairs is his boss. If there is any chink to be found in Mr. Bacu's armor, it would be through the minister, who is a much more reasonable man. Here is his name and private number." She spelled out the information in efficient cursive on a sheet of notepaper.

"I have one more favor, Maria."

"Anything."

"I was wondering if you have a secured phone that I could call the Canadian embassy with. I have information on the case that needs to be kept confidential for a bit. If you wish, you may even listen in. But it has to stay discreet for now."

Maria smiled, and patted his hand. "You've been a good colleague and a pretty good friend as well. Of course. You can use mine, and no, I do not need to eavesdrop." She pulled a new cell phone from her purse. "Do you need it for a day, or...?"

"Five minutes right now would work." He ordered a glass of wine for his guest and stepped out onto the street to make the call.

"Mr. Ambassador."

"Call me Rory. What have you found?"

"I'm in Bucharest. I've discovered that Bacu, the government rep we were chatting with the other day may be the culprit. He's been described by a trustworthy source as ambitious, self-serving, and not a nice man, to quote her. This isn't enough to incriminate the bastard, but it certainly points me in a certain direction. Here are the name and contact coordinates of his minister." He relayed them to Thompson. "He's supposed to be a decent sort, easier to get along with."

"That's not enough. What else do you have?"

"I have two handwritten instructions to the two truck drivers, in English, the first to intimidate the warehouse supervisor, and the second to kill anyone who investigates the potato spoilage. I'd bet the farm Ace Hendricks wrote both notes. And I have the murder weapons. No new fingerprints on any of the evidence since I took control of them. So if we can get the two truckers and Ace in a couple of interrogation rooms, I think we can get one of them to crack and spill."

"Well, that's a start. Don't tell anyone you have that, and don't lose any of it like we lost our two colleagues, for God's sake. Just know that I'm using our External Affairs to put as much pressure as I can on the Romanian government. But as they've told me twice so far today, these things take time." He rang off.

Donovan returned to the restaurant. Maria leaned over the table, her voice low. "I can't promise you anything, but I have no problem doing a little delicate inquiring about the agricultural side of this. This I will absolutely share." Her perpetual smile drifted off for a second. "I need to know with certainty that your friend is innocent of crimes, and that she did not harm any Romanian citizen. Can you make that assurance to me?"

"Of course I can. Here's the whole story, in a nutshell: A British woman sold the Romanian government a load of potatoes, which were artificially quarantined at the Constanta dockyards until they were sabotaged and subsequently rotted. When she came here to protest, a simpleton was hired to kill her. He succeeded, shooting her at the Constanta Shipyards and was immediately arrested. When our RCMP friend Jack came to investigate on behalf of the Canadian government, he was shot. At the same moment, a Romanian citizen was murdered for the crime of standing beside him at the wrong time.

"I came here with the Canadian Embassy's Director of Communications. We located the shooters, who by the way are from England, and the Romanian police let them go and arrested Beth. Now, you're all caught up. Except, I think all the Romanian players might be innocent bystanders, with the exception of Bacu. On that note, I would love to know as much about Bacu as I can, including his place of work, where he lives, his habits, everything I can get my hands on."

Maria's face paled. "Oh, my goodness, you said Constanta Shipyards. Stay here." She left her seat and hurried up to the front of the restaurant, returning with a newspaper. Opening it to page two, she jabbed a finger at the photo of a man lying in the street. "The paper says his name is Fyodorov, and he worked at the shipyards. Is he…?" Donovan nodded, and she sat back in her chair, flustered.

Donovan studied the photo. "When Beth last saw him, he had been taken into custody by the police, led by Bacu. A minute later, once they'd been marched out of the apartment, the two Brits and Fyodorov had all disappeared. We'd assumed they had been released. Apparently, only the two from England were." He took a moment, permitting her to absorb this shock.

In a minute, she told him everything she knew about Bacu, the Minister of External Affairs and his Ministry, promising to share additional information as she received it. Maria's smile returned, but her forehead carried a worry line. "This appears to be a deep hole in which you and your friends have been placed. I cannot overrule anybody, but perhaps I can tease out some information, very quietly." She placed a finger to her lips, signifying discretion.

"That would be greatly appreciated. Thank you."

"How do I get in touch with you, if I hear anything?"

"I'll contact you, if that's all right. I may be hard to get hold of from time-to-time. Perhaps I can call this number?" He pointed to her cell phone.

"I don't think so, Sean. If the profile of this issue rises at all, I wouldn't be surprised if a series of calls to my phone could draw some attention. Call this number, instead. It's my daughter's. And I'll get you a third cell phone number, if we deem it necessary. Am I being paranoid?"

"Unfortunately, no, you aren't. Listen, I won't pull you in too deeply, I promise."

"That's good. My daughters won't thank you for that. That being said, I'm going to leave now. You stay and eat. You've lost weight since we last met." She leaned over to kiss him on the cheek. "Take better care of yourself, my mysterious friend," and with that, she left him to drink her untouched wine.

When he left the restaurant, he headed back to the hotel and took a nap. He awoke at five o'clock, worked out at the hotel exercise room, and had a leisurely dinner. At seven, he strolled down the street to a payphone and called the number of the Bucharest metropolitan police. Asking for someone who spoke English, he left a message for Mircea Bacu. In it, he stated that the two Englishmen were being followed and would be picked up upon their entry into England. For more information about these events, Bacu could go to the Giurgiu Restaurant in Giurgiu, an hour's drive from Bucharest. *If he goes, that gives me a couple of hours to visit his apartment. If he doesn't go, he'll be sitting at his desk at the police station. But he'll be worried enough to go.*

He did an on-line search for a map of Bucharest and returned to the hotel, where he asked to have his car brought around.

Bacu's apartment on Magharu Boulevard offered a distinct contrast from Ava's apartment building in Constanta. While still a depressing gray concrete edifice, the gardens and walkways were maintained, and the lobby was lined, wall to floor with the ubiquitous pink Romanian marble. There were no security cameras. He buzzed four apartment numbers—all from a different floor than Bacu—before someone let him in without asking questions. He took the elevator to the seventh floor and walked down the stairs to the sixth, and spied the number he'd been given.

He walked straight to the door and knocked, lock-picking tools palmed in his left hand. There was no answer. After a couple of seconds, he solved the lock and entered without hesitation, pulling a mask over his face as he crossed the threshold. There was no alarm, and no one there to challenge him. Donovan didn't see any cameras, but saw no point in taking additional chances. It was obvious Bacu lived alone: his laptop was in the lone bedroom, and the apartment was decorated by a bachelor. There would be no use searching the apartment for access codes; Bacu wasn't that kind of man. He unplugged the computer, placed it in the dusty computer bag he found in the closet, and left, pulling the mask off, again, as he crossed the threshold on the way out. The whole process took twenty-two seconds.

Once back in the car, Donovan returned to his hotel, where he set to work retrieving a username and password, English-Romanian dictionary at his side. To begin, he entered every area that wasn't password protected. No luck. After that, he tethered his laptop to Bacu's, and directed his computer to gain access to all directories found on the laptop. Knowing it would take at least a half hour, he left the pair of computers to chug away, while he made a cup of tea.

His laptop's search through Bacu's laptop directory took nineteen minutes.

Donovan sat in front of the two laptops, thanking the American government spyware that permitted him to break into the personal computer life of strangers. He waded into the directory, searching for usernames and passwords.

This search took four seconds. Banking seemed like an excellent place to begin, so he checked Bacu's bank transactions. There were no offshore accounts, not even savings accounts. Apparently a simple man, his approach to finance was to dump all of his money into one spot and withdraw funds as his needs dictated, all from this same account. Activity from the previous thirty days revealed the two obvious debit and credit columns. There were no withdrawals in excess of a hundred dollars.

There were two, lone deposits into the account. The first, at the beginning of October, appeared to be a government paycheck. The second deposit, from an account outside of Romania, was for fifty thousand dollars. One transaction and one minute later, Donovan had relieved the account of its entire credit balance, except for one hundred dollars, the tiny balance left behind to delay the discovery by Bacu. At that point, Donovan checked for any email exchanges that might be pertinent to the case. Finding none, he programmed the laptop to suggest that the computer had been hacked by the Chinese government. Untethering took another few seconds, and he then closed the cover and stared at it, determining its fate.

He went to the parking garage and recovered the weapons as well as the notes from Hendricks. He brought them back up to his room, storing the notes under the rug that encircled his bed. The metal box of guns went into his closet, there being no easy place to hide them. It took a half hour to drive to the Danube River and drop the laptop off a walking bridge.

The bridge and embankment offered a calm place to think, so he took a stroll in the evening light. He'd made no contact with Beth since discovering her whereabouts. This was due in part to him not wishing to identify himself as someone interested in her case, and who, not coincidentally, happened to be in Bucharest. It had been two days since he'd heard about Jack's prognosis, and that news had come second-hand, from England. And what of Ava? Was she right this minute explaining to the Romanian government that he was the mastermind? Responsible for everything from the murders to the missing Brits? Was he to be on tomorrow's front page, the spy on the run?

For some reason, he thought of a time when he'd just moved—ran, actually—away from home at age sixteen. He'd taken some cash from his father and it had disappeared like popcorn at the movies. Tired, homeless and broke, he accepted a job as a bicycle courier in Montreal, working as many hours as they'd let him, and sleeping in a flophouse room at night. On one run through the business district, he watched a cab driver pull up to a waste bin on Sherbrooke and dump a leather briefcase, driving off with just a little chirp from his tires.

Young Donovan had retrieved it, checked it for identification and brought it to its owner, first thing the next morning. In addition to a reward, the owner of a security company, as it turned out, hired him on the spot, and mentored him in the business of locks, security systems, and, later, electronics. That was a while ago. It's funny how something so serendipitous can send a little homeless boy halfway across the world. He thought about that, as the cool zephyrs of air came up off the river, brushing up against his face.

He turned to head back to Ava's car. A police vehicle had pulled up behind it and two officers with flashlights were peering into the driver's side. Noting that there were no blue lights circling the top of their car, he took a chance and approached them.

"Good evening, officers. How may I help you?"

The senior of the two officers replied in English. "Is this your vehicle?"

"Yes. Did I park it in the wrong place?"

"Why are you walking in this area? It is dangerous."

"I had no idea. The city is so beautiful, I thought I could go anywhere without worrying about criminals."

"Well, that is not accurate. We would like to see your papers. We will look in the boot of your car as well, please."

"Of course. Let me open it for you."

The three men stood in the dim light, staring into the empty trunk of the car. Even the spare tire had long since disappeared. "That is fine. Thank you. You should move along. It's not safe here." The junior policeman slammed the trunk and the two officers walked away without further comment. Donovan realized he had been sweating in the chill November night air.

CHAPTER TWENTY-TWO

Bucharest

ON A PREVIOUS TRIP TO Bucharest, Sean Donovan had awakened to the sound of children playing in the street. He'd had few friends, and fewer responsibilities. Work and life at the time had been a steady pattern of exploring the landscape and sussing out opportunities for profit. Everything was reduced to the simple, selfish act of stealing for money, earning money, and stealing yet again.

This morning, he lay in bed thinking about Beth. Without making a single demand upon him, she'd become his sole preoccupation. She was in prison in a foreign country. He had to get her out. Jack Miller was in a hospital in a coma. Another form of prison. There was nothing to do about that. Gemma Trask was working a dangerous case in Manchester, essentially alone. Gaia wanted an art relic. Not now. Today was about Beth, and the rest would have to wait. He headed for the shower, working out a plan for the only individual he seemed able to help at the moment.

Later that morning, Donovan entered the offices of the Ministry of External Affairs, Romania. It took a gauntlet of a half dozen intermediaries to work through before he was permitted to speak with the Minister, Alex Blaga. The minister made a point of not sitting, a clear indication of Donovan's limited time.

"Good morning, Minister, and thank you for your time. I'll be honest, I'm here to advocate on behalf of Beth McLean, who is at this minute wrongfully incarcerated in a Bucuresti prison. Ambassador Rory Thompson has already been in contact with you, but his efforts are based on diplomacy and fairness, laudable efforts that will take time. I'm here to try another approach, if you will permit me."

Minister Blaga smiled, and Donovan was gratified to see it reached to his eyes. "Your colleague—friend? Ms. McLean has already explained she was trying to solve the murder of Ellie Campbell. As you know, that deplorable attack on Mrs. Campbell had already been resolved, and the attacker is in custody with no alibi and several witnesses. What more can you add to this scenario that would suggest Ms. McLean should be pardoned for interfering with Romanian justice?" Blaga sat on the corner of a desk, awaiting a response. His demeanor was calm, assured. It was as if he anticipated any question or argument Donovan might come up with. The minister had been prepared by staff—Bacu?—for an occasion like this.

Donovan met his gaze, and held it. "I've done my research on you, sir. My Romanian colleagues advise you are a fair man, who just wants what is best for his country. You are aware things aren't always as they seem. Have you personally spoken with the murderer of Mrs. Campbell?"

The minister paused. "No. But my lieutenant…"

"Bacu."

"Yes, Mircea Bacu personally conducted the interview with the man."

"So, if Bacu can be trusted, I can certainly see why you would take his word."

A peeved look came over Blaga's face. "Of course, I can trust him. He's worked for me for almost a year. Well, six months, at any rate."

"I completely understand, Minister. I am equally loyal to my colleagues. But let's set that aside for a moment, and permit me to offer you a series of absolutely verifiable facts. One. The murderer is described by people who know him as a simpleton, with literally no connection to Ellie Campbell and therefore no motive, yet he lay in wait for her arrival, even though she came to Constanta unannounced. He was paid two thousand dollars, a year's wages for someone like him, and he was given a gun he didn't own the day before he shot her. So there's motive, but not in the sense we are speaking about it. He was paid to shoot Mrs. Campbell. Who paid him?

"Two. My colleague, Jack Miller asked one simple question at the Constanta Dockyard, relating to Mrs. Campbell's potato shipment and was shot by two men, five hours later. Three. My colleague Beth McLean was with a Bucuresti citizen, the widow of another Romanian citizen who was murdered by these same two men and their driver. Both attest that two British citizens and the dockworker, Fyodorov were arrested by Bacu yesterday, yet there is no record of these men having been taken to jail with Ava and Beth. And now we find Fyodorov on page two of the papers, conveniently murdered shortly after being released into the custody of our Mr. Bacu. And what is Ms. McLean's alibi during Fyodorov's murder? She was being held in custody en route to Bucharest by the police, with Ava Pitu as her witness. Between him and Ms. McLean, one of these is a liar, and I know the easiest thing to do is call the one in jail a liar and sweep this under the rug. But as an international incident is developing here, the evidence against Bacu is mounting."

The minister had begun to pace. "Hearsay."

"No, sir. That's my point. This is not hearsay. What do you think the two police who accompanied Bacu might say, if they were presented with evidence and photos of the two British murderers? I bet it wouldn't take long before they recanted. Let's share one more little bit of information.

"I happen to be in the security business, and I make it a point to do background checks on people who, shall we say, aren't behaving in an entirely legal way. I believe if you were, say, to do an audit of Mr. Bacu's bank activity for the past month, you'd see a significant sum of money enter his personal account at the beginning of the month, and magically fly out of the country very recently. Do you believe a government worker like Bacu would reasonably receive fifty thousand US dollars for doing something legal? I do not believe it came to him in the normal course of his duties as a public servant. What I'd like to draw to your attention, sir, is at the time Bacu received that money, a month ago, the only information available to us was Mrs. Campbell was becoming upset because her potato shipment was being artificially held up in a Romanian dockyard."

Blaga didn't reply. He paced some more, rubbing his temple with the tips of his finger. "But there is no evidence of these…British men being arrested, or even being in Constanta. This is getting complicated."

"Yes, Minister. It is complicated, and that's another reason why you need Beth McLean on the outside helping with this case, instead of locked up, raising international tensions. There's already two Romanian citizens shot to death, a British woman shot dead, and a Canadian in one of your hospitals, victim to all of this. Frankly, you can do worse than to have specialists like myself and Ms. McLean actively helping you with this case, especially if we are convinced non-Romanians are the murderers.

"First, though, I'd look into Bacu's situation and see to it he is placed into custody so he does no more harm, especially to Beth. He'll be like a cornered rat, as soon as he sees the mask is off him. As for Ms. McLean, seize her passport and give her a letter of entrance to go anywhere she wants to in Romania. That way, you could keep her in the country until the case is solved." Donovan tossed Beth's passport on the minister's desk and waited. He assumed the single word the minister muttered was a curse at the position he found himself in.

"Mr. Blaga, you have an opportunity to turn this embarrassing, escalating situation around. Instead of receiving pressure from Canada for unlawfully imprisoning one of their citizens, you now have the opportunity to crow about an international cooperative action. Beth will make you look good, I assure you."

"Look here, who the hell are you?"

"I'm just a security agent, hired by the Canadian embassy in London. I do have a reference you could use, if you wish. I've done work, on behalf of Canada, for the Romanian Ministry of Labor. And I am known to Professor Roberto Umbra. Although he works ostensibly for Concordia University in Canada, I can tell you in confidence he is a national security employee of your government. He can vouch for me as well."

Blaga stopped pacing to stare intently into Donovan's eyes. "There is a lot at stake here."

"I know."

"If I follow the wrong stag, I'll be lost in the forest."

"Yes. But you won't. Because you listened to what I said and you know what I've said can be verified, even if you don't exactly trust me. I want to know two things. When can Beth get released, and what else do you need from me to reassure you? Because I am sincere. If Bacu catches wind of this discussion before Beth is released, you'll be party to her murder. He will kill her without a thought and without her ever leaving that cell, you know it's true."

"Don't threaten me, sir." But there was no energy left in his tone. He stared at the floor, chewing on the corner of his lip.

"This isn't a threat at all. It's just another fact you are obliged to weigh. So. What else do you require?"

Blaga hesitated, and then capitulated. "I will require the photos of the two British suspects."

"I'll have them to you in less than a week, but the Bacu and McLean situation has to be sorted immediately, for her safety. Get an audit on Bacu's bank account, place him in a comfortable office with no phones for the afternoon and then release Ms. McLean at four o'clock. You'll have the evidence on him by then. The photos of the murderers will follow. I'll request the Canadian ambassador to Britain to send them to you and, because they are not Romanian, you'll receive excellent press from all this. Now, let's go give Ms. McLean the good news." He pushed Beth's passport an inch closer to the minister.

* * * *

"What took you so long?"

Donovan found Beth two floors underground in the women's correctional institute, at the end of a long corridor. There were no inmates, including Ava within ten cells of her, and the section seemed to have been recently renovated, with a fresh coat of gray paint. Her cell was six by eight, with a pee pot in the corner and a single seven-by-twelve inch slot in the door. While the hall was well lit, the cell itself enjoyed only the light that entered from the window slot.

The guard with the AK-47 stood away from the door, his rifle raised but not pointed, while a second guard unlocked the cell door. He swung the door wide open, yet Beth waited inside the threshold, wary. Donovan entered, giving her a hug. "Sorry, I'm late. I had to use words to spring you, and you know I don't like talking." He kissed her forehead, drawing her out of the cell.

On the way upstairs, Donovan told her of his recent activity, ending with the caution they were about to meet the Minister of External Affairs, and that, while she may wish to punch the man in the face, she was to thank him for this opportunity and agree to everything he said. "Oh, and I've updated your boss, Bacu has murdered Fyodorov, I lost you your passport for a bit, the minister is in a bad mood because of me, and I'll be leaving Romania without you in two hours."

"Sounds like it'll be you getting punched in the face." But her hand crept up to grasp his elbow, and she rested her head on his shoulder. They entered the office the Minister of External Affairs was using.

After introductions, Beth had one simple question. What was to happen to Ava?

He shook his head. "No. You are being too aggressive. Very pushy." Minister Blaga had his arms folded and his face wore a don't-mess-with-me countenance. "Ava Pitu is a Romanian citizen. You cannot presume to tell us what to do with our own citizens."

Donovan leaned forward in his chair. "You've been very helpful, Minister. And of course you are empowered to do what you think is right, but I'm asking you to rethink this. Although she's been living here for years, Ava is also a U.S. citizen, has recently been widowed and she's trying to get her life back together. And she's done nothing but try to catch the murderers of her husband. She was arrested by Bacu, who has since been discredited—"

"No. At least, no for today." He threw his hands up, having no more ammunition with which to fight. "But there is always another day. Why don't you ask me tomorrow, let us say," he looked at his watch, "eleven o'clock? That will give me time to prepare notes regarding you and Mrs. Pitu, in the event I am challenged by the media.

"I have a meeting to go to, so I, ah, must leave. Thank you for bringing this to my attention. I would ask you to refrain from discussing this with the press. Ms. McLean, let's meet in two days to discuss your passport situation. In the meantime, if you have any news on the murder, please call me immediately." He rose and exited the room, leaving Beth looking at Sean.

"Now what?"

"I take you back to my hotel, we get you showered and fed, and you tell me what you'll do here while you're waiting to get your passport back. I'll tell you my plans and then I head for the airport. Let's get the hell out of here."

* * * *

Donovan had a cup of coffee and a tray of food waiting as Beth exited the bathroom of his hotel room, towelling her hair. "Have you thought of what you can do, while I'm gone?"

"Why do you have to go, Sean? I'm feeling a little less—self-confident, without you, and with me being a brand new ex-con in a strange country. Also, I'm a little naked, without my passport."

Donovan smiled. "But you're one good-looking, naked ex-con. Seriously, I can't stay. Gemma is in Manchester and I'm worried about what Hendricks is going to do next. He's managed to stay out of jail because he's very smart. He's the key to all this and I have to get to him as quickly as I can. So I have to go. In the meantime, you have stuff to do. Ava's got to get rescued. I was really hoping you'd have a chance to check in on Jack. And are we sure we've uncovered everything about the Constanta Dockyards? Finally, I need you to rent a car. We have some murder weapons to store in the trunk, just for a few days. I've got Ava's car here, but it might not be the best idea, hiding murder weapons in the car of a Romanian citizen still in prison and under suspicion herself."

Beth paused. He was sure she was going to balk at getting involved with the weapons cache, but after a brief moment she nodded. "Sure. Least I can do."

"If there was any other way…"

"No. I'm all right. You go. What did you get me to eat?" She glanced at the tray. "Never mind. You have to leave in two hours?"

"Yes."

"Then let's go to bed. Honey, I need you more than food."

CHAPTER TWENTY-THREE

Manchester

Gemma returned to consciousness the hard way. Her face rested on a loose bolt that lay on the concrete floor, leaving her cheekbone throbbing with pain. Her arm had gone numb, asleep somewhere under her, her head felt like it had been caved in, as indeed the effort had been made. The gash from the pistol barrel cut her for two inches above the right ear and the impact of the gun barrel, together with the fall from the trap door left a concussion to push all other thoughts from her head. She cracked one eye open, just a slit. Nothing. She opened both eyes wide, peering out, and then upward.

Nothing.

She dragged herself to a sitting position, fighting nausea. *Am I blind? Why can't I see anything? And how did I get here?* Placing bare hands flat on the cold floor, she made a tentative sweep to the length of her arms. Clumping dust and grains of dirt. Dampness. It took her what felt like five minutes to find the courage to get to a crawling position and explore her new world. The only light came from flashes whenever she moved her head too quickly, resulting in complete upheaval in her stomach. Three crawling motions and her fingertips brushed up against chicken wire. She put her back to the mesh, gasping at the headache pain. Once the shock subsided, she hooked her fingers in the chicken wire and counted sideways arm lengths, moving right to left.

The exercise took ten painstaking and painful minutes. Gemma was in a cage, perhaps a dozen feet square. Two walls were comprised of chicken wire supported by two-by-two studs. The remaining walls were chipped, greasy concrete cinderblock. In her travels around the inside perimeter of the cage, she found a single, half-inch crack in the concrete floor. It went from one part of the cinderblock wall to the other, a distance of three feet. This was her new world.

Why didn't I ask for a full squad, instead of just Max? He might be alive, if I'd only...been able to see the future. Shit. But I didn't see this coming. At all.

Again, she sat with her back to the concrete wall, touching the length of the wound along her scalp, rubbing her fingertips and tasting them with her tongue after every inch. The bleeding appeared to have stopped. She listened with all her might, willing her heart to stop. Some distance away—perhaps thirty feet?—she could hear scurrying. Rats. *Least of my problems, for the moment.* Gemma looked up into the void. *I have to climb that, just in case it's open. Got to wait for the hammering to stop in my head, first. Ditto for kicking out the wire at the bottom. But am I blind?*

She'd been conscious for almost half an hour, with not so much as a spark to enter her retina. The good news was the feeling had come back to her arm and her strength was returning, even as her headache receded to something manageable.

She took a minute to think about her cage. Where are the weak spots? Are there any? She knew nothing about the ceiling, so that had to be explored. How secure was the base? She felt an arm's length of chicken wire. Two-by-two, shot-nailed into the concrete. What was the gap between nails? Thirty inches, she guessed, again grateful for her teen years working in construction for her father. She confirmed the location of the nail heads and sat, knees curled up, heels near the board at the fifteen inch mark. She kicked, heard a faint crack. Encouraged, she redoubled her effort. The board broke at the halfway mark, and separated where the concrete nails held the board down. A howl echoed through the greater room, and she realized as she held her head it was coming from her.

What's on the other side? *I'll burn that bridge when I come to it.* She pushed the board aside and pulled upward on the wire mesh, cutting the palms of her hands. In a minute, she'd got a gap almost a foot high. She crawled under it and lay on her side, stomach roiling, gasping with the effort she'd expended. *Still blind. Still don't know where in Christ I am, or why.* She rolled over and vomited on the floor, breathing hard and with sweat stinging her eyes.

Gemma tried standing, and banged her head for her troubles. She reached up and met a cold hand, which elicited another scream. Her hand brushed a stone-cold thigh, and she gathered she'd happened upon a life-sized statue. Beside it, she felt a wooden crate, and then another. By moving hand-to-hand and protecting her useless eyes, she was able to ascertain she was in a storage room. It seemed narrow—perhaps ten feet deep—and carried on for at least twenty paces. At the end, she met another greasy cinderblock wall.

She was in a warehouse of some kind, but of the queerest configuration imaginable. Who would build a storage facility twelve feet by not more than forty feet? It made no sense. And where was the door? She retraced her steps, palms flat against the wall. Nothing. Nothing! "Christ."

Snippets of thought crossed the landscape of her mind's eye. *Max is dead. And then, I was walking along the roof, followed by Hendricks when I saw a flash of lightning, blinding me. After that, nothing.* And she asked herself, again, where exactly was the bottom of this well that she found herself in.

CHAPTER TWENTY-FOUR

Manchester

SEAN DONOVAN SAT IN THE window of an old pub on Bullard Lane in Manchester, drinking coffee and trying to get warm. A period of unseasonably warm, dry weather had ended for the British Isles, and true fall had descended upon England. Inexorable sleety rain descended at a forty-five degree angle outside his window, and the comfy seats around the soot-darkened fireplace were the first to be snapped up. The weather dictated his mood as if they were twinned.

He'd spent five minutes staring at his phone, debating whether to message Beth. Gemma wasn't answering her phone, Hendricks wasn't anywhere to be found and Sean was getting nowhere fast. The only clue he had relating to this city was a text he'd received almost a day earlier, but had no opportunity to respond to until earlier that day. Gemma had sent him a curious note, accompanied by a photo of a flat rooftop. The rooftop appeared to be one tone of black for several feet leading inward from the roof edge, and at one point there was a demarcation where the remainder of the roof was several shades lighter. The accompanying text merely said 'Hendricks' warehouse. What do you make of this?'

I don't know what to make of it, Gemma. I wish you'd been clearer, or in a position to answer your phone. He wasn't concerned about the lack of communication per se, assuming her phone to be turned off for privacy or discretion needs. But his impatience was turned inward. *I'm stuck. I need just a teeny push, something to get me started in the right direction.* He activated his phone and texted the message to Beth, including the photo. 'Thoughts?' was the only word he added. He pushed the remains of his coffee away and headed out in search of a building contractor on the opposite side of the city from Hendricks' neighborhood.

The sign said Jones and Sons, and the shop was empty of souls, and after waiting a full minute, Donovan went around the service counter and raised his voice. "Hello. Percy Jones?"

"Hullo. Be right there." A moment later, a man of about sixty-five years shuffled out of the back office. "Just warming meself by the fire. Not looking forward to the winter, I must say." He took off his reading glasses to meet his customer's gaze. "What can I do for you, now?"

"I'm thinking about buying an old storage building and I wanted you to look at the roof and tell me what you think is going on."

"A building in the city? It's a bit wet for climbing on roofs today. Can this wait?"

"Actually, I brought a photo. Can you take a peek?"

The man smiled. "That sounds wee bit more reasonable than climbing up on a roof in the fall rain. Cheaper, too. Have over then." He offered a hand to take the phone, and studied it as a jeweler would a cut stone. In a minute, he looked up, his smile gone. He shook his head. "This is a repair job, and it doesn't look like a first-class one, at that."

"What's going on?"

"It appears to me that end of the building was compromised, somehow, and rather than doing a new roof, they just patched up the end of it. I don't like it." His eyes narrowed and he offered up a shrewd look. "That having been said, my boys could put a new roof on the full length of 'er, repair whatever ails the rafters and roofing, and put a new coat o' rubber on her. I'd treat you proper, cost-wise."

"You can't tell, by looking at it, why they did it that way?"

"Other than to cut corners, no. That would be my best guess."

"All right, thank you, then. How much do I owe you for the consultation?"

The man smiled and waved, heading back to his fire. "You know where I am, if you need a better job than that lot did."

Donovan took a cab back to his hotel, feeling dissatisfied. The man clearly knew what he was talking about, yet he could not answer the only question that was asked. Why was the warehouse repaired in that manner? It must have been important to Gemma, or she wouldn't have passed it on. Shrugging, he put his phone in his pocket, leaving the problem to stew for a bit.

And where was Gemma? The police station said that she and a detective from the local office were undercover. They were to check back in on Wednesday, almost two days from now. She was smart and had backup. She'd get out of this muck. What about Hendricks? He'd disappeared as well. Were they together? Was Gemma tailing him? Donovan hoped so. He glared through the window at the rain on the other side.

Two more hours of thinking yielded nothing. In that time, he'd received two text messages and a phone call. The call came from Rory Thompson, thanking him for getting Beth out, and asking if he needed additional help in getting Beth's passport returned. Donovan told him the passport issue was a ploy to keep the Romanian minister aware Beth was working in the interests of getting at the truth. Rory rang off, a tone of approval in his voice.

The text messages were also interesting. The first came from Dieter Schmidt, which made him smile, because it appeared to have been sent at two in the morning. *I must be keeping him awake at night, worrying about the winery decision.* In the message, Dieter said they were still mulling over the offer, and Claire appeared to be a sweet, smart young woman with a nose for the business of wine production. It was just as well the decision was being deferred a bit. Donovan had no time to think about anything but Hendricks.

The second message was brief and to the point. Gaia had heard of the entire room's worth of goods disappearing. Was progress being made on locating it? Donovan frowned when he read this. He'd had no time to do a proper search for it, hoping it might turn up in Manchester. A fresh trail was always easier to follow, but there was no time! He wished he could just sit each of his problems on a chair, scold them for being so noisy and tell them he'd be back for them later. But that wasn't how life worked. Addressing problems was more like juggling fire sticks, and sometimes, it was more like bumper cars, but less fun.

None of this was getting him anywhere. When he'd called the police station to inquire about Gemma, he'd also asked if there were any developments on the Campbell murder. There were not. Beth hadn't replied to his question, so that left him with a fat zero to work with. A trip to Ambleside might not hurt...

* * * *

On this visit to the Lake District, Donovan strode up to the portico of Noel Rigg's house, rang the bell and hoped the man was in. He was, and a moment later Donovan had introduced himself as Devin Koulos and was seated on a cheaply-made lounging chair in the barrister's barely-furnished sitting room.

"A bit spartan, I'm afraid. I've had to replace all my furnishings recently and, well, one cannot do justice to the entire shopping experience without benefit of time and, well, other resources."

Donovan nodded, smiling. "I understand your house was relieved of everything but the bed and a wonky chair. That must be unsettling, no pun intended."

Rigg's eyes narrowed. "How did you...? Who exactly are you, Mr. Koulos?"

"Gaia sent me."

At this, Rigg's eyes widened and his hands rose in front of him, as if to ward off a wooden stake to the heart. "You—he understands this had nothing whatever to do with me, doesn't he? I took my eye off the products for a few hours…"

"Actually, it was a long weekend in London, as I heard it."

"All right. Two days. And upon my return, the place was cleaned out, with nary a scrap from pantry to closet. Everything that wasn't nailed down…gone. They would have killed me, had I been here, sleeping in my bed. Slit my throat in the wink of an eye." At the consideration of this, Rigg began to tear up, his lip quivering.

"Let's not think about that. I want to know what you know about the actual theft. Who might have done this, or known about this having been done?"

"No one." His head shook enough to make his jowls wobble. "No one at all."

"Let me come at this from another angle. Manchester isn't very far away. Who do you know there, who might be capable of this?"

At the name of the city, Rigg became fascinated by a spot a little to the left of Donovan's head. His eyes darted to the floor from time to time and his face alternated between going pale and flaming up, but his gaze couldn't seem to meet those of Donovan. "I dunno what you mean. Of course I know plenty of people—colleagues—in Manchester, but they're all on the up-and-up, if you know what I mean. Classy folks, like." The eyes roamed a bit farther afield.

Donovan's voice lowered, and the barrister leaned forward to catch the words. "Rigg, you're lying to me, which is really not a problem, since you don't know me from Adam. But when you lie to me, you do know you're lying to Gaia, since I am his agent, right? Me, I'd be scared to death to lie to Mr. Galen Attanasia. Can you picture a hundred million dollars' worth of angry, chasing you across the Lake District moors? I'm not sure even I could run fast or far enough to evade Gaia, and I'm probably a bit more nimble than you. Let's face it, your feet wouldn't brush up against the first batch of heather before he'd have you by the scruff of your considerable neck.

"Let's begin again, shall we? And this notion might just have entered your mind a minute ago, but it's there now. Might as well say it as think it. I'll give you a first name, and you say the family name, okay? Here we go." He watched Rigg. "Ace."

The barrister began to stammer out 'Hen…' and his lip began to quiver again. "I…I can't. It would be more than my life is worth."

"I'll say it for you. It's Hendricks. You, sir, are in a pickle. You have to choose between incurring the wrath of a cut-throat gang bully, or Gaia, the representative of a consortium worth hundreds of millions, and your employer, by the way. I don't envy you." Donovan leaned forward in the chair, his elbows on his knees, watching his host begin to shake. "Let me play out a few scenarios. In the first one, I leave and you sic Hendricks on me. He may or may not catch me, and if he does, I'm dead. Or, I get away. In one case or the other, numerous replacements, or I, will show up on your door. Neither of us will be happy, because this doesn't just go away if I was to disappear."

Donovan didn't move a muscle other than his jaw. "In the second case, you share as much as you can to support Gaia retrieving his consortium's property. In this instance, Hendricks might get to you before we get to him, but if I were a betting man, I'd bet on me taking him out first. Are you a betting man, Mr. Rigg?"

"Oh, you know, a quid here…and there…"

"There you have it. We chat a bit more, you tell me as much as you can and I apply that knowledge toward saving your worthless life. You breathe a word to Hendricks or his associates, or even your associates, for that matter, and things will not work out for you, I promise. Don't even advise the police. The ones I'm working with are under cover, and it would be a shame if a few careless words from you jeopardized things for them. So, it's no comments to anyone, got it?" Donovan sat back in the uncomfortable chair. "All right then. Need seven seconds to collect your thoughts, or can you now begin with who might be interested in your comings and goings?" He leaned back. "And while you're at it, how about you tell me how Hendricks found out about your stuffed back room?

Rigg alternated between blanching and huffing, and Donovan was reminded of a cartoon teakettle, puffing and boiling. Rigg tried three times to say something, but nothing came out. After a long minute, the barrister decided that a murderer in the hand was worth a Manchester gang down the road. And the words flowed forth.

"I am a property barrister for a certain Spence Hoddle, and his wife, Norah. They live in Moss Side, an area of Manchester not known for its millionaires, shall we say? After two or three affordable commercial properties were acquired by Mr. Hoddle, I noticed the same co-signer on every transaction. I learned this co-signer, a Mr. Hendricks, was actually the money behind these transactions. Relative to typical Manchester sites, these purchases were bargain basement. I assume he was flipping properties. You know? Buy low, tart them up a bit and sell them for a quick double up of profits. I didn't ask.

"At any rate, one day, instead of Norah accompanying my client Hoddle, there was this…large man who quickly commandeered the conversation, shortly after stepping through the door. He brought a letter, already signed by Hoddle, advising he was relinquishing all rights and chattels to this man, who identified himself as Ace Hendricks."

The words were cruising out at a steady pace, as if Rigg was finally relieved to be sharing them. "Hendricks was in a very good mood, and told me I'd be doubling my Manchester business from here on in. Instead of the name Hoddle or Hendricks on the deeds, I was to look for a numbered company from now on. I have it at my office. At one point I, erm, invited Mr. Hendricks to lunch. I may have invited him to look around while I saw to the food."

Rigg shrugged. "After that day, the business kept coming in, and the business was good."

Donovan raised a hand, just an inch. "What were these properties? Rental units?"

"Oh, no. They were derelict warehouses, tiny workshops long since closed, that sort of thing. Mr. Hendricks mentioned he needed temporary storage of his home and office furnishings. He has a couple of moving companies."

"One more question. What was in that room?" Donovan pointed to the large room upstairs, at the end of the hall."

"I have no idea." But Rigg's eyes studied the floor, and there was no degree of certainty in his voice.

"Look at me." Rigg couldn't. "I don't really look like the murdering kind, but as you can imagine, I feel as if I'm about to meet our Mr. Hendricks down some dark alley. It will be soon, and I assure you, I'm going to have every tool and trick that I can muster at my disposal. You can consider me a desperate man. What, in your experience, do you believe desperate men to be capable of? I'll answer it for you. We're capable of anything. So, do I have to ask this question again?"

"The inventory list is in my office. In a file."

"Of course it is. Let's go get it now."

"Now? It's seven o'clock."

"Rigg, you didn't expect me to say anything else. Let's go." On their way over to the office, Donovan asked for the address and description of every property purchased in the name of Hendricks or Hoddle. As he gathered the information and put it into his messenger bag, Donovan reminded Rigg, Ambleside was small enough to keep track of the comings and goings of strangers. "I might not leave town for a week or so, if I was you. You know what's safest? Home is safest. Well, home with your big mouth shut is safest. Remember. A hundred million dollars' worth of pissed off, if you say boo. You're not a smart man, but you're smart enough to know that. I'll be calling Gaia immediately to explain how helpful you've been. Let's hope it stays that way."

Donovan paused. "One other thing. If a young man enters your house from a rear window, I want you to tell him his services are no longer required, and then pay him five hundred pounds severance pay. I'll be checking with him to see you make this happen. Cheerio."

He headed for the train, waving over his shoulder at the rotund man standing in the rain on the empty Ambleside street.

CHAPTER TWENTY-FIVE

Bucharest, Romania

AVA PITU STEPPED PAST THE final steel door of the Bucuresti Correctional Institute in Jilava. She carried a single meager possession, a jacket in one hand, with nothing in the other. She was greeted with a sympathetic smile by her new friend, Beth McLean. "Here's your purse. Let's get out of here. When I got out, I needed a shower before I was even willing to say a word. Let's get you cleaned up first, and you can eat later." Their footsteps echoed behind them, the remaining traces of their presence fading to quiet.

Over an early supper, Beth brought Ava up to date on events over the previous two days. Donovan was gone for the moment. The Minister of Foreign Affairs was beginning to understand the extent of the corruption from within his office, and the corruption began with Bacu. Finally, there were a few things they could tidy up, if Ava was still willing. She appeared to be, based on her words and the white fire in her eyes.

Ava's borrowed car was parked in the city, but Beth had Donovan's rental. They headed for Regina Teresa Hospital, taking the elevator to the third floor. The women were greeted at the reception desk with a warm handshake by Dr. Marie Kevler. The Canadian doctor sent by Rory met Beth with a tentative smile.

"Any news?"

"Yes. Good news. Jack eased out of his coma early this morning, and I have reason to think he's going to recover. He's very weak, of course, but he cursed at the tea we brought him. I'm thinking that's a good sign."

"Is it too early to ask of any…lingering or potentially fatal challenges, from here on in?"

Dr. Kevler's face became more serious. "There's always that worry, of course. Blood clots, weakened heart, things like that. But he's past the biggest hurdle by waking up on his own this morning. I don't have the champagne out, but it's in the back of my mind." Her smile returned.

Beth took Marie's elbow and tugged her away from the reception counter, leading her to a corner. It was clear Ava wanted to listen in, but she stood at the end of the counter, waiting.

"On a related note, I have a request. You weren't here for the initial operation, but I'm hoping the slugs have been retrieved from Jack and, hopefully, from Pitu's body. Do you have them?"

Dr. Kevler shook her head. "But I do know they've been kept locked up in a safe, here on the premises. And the way things work around here, it would take some kind of extraordinary government warrant to get hold of them. Maybe Ambassador Thompson…?"

"Yeah, we're thinking the same way, here. I'll work on that. Now, let's discuss the real reason we're here. Can we see Jack?"

She chewed on her lower lip. "I think it would be the best tonic for him to see you." Her eyebrows furrowed as she hesitated. "Perhaps not Ava. I understand she's the widow of the gentleman who was with Detective Miller when…We don't want him to relive painful thoughts at this time. I'll take her to the cafeteria for tea. But listen." Her voice carried with it a stern command. "You must literally be in and out in three minutes, and do not stretch it to four. Got it? And don't say anything inflammatory. If you want to talk about the weather, don't even bring up the onset of winter. I'm exaggerating, but what I'm saying is, don't talk about the case or anything like it. Letting him see your face will be the medicine he needs right now. Fewer words and more hand-holding, right?"

Beth pushed the door open, worried about what she'd see. Jack was lying on his back, a tube up his nose and thin sheets tucked so that his body was wrapped, but his arms were freed. He offered a wan grin when he recognized Beth. "Took you long enough. I've been awake for hours."

She pulled up a chair, took his hand and kissed him on the cheek. "You're boring when you sleep. I thought I'd wait until you could tell me some tall tales. I hear you can't stay out of trouble. Is that true?"

"It may be true." Jack's voice was frail, and it was as if he was operating on a quarter of his lung capacity. "So, the word on the street is I didn't die, yet. What can you tell me about that?"

Beth squeezed his hand. "I can tell you all you need to know with one small sentence. Dr. Kevler greeted me with a big smile and may have mentioned champagne. There."

"So, you're here to spring me out?"

She grinned. "Not quite. In fact, I have to leave in two minutes. But I'll come back this evening. They don't want you to become overexerted."

"Tell me what I need to know." Jack's focus was as sharp as ever, and his jaw was set at a stubborn angle. He made a faint attempt to squeeze her hand, and she leaned in to whisper in his ear.

"Here's what we have: the rifles used to shoot you are in our possession, but we haven't dusted them for prints. The hospital has the slugs they pulled out of you. They're locked up. A Romanian official released the two Brits who shot you, and the Romanian driver of the getaway vehicle, who turned out to be Costin Pitu's boss, is now dead. Murdered. We believe the shooters are back in England. Costin, didn't make it." Beth saw the pain on his face. "We figured out why the potato shipment was quarantined, something that wouldn't have been solved without you being so nosy.

"Donovan is back in England and I've got a new partner while I wait for you to heal up. It's Costin's wife, Ava. I have to go, now. You concentrate on getting better, and I'll be back to see you this evening, as I said. Need anything?"

"No. That doctor the embassy sent me is crackerjack. You go, and I'll get some rest." His eyes were already closed.

"Sounds good. I'll see you later today. Oh, and Jack? It's good to get you back." She closed the door on her way out, and then headed to the cafeteria to pick up Ava. When she arrived to greet the two women, the cup of tea they'd ordered for her was still hot.

* * * *

They sat in Donovan's former hotel room, sipping tea and chatting. Beth brought Ava up to date on her brief conversation with Jack and the doctor, omitting the part where the doctor had advised against Jack seeing Ava. "I'm glad he's going to recover. But I am a little concerned. Beth, we don't seem to have any leads we can look into. Any ideas as to where we go next?"

Beth shook her head. "But let's talk this through. What have we got right now?"

"We had two British guys who were probably the murderers. You should have let me kill them. At least Fyodorov is dead, one less for me to shoot. I probably should have killed him while I had the chance. I don't know if that official, Bacu, would be of any use to us. That's all I've got. What about you?"

"We've got their weapons, and we know where the slugs are that were used." Beth nibbled on a day-old croissant. "If we thought there was something to be found at the Brits' place in Constanta, we could toss it. I could find the place again, with a little advice from Donovan."

"Toss? I grew up American, but I don't know that word."

"Yeah, that's because you were a good girl, unlike me." Beth grinned. "It means to go over an apartment or a room, looking for clues and not caring what the place looked like after we're done." The grin morphed into a self-conscious smile in mid-chew. "Gangster talk, I suppose. Too many movies when I was going to school. Another possibility is Fyodorov's wife. Might she know anything?"

Ava shook her head. "Aside from the weapons, which have already told their story, I'm not holding much hope out for the other leads."

Beth frowned. "My dad was a forensic anthropologist, back home in Nova Scotia. When he wasn't checking the Parrsboro area for Jurassic dinosaur bones and the nearby Joggins area for Pennsylvanian era bones, he'd be called in on all sorts of police cases."

"Police?"

"Yeah. They'd find a human skull and wonder if it was some teenager who disappeared ten years earlier, or if it was the remains of a First Nations native buried there in some ceremony six hundred years ago. He had the skills to know the difference. Anyway, he always used to say solutions are always found somewhere on the road, but every road has two entrances. If you go down the one road and don't get anywhere, why not look at the other end of the same road?"

"I'm not sure what you mean."

"What I mean is, one end of the road is Romania. But the other end is in England. Maybe the answers we need are not in Romania. I think I have to go to Manchester. Everything seems to be pointing to this bastard and his gang in Manchester. So, everything seems to be tugging me out of here, to the other end of this road."

"Isn't Sean there now, looking into things?"

"The Hendricks gang has probably forty people in it. Sean's got one detective working with him, and I haven't heard from her in a while. I don't like the odds." Beth grinned. "Besides, we've got you here. If something needs poking, you can go get a stick. And with Bacu put away, and the two Brits gone, you'll be fine. Which reminds me." She reached into her purse. "Here's the second advance on your detective allowance." She handed over a thousand dollars in U.S. cash.

Ava looked at the folded bills. "I don't need that."

"Too bad. Take it. We're both working on this, we both landed in jail for our efforts. Why should I get paid while you don't? Take it," she repeated the gesture.

Ava looked at the cash in her hand. "Half the population of this country would gladly go to jail for a week for this kind of money. These days, I have to think twice before turning up my nose at it. I think I need to get back to the States. Back to what I used to call normal." She stuffed the bills in her coat pocket. "What else can we do, at this point?"

Beth thought for a second. "I need my passport back, and although it's only been a day, I need to get back to England. So first thing tomorrow, I'll go throw myself on the minister's mercy. For now, though, I have something to show you, just to get your opinion." She retrieved a cell phone, pulling up the image of an industrial rooftop.

CHAPTER TWENTY-SIX

Manchester

How black can black get? Gemma Trask was only able to see relief from the unremitting ink of her cell when she rubbed her eyes too vigorously, causing an imagined blue streak to glide in front of her. A moment later it, too, was gone, replaced by an empty, absent black unlike anything she'd ever experienced.

If I can't see, what else can I use to learn about this hole? She placed her hands on the floor. *I just learned the weather changed. It's colder than when I came to. And damp.* She heard scurrying in the distance. *I wonder which side of the wall they're on? Doesn't matter; rats can get in anywhere.* Earlier, she'd found a delicate table and snapped the leg off it. She reached for the makeshift weapon, drawing it near.

Come on, Gem, what's the plan? There's got to be a plan. And sitting here doing nothing'll get you nothing. Get off your arse and find a way out. She stood, her table leg playing the role of the white cane. She knew her previous cell was a chicken wire cage, eight feet by ten feet. Having broken through the wire, what was she facing now? It appeared to be a longer version of her previous confinement, but made with concrete cinder blocks. And it was filled with furniture, as far as she could tell. *How big?* Ten feet deep, she reckoned. *How wide? Let's find out.* Using her table leg, she moved along the concrete, pushing tables, chairs, chests and paintings aside as she inched along the wall. *Thirty feet, and nothing but a corner that will bring me back to where I started.* She hadn't touched anything resembling a door, and recalled how stale the air seemed. *Jesus Christ! No entrance or exit. Seriously?* The thought of being bricked in took her breath away, and she sat down, fear calling sweat to her forehead in cold trickles. *But how did I get here? I didn't just drop from the sky, did I? Did I?*

Her breath caught, and then accelerated. *Maybe I did.* She looked up, staring with all her might. Dead, unrelenting, deep space, inky blackness pushed down on her in waves, chilling to the bone. But, what if the door was right there, a few feet above her upturned nose?

* * * *

Sometime later—she had no idea how long each effort cost her—she stood approximately where she remembered regaining consciousness. By throwing the bolt she'd found on the floor, she'd ascertained the ceiling to be about fourteen feet from the floor. Because she lost the bolt every time it descended from the ceiling, this effort took what was for her a frustratingly long time. She'd dragged a chest of drawers up to the edge of the chicken wire cage, as close as possible to where she'd regained consciousness, and inched her way onto the top. She'd brought a pole lamp, from which she'd ripped the bulb and bowl. She'd also unscrewed the base, leaving her with a five-foot extension to her arms. Was this taking hours? Was there anything else to do?

Despite the drop in temperature, Gemma was sweating, and her head ached as if someone had beaten her with her table leg. Conscious of making too much noise, she pushed upward, as gently as possible. Solid resistance. She made mental note of the approximate location, and pushed against the ceiling, one foot to the right, trying to establish a matrix of points to test.

On the seventh attempt, she felt just the least bit of resistance, and in her excitement, the pole slipped and fell to the floor. Resisting the urge to weep, she sunk to her knees, and slid off the edge of the chest. By groping around, she found the pole and climbed back onto the chest. It took her another minute to relocate the spot, and she pushed harder, using her better shoulder and arm. An angular crescent of soft light appeared around three sides of a small trapdoor. Upon seeing it, Gemma lowered the pole, tears flowing from both eyes as she stood on the dresser in the pitch dark.

No. Not blind.

She stood there, wiping her cheeks, thinking. If she managed to push the trapdoor completely open, would she be able to jump to the edge and swing herself up? Would her repaired shoulder hold up? *I could do it if I had to. I think.* But if she crawled down, shifted the chest a foot or two to the left, and found another chest to place on top of it, she wouldn't have to jump more than a foot, if that.

It took her more time to round up an appropriate extension to her chest of drawers, and with adjustments, she was able to stack the one upon the other. Ignoring the pole this time, she crept onto the first, and then the second piece of furniture. The new height forced her to take care of banging her head against a metal ceiling truss. Another few moments and she located the makeshift trapdoor. It's now or never. She lifted the panel halfway and, hopping up, was able to peer up, into the chill evening air.

The square panel was torn from her hands and a meaty fist caught her on the temple. Down she went, her sternum catching the chest of drawers on the way. Breathless, she hit the concrete floor, her right arm, shoulder and hip absorbing the brunt of the punishment. Just before the trapdoor slammed, a thick Manchester accent advised her he'd come down and pound some sense into her, if she tried anything like that again. And, one more time, complete and utter blackness.

* * * *

Ace Hendricks drove his cell phone across the office, watching it explode off the wall and into a dozen pieces. "Shite! I'll end her useless life early, Neil, I swear."

The other man in the room, one of his truck drivers, looked over his drink and raised an eyebrow. "Is this about that girl you've got stashed away?"

"She found the trapdoor in the roof and just tried to escape." He fumbled with another cigarette. "She witnessed me killing her bloke, she knows how my warehouses are configured and she won't go away. Three strikes and you're out, isn't that what they say in baseball? Well, she's out, cop or no. She goes away tonight."

"You won't need her for, what's the word, leverage? What about that Canadian guy, the cocky one who came 'round your place last week? It's always good to have a bargaining chip."

"He's the one I killed the other night. No. I have a sophisticated operation going. Very complex. A lot of people, you included, rely upon me to put bread on the table. We can't have a stupid cow stumbling in, ruining things for a couple dozen men and their families, can we? It's really her fault. And she couldn't have picked a more…delicate time to put her nose in my affairs. In one day, I'll be shipping off a dozen truckloads of artwork, heirlooms, mementos and collectibles to Italy. I'll make enough with it to finance operations for years."

"You could buy an island in the Azores, put me in charge here." Neil smiled.

Hendricks strode over to his employee, hands on his hips. "Not a bad idea, Neilie. Here's the problem. I like my job. It's all I know how to do. Can ya picture me in a bathing suit, sunning meself on a tropical beach? Nah. I learned the business from my Da and my uncle, and I'm damned good at it. Nothing and no one stands in my way. That said, there are times when I can't be in two places at once, so I need to rely on my lieutenants to watch over things. Good job in Romania, by the way. So, from today, even though I'm sticking around, I've decided to promote you to Manager of Logistics. Congratulations."

Neil didn't flinch. "That's brilliant, chief. What does it bloody mean?"

"It means, arsehole, that when I'm not around, you're it. You're in charge. And the job comes with a hundred grand salary. That should keep you in Guinness and crisps, what?"

Neil's grin became genuine. "Thanks, Ace. Seriously. You won't be sorry."

"Good. And your first job is to shoot that stupid cow I've got penned up. Two o'clock tonight. And don't muck it up, Neilie." He pulled a revolver from the back of his waistband and slapped it into his new manager's hand.

CHAPTER TWENTY-SEVEN

New York City

THE SHEIK AND THE RESIDENCE owner stood in front of the drapes that had been pulled away from the window of the brownstone on the Upper West Side of Manhattan. Both watched the departure of a half dozen executive luxury model cars. Their drivers had sat the afternoon behind the wheel of each one, reading the paper or listening to the radio, waiting. Autumn leaves swirled around the sprayed-and-polished tires of each vehicle as each driver opened the door for each passenger, and pulled away. Each driver side window, that had been cracked open for fresh air, closed as they drove off. A minute later one of two cars, a white four-door Maserati Ghibli, sat waiting, a burly bodyguard parked in a grey BMW directly behind the luxury car.

Within the brownstone, Gaia continued his conversation with the sole remaining guest. The man, Sheik Saleh Ali, Chair of the Omega Group consortium, had stayed behind to direct Gaia's actions. Ali recapped the conversation that had eaten up the afternoon.

"We've heard from the board. They want answers regarding the loss of an entire shipment of fine art and antiquities, not to mention a satisfactory resolution to this mess. It's only a few million, but there is a principle, and our reputation, at stake here." Ali was not a tall man, but his grave demeanor and the cut of his suit suggested he was not to be trifled with. Balding and with a salt-and-pepper goatee, his piercing brown eyes absorbed whatever they landed on. It was evident his mind never rested. He picked the espresso cup from the edge of the library table, sipping while he paced. "You've heard my recommendation."

"Yes, we all heard your recommendation." Gaia sat behind his desk, trying to be patient. His fourth cup of espresso was served, but sat untouched. "Round up the thief and his gang members, drug them and burn the building in which they will die. And I repeat, it would probably work."

"Well? What is wrong with that?" Sheik Ali appeared to be growing tired of the circular discussion.

Gaia offered a dry smile. "It's that nasty little word, 'probably'. This group's unique advantage has always been its capability to remain absolutely discreet. We have a myriad of resources at our disposal, yet you propose using a hammer to swat a fly. We don't have to be personally and directly responsible for eliminating a score of armed men who have never heard of us. What's wrong with using a little…finesse?" Gaia leaned his seventh-of-a-ton bulk forward to grasp the tiny espresso cup in a ham-sized fist.

He continued. "As I told the group, I have an operative on the ground this very minute. He has this quality of being able to remain invisible, while mopping up these very unsightly messes. I trust him. But here is my selling point to you, Sheik. If anything goes wrong, he will be the one taking the brunt of the fallout, while we have the opportunity of swooping in behind him, and doing whatever needs to be done. So we can execute your proposed action, once he fails. If he fails, which he won't."

Ali had stopped pacing, his attention riveted on his host. The genesis of a smile began to form. "What I am hearing, my friend, is you are taking responsibility for this operation, putting all your eggs, so to speak, in this operative's basket?"

It was Gaia's turn to smile. He wagged a bejeweled finger in denial. "You know very well that's not how the Omega Group works. We decided"—he swept the room with his arm to encompass the departed board members—"as a board, to do something about this. We decided and we as a collective will support this decision. As a group, no? So it's not me, it's we. If you don't support Donovan going in first to guarantee our invisibility, it doesn't happen. All or nothing, my friend." Gaia sat back, his eyes never breaking with those of the board chair.

The sheik relented. "Very well. The operative has two days to tidy this up and retrieve our property. On the third day, you will deploy a team of assassins to mop this up. Gaia, my friend, you are counting on a lone operative to defeat an entire criminal group. And I am counting on you. I hope you know what you are doing."

Gaia gestured with the fingers of one hand. "This is a chess game, nothing more. What's at stake here? The lives of twenty strangers, ten or fifteen million dollars? Please. I make decisions like this every day. And so do you. Let's not raise our blood pressure over day-to-day business."

Sheik Ali smiled. "Yes, yes. You're correct." He returned his demitasse to its saucer. Business was through. "Good luck, my friend. Can I interest you in a box seat at the opera, this evening?"

Gaia demurred. "I don't believe so. My niece is coming over to play backgammon, and we'll have dinner. I'm thinking it will be grape leaf-wrapped rice dolmades, baked moussaka, and grilled fish. I'm partial to saganaki with honey drizzled over it, for my dessert, so I'll have that as well. And I'm opening a hundred-year old bottle of single malt scotch. It should be very pleasant. Another time, thank you."

He stood at the library window, watching the last two cars, the chauffeured limo and the bodyguard car depart. Alone, he permitted himself a trace of concern. Could Donovan pull this off? No sensible man liked twenty-to-one odds. Should he send a second operative over, as insurance? Where was Kianna? He opened a computer screen. Ah. She was protecting the son of a shipping magnate, presenting herself as one of the 'flowers' decorating his entourage off the coast of Villefranche Sur Mer, in the south of France. That option closed, he shrugged. *My friend*

Donovan will rise to the top, like olive oil. Or he won't. And he'll call if he needs help, or he won't. It's like a story. I'll have to follow it through to its conclusion, and turn the last page to see how this one ends. He let the curtain to the library window fall, shivering just a little at the November drizzle that fell against the panes.

CHAPTER TWENTY-EIGHT

London

BETH MCLEAN PEERED OUT OF the floor-to-ceiling windows of the fourth floor of MacDonald House, overlooking Grosvenor Square in Mayfair. There was no one in the park across the street, and the few automobiles in sight did not move. It was as if the city was hunkering down for winter. She shivered, wondering if a ghost had crossed her grave, or was it concern for the events of the next few days? The click of a door handle pulled her attention away from her thoughts.

"Beth! So good of you to have come directly from the airport. You look exhausted. Are you all right?"

"I'm fine. I wanted you to know what's going on, and…to ask for a leave of absence." She waited, her forehead a knot of worry.

"Of course you may. Is it your shoulder? Does this stem from your visit to Jack?"

She shook her head. "No. You may be aware that Sean and I are… seeing one another. This has in no way compromised my professionalism, with regard to my position here, but he's gone to face an entire gang in Manchester, and his partner, Gemma hasn't surfaced for a day. Now, I'm not worried about her. She's Scotland Yard, for goodness' sake. But it places Sean at a decided disadvantage in terms of numbers, in a city where the bad guy, so to speak, is on his home turf. Sir, I'd like to go there, now, and see if there's anything I can do to help matters. I'm well-trained in self-defence, I am smart, and I, well…I'm angry. I have to go, and this just doesn't look like anything I've seen in my job description. So, I can't very well pretend it's business as usual."

The ambassador focused on her, thinking. "You mentioned self-defence. I knew you attended a gym or some kind of facility. How, exactly are you versed in self-defence?"

"I'm an instructor in Krav Maga. It's–"

He finished her sentence, his voice soft. "It's the Israeli martial art. From what I can recall, you learn everything from where all the sensitive organs are, to how to take a gun away from an attacker at close quarters. That allays my worries a bit, I must say."

"You have it almost correct, sir. I'd like to emphasize that I haven't just learned Krav Maga. I teach it."

"Ah." The ghost of a smile crept onto his face. "I can see why you'd wish to correct me in that detail."

Rory jammed his hands into his pockets. "Let's take this request one part at a time, beginning with the last comment. At the bottom of your work description—and this applies to that of every public servant I've ever met—there's a single clause we in management call the escape clause. It states, and I quote: '…and other related duties, as interpreted by management.' Now, there's a lot of wiggle room in those eight words. Managers can read damn near anything into it they like. So, if I thought your presence in Manchester was to the advantage of the Commission's operation, then I could go ahead and sign off a travel claim for a train ticket and a per-deim allowance.

"But let's be a little more serious, here. Everything you've done day and night this past month has been out of deference to the Commission here, including a stint in international jail. Your request to travel to Manchester is in service to this case, of that I have no doubt. If you feel your time would be best served by going up the M1 and M6 a ways, then I think you should do that. I'll sign the request off, no further questions asked. I'll be worried about you. I'd prefer you let the police do this part.

But the thing is, I understand that the team of Beth and Sean might be better than Beth or Sean. Request for leave is withdrawn, but I'll sign off a travel request, leaving you on duty." He grinned. "At least, this way, I can ask for updates every six hours. You'll do that, won't you?"

"Yes, sir."

"Do you have time to bring me up to date on what you saw and heard in Romania? I'll arrange for a chopper to speed up your trip, in exchange. It's over two hundred kilometers…"

"Of course, and thanks. I can shower once I get to Manchester. Or tomorrow, perhaps." She stared down at a pair of scuffed running shoes. "I must say, I've never looked so much like a hobo in my life. This business of getting thrown in foreign prisons certainly gives you a perspective on what's really important in life, and high heels might not be too high on the list. At any rate, here's what I know at this point. To begin, I want to chat with you about a new friend of mine, named Ava Pitu. She's an American living in Romania, a recent widow as a result of this…business." She opened her hands wide in frustration. "Anyway, she wants to go home, she has portable skills, and nothing left for her in Romania. I was hoping we could…think of a way to get her back to the States. Now for the debrief."

Beth's presentation was concise, with few interruptions from the ambassador. In fifteen minutes a government limo was motoring to Hammersmith, where she took but a minute to re-pack her overnight bag. As they sped down the Tywardreath Highway to the Biggin Hill airport where her helicopter waited, she yelled to the driver to stop the car. They were passing through a warehouse district, and she'd spied a derelict building under reconstruction, in the failing light.

He pulled onto the shoulder of the road and she jumped from the almost-stopped car, running like a madwoman into the ditch to get a closer look. The wall facing the road wasn't completed, and she could look directly into the building. Three-quarters of the edifice was chipped cinder block and rusted steel. The new section seemed out of place, the quality being so much better than the original section.

What caught her attention was the stack of furniture, peeking out from tarps in the old part of the building. "That's it!" The driver's head turned at her shriek. She ran for the car, encouraging him to drive as fast as he dared. The car roared off the shoulder, spitting crushed rock, and gained speed. Beth pulled out her phone, thumbs darting across the screen.

Sean, your photo shows a sketchy warehouse, with a new section added on. The new space is for hiding the stolen stuff!!! And the safest place for a door is the roof, to keep it from nosy folk (like us). Hope this helps. I'm on my way. Let me know how I can help.

She sat back in the seat, somehow breathless.

CHAPTER TWENTY-NINE

Manchester

Ace Hendricks left his Dover Street headquarters, and drove to his company's garage in Tankersley. The loading doors were shut against the weather, and he entered by a side door, standing close to a propane heater to warm up while smiling in proprietary interest at his operation. The smaller trucks used for the tiniest work were all out on jobs. Nearest the loading doors, his three-ton, big box lorries were serviced and ready to move out at nine that night. Together with the time of day and the rain that was predicted, few people would be lolling about, observing things they shouldn't. The floor manager popped his head out from under a hood and made as if to join him, but Hendricks waved him off. He wanted a moment to organize his thoughts.

Neil's comment about Hendricks retiring and moving to the Azores struck a nerve. For the previous eight years, it was as if he'd led a charmed life. Every police raid ended in all charges being dropped, if they had even been laid in the first place. None of his men were in jail. His effort—and that of his father before him—of building the capacity of his community to protect his operation had met with nothing but success. Last year's receipts, a word that made him smile, were the best yet, and tomorrow's sale of twelve truckloads—twelve—of loot would make him a very rich man. He was cock of the walk.

But, why was he not sleeping lately? If he was honest with himself, things had begun to unravel with his most recent visits to the barrister, Rigg. It was shortly after happening upon Rigg's room full of treasures, and then lightening him of that burden, that things began to get more complicated. He may have to arrange an accident for a country barrister. But was it the Ambleside job that got the Manchester police interested in him once again?

And then there was the god-damned Campbell family.

Campbell the husband had been no problem at all to manipulate. As soon as Hendricks discovered Jesse and Ellie Campbell were considering adopting the blonde waif from the projects, it was dead-easy to push Campbell to doing anything. All it took was suggesting Campbell might be in a position to save the little girl and her ditsy mother, Nikki. Especially after he'd done away with Jesse's wife. Take the backbone out of someone and they can't very well stand up for themselves, can they? He scowled. But then the two cops came around, mucking everything up. That saga's almost done with. The Canadian cop's done in, and in a few hours, his partner's going to follow him down that one-way road. Done and done, just like that.

Still. Someone had broken into his house—his bedroom, for God's sake—and made off with a couple hundred grand of money and collectibles. Who'd done that? No one saw it. No one. Yet, his home was in the heart of his stronghold, with two generations of neighbors standing guard. Was he as impermeable to strikes as he always thought? What else had he underestimated? He shifted his mass to the other leg.

"I'll be glad when this shipment leaves town, better yet, leaves the country." He rubbed his hands over the heater, suddenly feeling November's chill. Maybe it is time to pack it in, buy a caravan and move to Wales. After a minute, he called Stokes, the floor manager over. "I know I said one man to a truck, but I want two." Hendricks jammed a crumpled piece of paper into Stokes' hand. "Here's the list of who travels with who. No changes, got it? Weddings, home births, grannie kicking off? No excuses. The trucks leave the shop at nine tonight, with two men in each. That's the lot of my men, except for you and Neil. The lorries will hit the tunnel and the ferries to France at half-hour intervals. They'll change drivers with the purchaser's team in Strasbourg and I don't see their faces on this side of the Channel for at least a week. And Stokes: have you ever heard people say, 'Do exactly what I say or you'll wind up dead?' You see that you put that thought in their 'eads, as you send these bastards off." He jabbed his finger in his floor manager's chest, a sturdy poke with each of his last words.

"Yes, sir."

"Now, I need your office. I have to call the buyer, make sure everything's still peaches and cream." Without waiting for an answer, he strode over to the dusty office, closing the door in the face of his floor manager, who'd been following at his heels.

CHAPTER THIRTY

Manchester

DONOVAN'S CELL PHONE BUZZED JUST as he left his hotel. The call would be important. He laughed at himself. What calls, at this point in the game, weren't life and death? Resenting the icy November rain assaulting his face, he turned around and found a quiet corner in the hotel lobby. The dark cold of November brought with it a profound sadness, as if he'd lost someone. He received a text message from his sister, Madeline. It was newsy, filled with grammatical errors and unremittingly cheerful. The mood he was in, he fully expected the call to have revealed bad news. *Must be the weather. That's enough to get you down, in and of itself. England's weather in November is like an Elliot Smith song: enough to make you want to quit everything.*

Beth had messaged him. She'd figured out the warehouse mystery, as well as advising him she was on her way. He remembered telling her last summer he didn't need a partner. He preferred to work alone, risking only himself.

He had to laugh. Here he was, not a loner at all. He had an embassy staffer, an RCMP officer, and a Scotland Yard chief detective, for god's sake, all working with him. What a difference three months made. Sure, they aren't to be found right this minute, but some of them will be around. Soon, I hope. Truth be told, he felt some comfort having Beth nearby. Under stress—what was it Hemingway defined as courage?

Grace under pressure—Beth was able to rise up. She could find a way out of things. In Gemma's absence, he asked himself if there was any resentment at her disappearance. No. She'd gone under cover before he could get back to Manchester. She was doing what she had to do. Whatever that was. Maybe there's just a spark of resentment, he thought.

Donovan recalled the plot plans he'd acquired from Rigg. It was time to look them over once again, this time for additional information. He returned to his room, and hauled out his overnight bag. What if he could somehow match the photograph to one of the twelve plot plans he had in the bag? And what was the most efficient way to attempt the matching process? He grabbed the bag and headed for the Manchester Police Department. It was time for another favor from Chief Inspector David Singh.

Five minutes later he was ushered into the chief inspector's cluttered office.

Singh was waiting for him. "How may I help you, Mr. Donovan?"

"If possible, I need to borrow Officer Bryan Robertson again."

"Absolutely possible, he's in the office right this minute. Is this as a follow-up to the, erm, Campbell case?"

Donovan nodded. "Officer Robertson seems to have a knack with patterns, and I've got a particular puzzle for him to solve."

"I'll have him come right in. Do you need me for this, or shall I… carry on?"

Donovan could see Singh's interest had been piqued, but he also noticed the phone hadn't stopped ringing in the brief time he'd been in the office. "I can tell by the phone ringing, all by itself, you've got your hands full, sir. How about I brief Robertson and have him in turn get you up to speed when you have a spare minute? I have to dash back to my hotel as soon as Robertson knows what is needed. The embassy's Director of Communications is arriving any time now, and she'll want an update as well."

"Very good. Here's Robertson now. Go find a bare desk top somewhere and he'll chat with me; hopefully, in an hour or two." Robertson and Donovan left, and Singh grabbed the phone at the next ring.

They studied the dozen building blueprints first, followed by the plot plans and civic addresses. There was no common size or shape, and no pattern to their location, other than how spread out across the city each was to the rest. Both pored over each document, willing it to reveal all its secrets. Each building appeared to have been chosen so it wouldn't be associated with any mass purchasing. The plot plan revealed each property to have a rear alley entrance, accessible by vehicle. In most cases, the blueprints suggested the rear driveway did not appear to lead to a door or opening to the building.

Most of these building documents had the words 'condemned', or 'scheduled for demolition' in the property description. But a ten-grand reno for each building would generally keep the city properties folk at bay. Not a large price to pay to hide stuff.

Donovan looked up. "I have to go. You could keep looking at this, but I'm wondering if there might be a faster solution, although what I'm proposing is more expensive. What if we get the police helicopter to visit each of these addresses, taking a photo? Couldn't you then apply photo pattern recognition to match this picture to the applicable roofline of one of these twelve buildings?"

Robertson offered an admiring glance. "That could work brilliantly, in fact. They'd need to use night vision photography, but that's possible. Let's go get permission." He hesitated. "I expect you'll have to do the sales pitch, Mr. Donovan, budget being the issue."

"I can do that. Let's go." They entered Singh's office, made the pitch and received concurrence, after a brief discussion of Gemma's safety. Donovan explained, "If there's a hub-bub from the chopper, and if Gemma's captured or nearby, we run the chance of exposing her, or rousing suspicions. It's got to be quick and as low-key as possible.

"We could issue a media release, advising of a missing child." Both Singh and Donovan gave Robertson an approving nod at this suggestion, which had him beaming.

"Yeah. Here's what we need. You give the chopper crew twelve civic addresses, getting them to photograph the rooftop profiles of the buildings they find at those addresses. Infrared cameras, I suppose. No hovering. It's got to be fly over and get out, without arousing suspicion. The addresses are spread out all over the city, so it will be a tedious job, but not too disruptive, I suppose."

A moment later, Donovan was headed back to his hotel room.

* * * *

He heard footsteps padding on the carpet outside his door, and then a knock.

"It's me. I'm alone."

Donovan opened the door and Beth leaped into his arms. "I know what you're thinking," she whispered into his collar, "Hard time in prison has reduced all my inhibitions."

He kissed her, and then eased her away to arm's length, studying her. "You look like shit, sweetie. Especially around the eyes. And you've lost weight you can't afford to lose. Should I be worried?" He pulled her back in for another hug.

"Nah. I'll be fine, after I shower. Anything to eat here?"

"I'll order something."

"No, I'll eat later. Sean, I have this awful feeling we're running out of time. And Rory's been wondering where Gemma is. Neither she nor her partner is responding."

"When were they supposed to check in?"

"Not until tomorrow morning at six, but the detective's wife told his supervisor their secret message didn't arrive at dinnertime today. The supervisor's checked in with Rory. I think they're going to send out a team from Gemma's shop to check out Hendricks."

"Was the detective allowed to have secret messages with her?" As he spoke, he began to guide her backwards toward the bath, undoing the buttons of her blouse.

"Not really the issue, baby. Anyway, like I said, I'm feeling an asteroid heading straight for Planet Sean, or whatever. You know what I mean." She swivelled to permit him access to her bra fastenings, while she kicked off her runners and undid her jeans.

"I agree. How fast can you shower? We've got work to do."

"Five minutes." Her panties pooled around her toes and she stepped into the shower. "Four minutes. Line up your thoughts. I'll be right there." He closed the bathroom door and ordered a glass of milk and a sandwich from room service, returning to the property documents.

* * * *

"What time is it?"

"Almost nine o'clock." Donovan started toward the bathroom door, and it opened, halting his approach. Beth stepped out in bra and panties, a small puff of steam chasing her. Her auburn hair was still wet—she hadn't bothered to dry it, opting instead to tuck it behind her ears for the moment. She sat on the bed, tugging at slim jeans that fit her tight at calf and thigh, and she slipped back into her dusty runners. She wore no jewelry.

"I need a sweater. November England is frigging cold." She opened her overnight bag. "Whatcha got for weapons? Seriously. I need something." She turned to face him, hands on hips.

Donovan rooted around in his overnight bag. "Hmm. Okay, I have two things. One is this mouse gun. It's a Beretta 3032 Tomcat. It's small enough you can conceal it in your hand. Seven shot clip and room for the eighth bullet to top-load straight in." He inserted the clip, and showed her how the gun was loaded from the barrel. "This exposed hammer here—" he pointed to the piece of metal sticking out of the back, behind the barrel, "means that if the safety is off, you either pull the hammer back or you can just pull the trigger hard to fire it. It's safer, because your trigger finger is actually drawing the bullet up into the chamber and pulling the hammer back at the same time. Little to no kickback. I'd carry the eighth bullet in my pocket, and load it once I got close to danger. If the bullet is in the chamber and the hammer's back, it's easier to fire, because your finger is only performing one action. The safety works great, by the way." He clicked it off, and then back on. "Got it?"

She nodded, silent, and put it in her purse, and slid the eighth bullet in her front jeans pocket.

"Next is this." He handed her an implement the size of a carrot peeler handle. "It's for up close and personal. It's a ViperTek stun gun, fully charged. Lots of volts at your disposal, so don't test it. There are only two things to know. Those two points at one end? Press them hard against your assailant. And the trigger's that red button. That said, if you poke it in his arm, it will probably do the trick, but it'll be less effective than if you stick it in his eye, say, or his groin. You've studied Krav Maga, so you know all the best points, but it works anywhere you can get close to skin. Just push here and it does the rest." He pointed to a discreet button on the side, and into the purse it went, to rest beside the first gift.

"Did you keep any toys for yourself?"

"Donovan grinned. Did you see the size of that bastard? Look at me. Do I look like I'd prefer to get in a cage match with him and his entourage? I don't think so. I'm armed, I'm good."

There was a knock on the door and he retrieved a tray. While she wolfed down the food, Donovan shared his growing concern for Gemma and her partner. "I'm wondering where they've gone off to. It's a little thing, but cops' wives often have…instincts. I know they're not due to report for another half day, but I'm—" he let the thought trail off.

"So, what can we do?"

"I think we have to act now. Police are going to look around for them after midnight, if they haven't checked in by then, so I hope they'll find their way back to the station. Here's the problem: with the police, we can find them faster. But with the additional manpower, the chances of a local alerting the gang are multiplied, and we'd absolutely be risking Gemma's life. In the meantime, though, a single body like you might be able to locate her first."

She looked at him, eyebrows raised.

"I've given the photos of the warehouses to a forensics team, together with the one you sent me from Romania. We need to know which one of the dozen warehouses matches the photo Gemma sent us. But in the meantime, here's the address of one of the storage sites. It's a condemned machine shop. I'll get you to start there, but once the chopper team working on the photo match get their results, you have to drop what you're doing and go straight to where they say and get her out. We'll get Scotland Yard to back you up, but every second will count."

Donovan's face was as serious as she'd ever seen it. "So, that's where you're going. I have to find Hendricks. Tonight." His chin set. "We know what he did to Nikki and her daughter. We suspect what he's done to the Campbells, and to Jack, and to Ava's husband."

"And maybe Gemma." Beth murmured this under her breath.

As if reading her mind, Donovan continued. "I'm really afraid of what he might have done to Gemma and her Manchester cop partner. And I'm getting angry. Not stupid angry, but maybe righteous anger."

"All right, then. I'm on it. I'll let you know once I head for the warehouse in question."

"Good luck." He kissed her, lingering a moment.

She paused, shaking a wet strand of hair. "Why is that particular warehouse the place to start?"

"That's the last place we think Gemma and her partner were at. You'll be looking for clues as to where she might have gone off to from there."

"Okay. Well, off I go." He heard the door click shut, but his nose and his mind were in his overnight bag, looking for weapons. The first item he came upon was a cell phone. He picked it up, staring hard at its face. After a long minute, he punched in the numbers to a by now familiar residence on the Upper West Side of New York City. One brief ring and he heard a familiar voice intone one word. "Yes?"

"I need a favor that will result in some mutual benefits."

Once he'd discussed things with Gaia, Donovan sat holding the phone tight, weighing things. At nine fifty-five, he punched in a new set of numbers. "Scotland Yard? This is Sean Donovan. You need to send a car to this address. My partner is there, trying to rescue Chief Detective Gemma Trask and her partner, also a Scotland Yard detective. My partner may not be enough to get them out. Can you send armed backup?" He gave them the address.

CHAPTER THIRTY-ONE

Manchester

Gemma didn't quite descend to unconsciousness this time. She felt the furniture edge tear at her side, had time to cringe in that second before hitting the unforgiving concrete floor; heard the crack of her head, as it bounced, once. Ominously, she heard her shoulder pop. The impact of her head on the unyielding floor sent screaming blue and red lights across her line of vision. But that calmed after a minute, leaving her in the inky well she was becoming oh-so familiar with. The ache in her left shoulder was getting worse. She thought about a movie she'd seen, where some tough guy used a wall to brace himself as he bullied his shoulder back into place. Not understanding the anatomy, purpose, or process to employ, she shook her head and cursed her luck. And she cursed Ace Hendricks.

Drawing herself up to a sitting position, she took stock. The shoulder was broken and she had a minor concussion, but her eyes worked just fine. Aside from small pangs of hunger, there appeared to be only one sensation over-riding everything else.

Desperation.

To her knowledge, no one knew where she was. Both of her partners —not counting poor Max—were in Romania, and someone from the gang would come hunting her any time, of that she had no doubt. Who was left to help? No one. Gemma had lost track of time at this point. She knew the police would begin to search for Max and her, but not before midnight at the pre-determined date. She bit her lower lip, clenching her fists.

Can I get out of this by sitting on my arse, waiting for Hendricks to come?

No.

With her good arm, she raised herself, feeling the chicken wire, finding her bearings. What was there to be found among the items stored around her? She shuffled to the end of the room, following the greasy cinder blocks, listening to the rats. Were they getting bolder? She couldn't tell. But it was getting colder, and she shivered in acknowledgement of that. In nine paces, roughly half the length of the building's width, she reached the corner. *I'll begin here. What can I feel?*

Placing her bad shoulder against the wall, she reached out to the stack of antiquities atop a dresser. First up, she found a metal mask, not too large and sporting a leather strap across the back and over the top. She put it on, to reduce the chance of something poking her in the face or throat. Sensing there was nothing more to be salvaged from the dresser top, she proceeded another three feet. Her outstretched arm happened upon a rack of clothing. Gemma searched for, and found a heavy serge jacket. Probably military and therefore warm, she thought, feeling the braid loops around the cuffs. Taking care, she managed to pull it on, after squishing the outside of each pocket, checking for creatures.

Moving along, her hand located a storage chest sitting on a table. She opened it, swallowed feelings of revulsion, and then reached into the box. Something pointed. Sharp. She traced out a dagger, and then another that felt identical. Her mind returned to her childhood, to a time when her father had taken her to a forested area near Sussex. He picked out a broad oak tree, pulled out what looked like a traveling backgammon box, and withdrew a set of five weighted-and-balanced throwing knives, the kind you'd see in a midway carnival.

Father didn't know much about throwing knives, but vowed they would learn that day. They'd spent the afternoon taking turns with the knives. The goal was to throw a knife from such a distance the blade would tumble end-for-end at least twice. He'd shown her how to grasp the blade with the soft muscle of her thumb on top, and the side of four fingertips underneath it. After a bit she could throw it both overhand and up from under with equal ease. At some point, she noticed she had better success with just the side of the thumb and two fingers under the blade. Having no trouble achieving a single spin of the blade from six feet away, she backed up to nine feet.

She'd done it first. Then, she bested him, three out of five. He'd given her the knives on the way home, exacting a promise to never throw them at anything breathing or expensive. Within a week, a one-inch thick plywood target with a full-length man's silhouette magically appeared at the back of the workshop. In a month, a hole the size of a grapefruit appeared in the plywood, where the heart had been drawn. The area around the genitals and the silhouette's left eye were torn up as well, a result of 'misses', according to the thirteen-year-old girl.

Gemma hefted the daggers, and then slipped them into her waistband within reach of her right hand. A fumbling search around the bottom of the chest yielded nothing else but a knitting needle. She placed that through the eye of the mask, having the entering tip come past her temple to rest over her ear, while the other end stuck out in front of her face. The jutting needle would give her six inches of warning, should something pointy approach her eyes in the blackness. She invested another half hour to search for anything else resembling a weapon, but came up short. After that, she crossed the room again and again, memorizing the location and shape of the objects, as well as the holes big enough to swallow her up in the dark.

* * * *

Neil walked the brief length of his employer's floor, glanced at the clock on his cell phone, and then continued pacing. Nine o'clock. He'd left the house at eight to get some cigarettes, and returned a half hour later to find a note on the kitchen table. 'Gone to meet with my clients. Be back at midnight to celebrate. By then you'll have done the police cow, and I'll have gotten rich. We'll go out for a brekkie fry-up. Call me if there's a cock-up. 888-6565.'

Neil stared at the paper, and then at his wristwatch. And then back to the paper. Midnight. A bloke could have a good time with a woman in three hours. Why couldn't he just nip over to the warehouse, hit her around a bit, and then have some fun? He pretended he was still mulling it through, even as he picked up a flashlight and his boss' pistol. A half glass of gin later, and he was out the door.

* * * *

Not long after Neil left, Sean Donovan breached the lock at number forty-five Dover, and entered the kitchen of Ace Hendricks. This time, he didn't wander about the house, looking for things to steal. He went right to the table, studying the rough note from Hendricks to his thug. He memorized the message without touching it, and left within a minute of having arrived.

Halfway down the block, he ducked into the lee of a building, it having begun to rain again, and called Beth. His first message was to warn her of the threat to Gemma, and to be on the lookout for at least one man. His second call was to Scotland Yard, asking them to share the GPS tracking he'd put on the cell phone with the number 888-6565. Could they call his cell and tell him what part of the city that phone was at this moment? He hailed a cab and sat in the back, waiting for his phone to ring. In a minute it did, and with a few hurried words to the cabbie, he was on the move.

* * * *

Neil sat in his car, finishing a cigarette, staring at the droplets of rain that hit, and then slid down the windshield of his car. *A hundred grand a year. I'm set. And the job comes with...enticements. Like the one I'm about to enjoy.* He remembered her, hovering upside-down over the hole in the roof of the machine shop, remembered how small her ankles were, how little she weighed. Yes, it was going to be fun. Would she fight back? All the better.

He rubbed the scruff of his whiskers. Almost time. Neil exited the vehicle and crossed the street to the side door of the machine shop. Hauling out a massive ring of keys, he picked one and unlocked the padlock that chained the door. He entered and, a minute later, came back out with an aluminum extension ladder. Climbing onto the roof took just a minute, the feel of the icy rungs of the ladder on his hands waking his senses, exciting him. He thought about being quiet, but the rain kept a visual and sonic screen between him and the neighbors. Would she hear his steps on the roof? Of course. They'd serve to wake his prey up; get her ready for him.

He unlatched the trap door, lifted it, and dropped the ladder in. "Hey, copper. I'm coming in. Got a blanket for us?" He shone the flashlight down the hole, confirmed there was no one at the foot of the ladder, and began his descent.

On the third rung from the floor, he heard the tiniest swish, the delicate sound of which called to mind something he'd heard as a boy. It reminded him of the wind in the trees at the top of St. Sunday Crag. The sound was followed by a punch to his kidney, eliciting a grunt. He smiled in the darkness, jumping the last yard to the concrete floor. "You can punch me all day long, girlie. Once I get my mitts on you, I'll shed the fight from you."

He reached behind him to his kidney, to where he'd felt the punch. His hand curled around the hilt of a knife, its blade nowhere to be felt. The hand was wet. He dropped the flashlight and it rolled under a stack of furniture, carrying with it all light.

He frowned, the aura of pain beginning to radiate from the punch. "Stupid cow. You're taking all the fun out of this." He turned in the direction the dagger had flown.

His words were absorbed into the ink, with no echo to comfort him. With deliberation, he pointed his gun in his best approximation of the direction from which the dagger had flown. He took a shot, and the flame from the end of his pistol relieved the darkness, just a little.

It was enough.

He saw her, a tiny silhouette figure half the size of the picture his memory had taken the night Hendricks tossed her in here. She was crouched on one knee, a second dagger just leaving her hand. He ducked, firing a second and third round in her direction. The blade of the second knife entered his chest, less like a punch and more like the incision it was. It sorted its way between the costae verae, and the metal came to rest in the lower lobe of his left lung.

Neil didn't think. On instinct, he emptied the remainder of his clip into the darkness, satisfied to hear her gasp with the release of the last bullet. He took a breath and was startled to hear a burbling sound. And where had his strength gone? Still strong enough to silence the little cow. He pointed his head, unseeing, toward a shuffling sound, and a chair or stool shifted on the floor. Neil was already stumbling toward the sound and in a second his foot booted something soft, causing a whimper.

He reached down and grabbed a shoulder, which caused another gasp, and dragged her up to his level. He wanted to call her a stupid cow again, but it seemed like a lot of effort, and his breath just wasn't there, anymore. Holding her in one hand, he drew a fist back and drove it straight at the space where he assumed her head to be. It connected, but met a textured sheet of metal, breaking his hand. Weakened by the loss of blood, together with the accompanying loss of breath, he dropped her, kneeling to put his weight on her hips. He spat a gob of blood to the side. Unable to see, he thrust his good hand downward, searching for the mask, to rip it off. To make her pay.

As he leaned in, something stung his nose. The stinging sensation became an unbearable halo of pain centering around his nasal cavity, and then bursting through his sinus cavity. His bowel evacuated and his good hand, not nearly as obedient as it was a moment earlier, rose to his face to bat away the stinging. He found a tiny hand, curled in a fist, the index finger and thumb pressed tightly to his nose. He wanted to push the tiny hand aside. He truly wanted to, but none of his appendages wished to obey him any longer. *My head is being held up by…something. And my arms won't obey me. How can that be?* She released…something from the area around his nose, after twisting it sideways.

His last action, prior to falling, was to note the presence of a knitting needle—just an inch or two—protruding from one nostril. He fell face first into the blackness, the concrete floor jamming the needle the rest of the way through his brain.

* * * *

Using her good arm, Gemma pushed the corpse off her hips and, noting the absence of anyone's breathing but her own, decided to take stock. But first, she needed that flashlight. Her left arm wouldn't perform, so she dragged herself along, supported by her right elbow. The bullet had entered her leg at the meaty part of the thigh. She couldn't tell if an artery had been nicked, but there didn't seem to be too much blood.

She needed that light.

The flashlight had to have fallen within a four-foot radius of the ladder, so that was where she started. Once there, she placed her back against the chicken wire, working left-to-right around the ladder. Three-quarters of the way 'round, she found it, and it was still working.

Squinting, she pointed the light at her leg. The bullet had entered the front of her thigh, six inches below the hip, and exited directly behind, apparently without touching bone or artery. That left her head and shoulder to review. The man's fist had stunned her, upsetting her sense of balance, so she suspected her concussion symptoms had worsened. And her left shoulder was completely useless. She caught herself laughing. How god-damned unlucky must a girl be, to injure the same shoulder twice in one year? No fair. The right shoulder was bruised but nothing to concern herself about.

What was worrying, however, was the fourteen-foot ceiling. The ladder stood there, taunting her. Could she climb it, to save her life? She hadn't tried, but the fact she couldn't even stand left her feeling fearful. Because, wasn't there almost thirty people on Hendricks' payroll? Getting the drop on one man didn't amount to much. And she guessed that, within an hour or two, someone would come looking for the corpse laid out five feet from her.

If. If another man came for her, what would she do this time? Quit wasn't in her vocabulary. That being said, what would she do? Pursing her lips, she crawled back to the body, and, with an effort, pulled the daggers from his kidney and ribcage, wiped them on his clothes and hauled herself, bit by agonizing bit, back to a spot not far from the ladder. The adrenalin she'd used to fend off her attacker was now expended, and she began to get cold. Shivering soon racked her core. But there didn't seem to be any way to get warm. She found the clothes rack, hauled down enough material to build a small nest, and closed her eyes. There'd be no sleep for Gemma, but perhaps she could stay warm, and rest enough to make the hammering within her head subside.

A foot kicked the top of the ladder.

CHAPTER THIRTY-TWO

Manchester

BETH MCLEAN PULLED UP TO the machine shop identified by Donovan as being the first one Gemma was to explore. She wished she had a police escort, but knew if there was any disruption on the street, and if she was there, people could spirit her away and Gemma would never be found. And she could call the police if anything smelled funny. She counted on the element of surprise, aware it might not be enough.

And she fretted about Donovan, as well. She knew there'd be a reckoning with Hendricks, and if it didn't go well, she might have more than one man to deal with, inside the building that stood before her. Dread washed over her, as she imagined Donovan's fate, if Hendricks got hold of him. Shaking her head, she focused on the padlock sitting unused on the ground beside the shop door. With the building as derelict as it was, there could be homeless people within it. It could have been broken off weeks earlier.

Or, Gemma's hunter could be in there. Shivering, Beth dropped the eighth bullet into the chamber behind the barrel. She pushed the door in and followed it, her light playing off the far walls. The machine shop was basically a filthy, but empty shell. She found what had been a wooden ladder, missing a few rungs, thrown up against a far wall, grabbed it and maneuvered it through the shop door. Taking care not to bang it against anything (and grateful for the cold and rain), she rounded the corner to the back of the building with the least amount of fuss she could generate.

Almost eleven o'clock.

It took her an eternity to climb the ladder in the frigid rain, making every effort to minimize noise while having to test every rung for support. Once on the roof, she noted the opened trap door and the top of the ladder, her stomach turning. Beth got down on her hands and knees, leaning over the edge of the opening, and listening. She listened for a full minute before swinging a foot onto the ladder and grimaced as her foot kicked the rung, making it clang. Not knowing what lay beneath her, she called out. "All right. It's the police. We're coming in. Have your hands up when we get there."

A tiny voice, weakened and filled with pain, returned the challenge. "It's over, Beth. Just get me out of here. I can't walk."

Beth shone the light from her phone on the floor, leaping the final five feet. She didn't spot Gemma immediately, turning at first to shine a light on the prone figure lying face down. Startled, she found a restless nest of clothing, a hand wiggling from its middle. She rushed over and offered Gemma a quick hug, before tugging at her. This elicited a gasp and a moan.

"We've got to get out of here." It was Beth's turn to emit an exhalation of air.

"You're bloody right, we do." Gemma tried to get up, but failed. "I can't walk. You're going to have to help me."

"Where are you hurt? You have to let me lean on that side, so you can use whatever you've got."

"My left shoulder, my head and I've been shot in the thigh. The shoulder's the worst, for now. My legs aren't badly injured, but my brain can't seem to order them about."

"Help me get you up. If you lean on me with your bad shoulder, it'll hurt like a bitch, but you can pull yourself up with your good arm. Let's go." Beth half-lifted her to an upright position, and then dragged her to the ladder. Once there, though, she felt Gemma slump.

"What's going on?"

Gemma's voice was slurred. "S'too much. Can't make my legs work."

Beth didn't reply. Her response was to pick her up in the classic fireman's carry, and began to ascend the ladder. Halfway up, she asked Gemma if she could hold a rung with her good arm, to give her a rest. Ten seconds later, Beth poured Gemma onto the roof. Not worrying about noise this time, Beth hoisted the better ladder from within the hold, and placed it beside the rickety one. They fumbled their way to the ground, and were almost out of the alleyway when a pair of men met them at the street, blocking the exit.

"Oy. What are you two up to?"

Beth didn't say a word. Handing the taser to Gemma, she'd already pointed the Beretta at the man closer to them, and waved them aside. But they, too, had a single pistol staring right back at them. Trying not to listen to her pounding heart, Beth kept moving toward the opening from the alley to the street, inching closer to the pair of thugs.

At six feet, Beth shifted her Beretta from the larger man to the smaller one who held the pistol. Pointing it at his face, she waved it, just a little. "One of us has killed a man tonight with a Beretta eight-shot, and it wasn't fucking you. Drop the gun and I promise not to spill your brains on your partner. I'll also remind you of the Taser beside me. One of us will take you out and that's the truth. You'll be dead and you won't even know why. Beat it. And take the simpleton with you."

The sound of a siren rounding the corner caused the men to back up, melting into the dark. The women hobbled toward the light as a police car screamed up, stopping in front of them.

"Get us to a hospital!" Beth leaned Gemma against the fender of the car, imploring them to hurry. Once in, they headed for the nearest hospital.

* * * *

On his way to the address identified by the GPS of Hendricks' cell phone, Donovan's phone rang. Hendricks was apparently on the move. "Can you tell me in which part of town it seems to be headed?"

"Tankersley. It's an industrial area. Your man Hendricks has a vehicle repair shop there. Here's the address. Do you need backup?"

"Not yet. Any word on Inspector Trask?"

"No, sir. But the results of the matching exercise are just in. It appears we have a match." The address corresponded with Beth's destination. He thanked them and called his Scotland Yard contact, who advised him a Manchester police team had already been sent to that address.

Donovan rang off, but hadn't put the phone down when it rang once again. This time, it was Beth.

"I've got Gemma. She's in bad shape, but not as bad as the bastard they sent to kill her. You'd be proud of her. Was it you who sent the police out to find us? They arrived just in time. Thanks, Sweetie. We're on the way to the hospital. Let me know where you're going and I'll meet you there as soon as I can."

"No. Stay with Gemma. Get two guards for the hospital corridor and stay with her inside the room, your back to the wall and gun loaded and pointed at the door until I get back to you. I have to go, now." He rang off, and then phoned Gaia. "It's show time." He threw the phone onto the seat beside him and accelerated.

* * * *

Eleven P.M.

The repair and maintenance shop in Tankersley was a tidy affair, nothing like the ratty warehouses Hendricks had splayed out across Manchester. Galvanized steel walls clad the sides, and the bay doors were sturdy barriers. From the far end of the building, Donovan had watched the last of a dozen furniture trucks pull out of the bay doors in the front. A moment later, the massive mercury vapor lamps dropped to black, row after row within the cavernous building. There were no lights on around the exterior. Once the last vehicle had gone, the only illumination from the building shone out of the office, close to where he stood near the back.

From what he could see, Donovan suspected Ace Hendricks was all but alone. He crept closer, to confirm this. One form, feet on the desk, thumbs busy with a cell phone in his lap. Hendricks was playing a game.

"What's this, then?" An older man had come up behind him, gun pointed at Donovan's chest. The man kept advancing.

Donovan said something too low for the man to hear, and as the man leaned just within reach, ear cocked, Donovan grabbed the barrel of the pistol, twisting it up and to the right. He continued approaching the man, turning the gun completely out of the man's hand. Rotating it end for end, Donovan finished what appeared to be a single motion by pointing the gun at the man's face. He raised a finger to his lips, motioning the man to silence. A minute later, the man was tied up and stuffed behind a refuse bin, not quite out of the rain.

Donovan rounded the building to the front and, using the key ring taken from the floor manager, let himself in. The roof reminded him of a warehouse version of the one at Paddington Station, Quonset-style, elongated and arched the full length. The overhead lights were extinguished and he made his way down the side past a half dozen hoists, courtesy of wire-grilled sconces that offered up paltry forty-watt lighting. He took a breath, cocked the floor manager's pistol, and walked into the office, gun barrel at eye level.

Hendricks' eyes popped as if he'd seen a ghost. But it didn't slow his reflexes an iota. The cell phone dropped and his right hand flew to his waiting pistol with surprising speed for such a big man. Donovan's first shot entered Hendricks' elbow, shattering the olecranon process on its way out. The second shot destroyed the phalangeal joint of his thumb. The pistol remained on the desk, pink droplets sprayed artfully around the handle.

"Bastard!"

"You know you got off lucky, Hendricks. It would have been so much easier, and given me so much more pleasure to have put the two slugs through that melon of yours. Now, get up. I want your seat." While he spoke, he drew the blind closed. Walking over to the side of the small room, he turned off the ceiling light, leaving them with just the desk lamp to view one another.

Ace hauled his massive bulk out of the chair and shuffled around to the side of the office nearest the door. He eased into a dusty metal chair, taking care to avoid touching anything with his right arm.

"Tell me this." Donovan waved his gun at the arm. "Why is it when a guy hurts his arm, he limps? I never figured that out." This elicited another curse from Hendricks, and his attacker tossed him a roll of paper towels, which he failed to catch. Both ignored the useless roll as it found its way into a corner of the office.

"I'm very interested to hear your story, Ace. You've hurt a lot of people, some of them my friends. Want to talk about it?"

"You go square to 'ell. My men'll be here in a minute, and that'll be the last of you, mate."

Donovan shook his head. "You have no more men. They're all dead. Twelve separate industrial accidents, is how I heard it. Plus the scum you sent to kill Gemma. She weighs one hundred-fifteen pounds, by the way. Just before she killed him with her bare hands, he probably apologized to every woman and child he ever bullied. Nope, all you have left is that old man, tied up by the garbage bin outside. And your millions. Um, nope, you no longer have that, either. Shit, you're not really in good shape, my friend.

"But here's what I can do for you. I can kill you, to save you the mortification of seeing your failure in tomorrow's headlines. Is now a good time?"

Hendricks shook his head, unsure if Donovan was serious. The cloth around his elbow had darkened, and a drop or two had begun to puddle on the floor beside him.

"Okay, then. Here's what I'm willing to do. I'll name a name, and you'll tell me the story. The more names you chat about, the longer you get to live. I have two pistols, which make six plus eight shots. The first thirteen will serve you pain, the last one will send you to hell. Ready? Let's play. The first name is Jack. Let me remind you. He's my friend who just came out of a coma in Romania. A coma caused by your men, under your orders." He waited.

"Fair enough." Hendricks put on a show of bravado, chin jutting out. With his good hand, he cradled the mess where his thumb had been. "I sent two of my boys, Neil and Gerry to Constanta, to intimidate my bought guy. Your fella came 'round, and, well, their hands were tied. I had to do summit to shut him up." He smiled at the thought.

Forcing himself to get the facts rather than exacting vengeance, Donovan called another name. "So, you had to do something to shut him up. Let's leave that for the moment and move on to Gemma. My partner who visited you again the other day."

Hendricks smiled again. "You're wired. I ain't saying another word." In response, Donovan lifted his sweater to reveal a bared chest. He waggled the barrel of the pistol to make a point.

Hendricks continued. "This one wasn't my fault, either. She and another copper, who I thought was you until a minute ago, were trespassing on my property. I was just defending my land. So, I shot the one and tossed the other into the storage cage of the old machine shop."

"Nikki."

The man's face assumed a stubborn look. "I'm not saying anoth–"

Donovan shot him in the knee, shattering the patella. The man rolled off the chair, clutching his knee and groaning. "Twelve more shots before I kill you, Ace. We're far from done. I said, 'Nikki' and you either tell me a story or say goodbye to your other kneecap. Now; ready, steady, go."

It took a few seconds, but, biting his lip, Hendricks began.

"She's my sister."

'What?"

"She's my god-damned baby sister. She grew up in the family business, and once she figured out what was what, she picked up sticks and moved into a tenement. Me da said good riddance to her, but she was being disloyal to the family. So I saw to it she never had a pot to piss in or a window to throw it out of. I dogged her every step of the way, making sure she never got ahead. Ya cannot forgive disloyalty, right?" He grimaced, groaning at the pain in his knee.

"So, when you came 'round, demanding I give her the packet of money Campbell had for her, I wasn't having any of it. So I sent the boys over to send her a message. She got the message, right? 'Cause she's no longer in town." He spat on the floor beside him. "I hope she's dead."

"Campbell's the next name. Why did they take in Lexie, your niece?"

"The Campbells were just nice people, in their way. Apparently, Mrs. Campbell used to get massages from Nikki, and doted on Lexie. I needed a way to ship valuables to Eastern Europe, and Constanta has the largest shipping docks in Eastern Europe. So when I found out about her business I began using her potato cargos to hide my collectible shipments. I'd get the artwork to the dockyards in Constanta, and from there the valuables would be shipped all over the world. Mostly to Russia, though. The new-rich Russians 'ave buckets of money to piss away on art they don't understand or appreciate.

"It worked well until her ship got quarantined. There was a corrupt official at the Constanta dockyards, and he tried to blackmail Mrs. Campbell.

"At that point, it was clear my shipping game was going to be exposed, so a couple of people had to get out of the way, the first being Mrs. Campbell. Again, I'm almost not guilty of her getting killed, either." His voice rose, as if surprised at how he was even involved in the mess.

"At the end of it, Campbell had nothing to live for. At that moment, he was dead-broke, he got it into his 'ead he could have prevented her getting killed if he'd gone instead. So, once she was killed he just didn't care anymore. The senior bureaucrat at the Canadian embassy was worse than useless. Since Campbell thought he was at fault for not going to Romania and the director was at fault for not fixing things immediately, he was willing to go kill him, at my suggestion, in exchange for me giving a packet of money to Nikki, for her daughter. I said I would, but... family loyalty being what it is..."

There was a pause, and the room—the whole building—seemed to hesitate. Ace's labored breathing was more audible, his face contorted in pain. "Give me another name, damn you."

"All right. Last name. Rigg. What is the identification number of the truck with the contents you stole from Rigg's house in Ambleside?"

"Rigg." Hendricks' face showed disgust. "What a pratt. Now, there's a man lost what he never deserved to have in the first place. I wondered where he got hold of all those valuables, though. Judging by his ass-ugly Chinese bed, he sure as hell wasn't the one who chose 'em."

Donovan ignored him. "The truck."

"The inventories are in the safe."

"Give me the combination."

"Go to hell."

"No problem. Give me your left knee." Donovan got up.

Hendricks put his good arm up to his face. "Thirty-six, thirty-three, eight."

Donovan took a moment to key in some numbers to his cell phone. A quick call to the police, suggesting they check out the workshop in Tankersley, and he headed for the safe to dial up the three numbers.

A second later, Donovan had emptied it of its cash, filling all of his pockets. The inventory sheets for each truck were clearly marked, and Donovan phoned Gaia with an untraceable burner phone, citing which one carried his personal property, together with that of the consortium. Powering down his cell, he stepped over Ace Hendricks on his way to the door.

"Police will be here in just a minute. I expect to see them in my rearview mirror, in a moment. You stay here. I see you've lost a bit of blood. Don't get up; I'll see my way out." He returned to the desk, destroying the cell phone and desk phone. He emptied Hendricks' gun, wiping it down, and left the room without bothering to close the door behind him.

CHAPTER THIRTY-THREE

London

RORY THOMPSON SAT AT THE head of a conference table on the fourth floor of MacDonald House, in Mayfair. To his left, Sean Donovan, his security consultant sat beside the communications director, Beth McLean. On the other side of the table, in a wheelchair, his Scotland Yard associate Gemma Trask sat, scribbling notes. At the end of the table, a flat screen monitor projected the smiling face of Detective Jack Miller, from his bed in Bucharest, Romania.

"So, congratulations are in order. You've ensured the end of what may have been the most notorious gang Manchester's seen in generations. I accompanied Gemma's supervisor from Scotland Yard to visit with the wife and parents of Manchester Detective Max Caldwell, to offer my condolences. I stated, from the heart, that he was a hero to England and to Canada, for upholding all that is good about the Scotland Yard." He raised a glass of champagne to the people gathered around him.

"And in a similar vein, I toast you, for doing a hard job with courage. One never wishes to boast, especially not in victory, but you were a formidable team. Thank you, so very much. Words can't do justice to speak to what you've accomplished.

"Time for updates. Jack, you go first."

All eyes turned from Canada's High Commissioner, to the opposite end of the table. Jack smiled on the screen. "You do recall I did most of my best work while unconscious." Everyone laughed, and Beth touched his image on the screen. "I'll recover nicely, it seems. I'm flying out of Romania to England in two days, and I've asked if I can get back to strength in Ontario. London's…wonderful, but I need to go home to heal up. I'll miss you all, though."

Donovan leaned forward. "Do what makes you feel right, Jack. But I'm buying a winery in Ontario and I'll need a manager of security. If it's time to move on, think about moving in my direction, buddy. It's not far from wherever you'll be." This got them both a cheer.

"Gemma?" Rory's voice was gentle, as if he worried about asking even this of her. But her response was strong.

"Most of this is in my statement, but I owe my new friends a verbal accounting, don't I?" She shifted in the wheelchair, the better to keep eye contact with Jack. "As you know, my team had their own fish to fry, leaving me to visit that bastard Hendricks with…well, with Max. We'd begun to sort out the whole warehouse thing, when we got caught and…" She paused, getting a grip on her emotions.

"So, I awoke with a concussion, in what felt like the bottom of a well. I tried to get out and got a separated shoulder for my troubles, thank you very much. I knew they'd come to get me so I prepared as best I could and, it came out in my favor. But by then, I'd also been shot and my concussion had worsened by a second fall. I was awake and aware, but unable to get up." She paused, becoming emotional. A moment later, she regained her composure.

"It was then that Beth came and rescued me. She literally threw me over her shoulder—mind you, Beth only weighs perhaps eight stone—and carried me up a ladder and off a roof, in the rain. And if that wasn't enough, she went all John Wayne on a couple of blokes putting their noses in where they didn't belong. I couldn't believe it, from such a wee sprite. Beth, you saved my life." Gemma reached across the table to clasp her hand.

"Which brings us to Beth. How did the case unfold for you?"

"It's too long to tell here, really. I knew Ian Gross, the director whose murder started it all. He wasn't much of a government administrator, and he was basically in pre-retirement mode. But he didn't deserve to be killed. Hendricks put both Campbells into untenable situations, resulting in their deaths. He, or his men assaulted his own sister Nikki and her daughter, Lexie. With the rifles and slugs, together with the notes in our possession, we can pin the Romanian murders and assaults on Hendricks." Her voice trembled, and then hardened. "He's a very bad man.

"The solution of the warehouses was determined jointly. It needed Gemma, Sean, and me to suss out how it all worked. I'm not exactly sure where all of the stolen loot went to, but the design of the buildings did get us Gemma back, as well as strengthen the case against Hendricks." Her voice was rock-solid, but her hand trembled as she withdrew it from Gemma's clasp.

"Sean, that leaves you. Where were you on that last evening?"

Donovan took a moment to meet the eyes of each person around the table. "After I left Beth to go find Gemma, I knew we needed more information from Hendricks. But first and foremost, we needed to ensure he didn't slip off into the night. With help from Scotland Yard's tracking team, I headed to his maintenance depot. It wasn't busy, so I overtook the floor manager, tied him up and entered the shop. I caught Hendricks in the office and a gunfight ensued. A couple of wild shots later and Hendricks was basically nicked in a couple of non-fatal spots.

"He knew the jig was up, so he told me some of the facts we had been missing. I phoned the police to come get him. I understand there were some gang members who've disappeared, and some of Hendricks' trucks that have also gone missing, perhaps even with some of the loot. I assume they used the trucks to get away to France, and I expect this'll clear up sometime over the next few months. Commissioner?" He focused on the ambassador. "Have you got anything else from Hendricks?"

Rory shook his head. "He hasn't said a word since we brought him in. Of course, anything he says will only deepen the hole he's already in.

What we don't have from him to this point will in all probability remain a mystery. He's finished, though. Taxation will clean out whatever remaining accounts and properties he owns. Many of the men he associates with have disappeared. Warrants have been issued, but we aren't even sure what country they're in. It'll sort itself in time. But Hendricks is done, Manchester's a better place, and you, my friends and colleagues, deserve a vacation." He raised his glass again.

Beth raised a hand, as if in class. "Sir? There's one other thing. Ava in Constanta. She's an American citizen who's helped Canada immeasurably, and given her husband's life to this case. She's an art dealer by profession, with no more ties to Romania, but quite possibly some enemies. I was hoping…"

Rory raised a hand. "I think I know where this is going. I've already made arrangements to have her stay in England on a visitor's visa until her papers get sorted. She can return to the States or come work in Canada. I arranged a job interview with a gallery in Toronto, and they say if her credentials are even close to what she says, they'll be pleased to have her. It would be a fresh start. I suspect, however, she just wants to go home to the States. "Now, all but one of you can rest. Beth?"

She pretended to pout.

"Your government needs you for the rest of the day, prepping your Comms team with media releases and ministerial briefing notes. I expect to see a leave form request on my desk at five o'clock. Two weeks, minimum, do you understand?" She nodded, smiling.

"Do you have any place special you intend to go to, or will you relax at home in Hammersmith?"

Beth reached under the table for Donovan's hand. "I've been invited to visit a winery in Canada, sir. It sounds very quiet. You should all come visit." That got a round of applause.

* * * *

Marseille, France

The last of a dozen furniture trucks arrived in Reims, in the north of France. They drove into the same nondescript warehouse a dozen military trucks had entered a day earlier, and both sets of trucks sat, waiting. The Manchester drivers had been caught before they'd left the city, shot, limed and then buried in the concrete footings of a new football stadium being constructed in Sheffield. The teams that had performed the hijacks had continued with the loaded trucks on to the border, crossing into France.

Once in the warehouse in Reims, the British furniture trucks were disassembled and their parts were sold to repair shops throughout Hungary, Slovakia, and Croatia. Their contents had been emptied into the military vehicles, and the new teams drove directly to the docks in Marseille. Once there, the contents were loaded into shipping containers, bound for New York City, and the drivers returned to the warehouse in Reims. The trucks were cleaned. All of the drivers promptly disappeared.

On December fifth, the sum of four million U.S. dollars was transferred into an offshore, numbered account, where it was subsequently moved to an account owned by Sean Donovan. One day later, a photo of a stone Grecian statue appeared on Donovan's cell phone, together with the words 'Thank You' beneath it. The photo erased itself, ten minutes later.

CHAPTER THIRTY-FOUR

London

Beth McLean sat on her sofa, a glass of burgundy in one hand, a copy of Natalie MacLean's book, *Unquenchable* in the other. "It says here Ontario's a fine place to learn about New World wines. I can't wait."

Sean Donovan continued to massage her foot, working from the toes back. His thumbs dug with expert precision into the arch of her sole, worked past the heel and a few inches up her calf. "And we'll have nothing on our plate except each other, and maybe a bottle of wine or two. I promise not even to have wine business. At least, not more than an hour or two a day." His hands wandered a bit up the calf and, in response, Beth switched feet.

"Half an hour, that's all you'll get. And what's with inviting Gemma and Jack? How can I have you to myself, if you're going to invite half the British Isles? Jeez."

"I thought it was you who invited them. I just repeated what I heard from you. Anyway, they won't come. We'll have the spa, the nightly entertainment and the food to ourselves. They aren't interested in traveling, in the shape they're in."

Her voice softened. "And what about us, Sean?" His hands slowed, and then stopped moving. "I only have a couple of weeks with you, three at most."

"First of all, I like that you're thinking of us as an us. That's a start. Secondly, it's three weeks, which gets us almost to Christmas. There's nothing much going on at the winery over Christmas, except for the restaurant, which rumbles along nicely without me. I was thinking of having an old-fashioned Christmas in London, if there's room for me in Hammersmith."

Beth smiled. "Lots of room. By the way, I was thinking of moving to a place a bit closer to the office. We can look for a flat, together. Are you interested, or should I put it off until spring?"

He lifted her up, placing her on his lap. "A spare bedroom for me?"

"A spare bedroom for guests, and a bedroom for us. Sound good?"

"Yeah. That sounds good."

THE BODY ON THE UNDERWATER ROAD

Donovan: Thief for Hire #4

All Donovan, a contract thief for hire wants is to get married, buy a winery and settle down.

But circumstances keep drawing him back into the life he has chosen to abandon. In this, the fourth novel in the series *Donovan: Thief For Hire*, old friends stumble upon a suspicious death at the home of their host, a rich New Yorker summering in quiet St. Andrews By-The-Sea.

As the event is investigated, Donovan and his new bride are invited to look into the who and why of the death. It becomes clear it is more than furniture and family that are brought from New York State to the tiny Canadian town.

Donovan and Beth follow the fishing community, the arts community and the small, powerful group of wealthy estate owners to get to the bottom of the woman's death. Was it greed, or secrets that have been hiding the truth?

Follow Donovan on his fourth adventure. He has skills he can use to navigate the dark side of society; will they be enough?

ABOUT THE AUTHOR

Chuck Bowie graduated from the University of New Brunswick in Canada with a Bachelor Degree in Science. He lives on the East Coast of Canada.

Growing up as an air force brat, his writing is influenced by the study of human nature and how people behave, habits he picked up as his family moved nineteen times in his first twenty one years. Chuck loves food, wine, music and travel and all play a role in his work.

His writing will often draw upon elements of these experiences to round out his characters and plotlines. Chuck is involved in the world of music, supporting local musicians, occasionally playing with them and always celebrating their successes.

Because he enjoys venting as much as the next fellow, Chuck will at times share his thoughts with essays and blog entries that can be found on his website: http://chuckbowie.ca

He is working through the fourth novel in the suspense-thriller series: *Donovan: Thief For Hire*. It's entitled: *The Body on the Underwater Road* and follows *Three Wrongs, AMACAT* and *Steal It All*.

Chuck is married, with two adult musician sons. He and his wife Lois live in Fredericton, New Brunswick.

Email: chuck.bowie33@gmail.com

Did you enjoy *Steal It All*?
If so, please help us spread the word about
Chuck Bowie and MuseItUp Publishing.
It's as easy as:

- Recommend the book to your family and friends
- Post a review
- Tweet and Facebook about it

Make sure to catch the entire series:

<u>Donovan: Thief For Hire</u>
Three Wrongs
AMACAT
Steal It All

Thank you